HE HAD DANGEROUS WRITTEN ALL OVER HIM

Kate stared down at the unconscious man on the bed. At the five tattooed dots on the soft flesh of his hand, between thumb and forefinger.

The spider web on the side of his neck hadn't been conclusive evidence, but this...this was unmistakable. Four dots forming a square to represent prison walls, a fifth in the center representing an inmate.

This man had done time.

Cold trickled down Kate's spine. Bloody hell. Just who—and what—had she brought into the house with her sister?

SHADOW OF DOUBT

LINDA POITEVIN

Michem Publishing, Canada

Published by Michem Publishing, Canada

SHADOW OF DOUBT

Cover design by Kanaxa
Interior design by Clara Stone

ISBN: 978-1-9894570-0-9

ONE

The late October rain swept across the windshield, obscuring the dark, narrow road ahead. Kate Dexter flipped the wipers to high and returned to clutching the hard plastic of the steering wheel with both hands. Even with the wipers slapping back and forth at top speed, the road remained mostly invisible. The car's worn tires slid sideways on the rutted gravel road that was rapidly turning into a series of lakes.

Kate eased up on the gas pedal.

Damn, but she wished she'd taken her own vehicle, a solid little four-wheel drive sedan, instead of the family's old boat of a station wagon. That would teach her to give in to the nostalgia of her youth.

Not that there was a lot of nostalgia to—

Another sideways slip on the road. Kate corrected her steering, then eased her neck to the side to stretch out the tension forming in her shoulder, feeling every one of her thirty-three years. The ache intensified. She sighed. As much fun as it had been to get together for dinner with the old gang, she and her shoulder would pay for this little excursion tomorrow. In spades.

And her physiotherapist would tear her a new one for the abuse she'd put her injury through over the last few days. Schlepping all those boxes around, digging through fifty years of accumulated stuff in the attic...how in the world had she missed the fact that her parents had been borderline hoarders? And what in hell were she and Laura supposed to do with everything now that—

She slammed her foot onto the brake pedal as jagged blue light split the night, illuminating a silhouette ahead. A person. Dead center of the road, mere yards away.

Frantically, Kate pulled at the steering wheel, aiming the station wagon toward the trees, but the car, so determined to ditch itself only seconds before, refused to leave the road. Another flash of lightning illuminated the figure. Details imprinted themselves on Kate's brain. Male, dark hair, eyes closed against the glare of headlights.

Then metal struck flesh with an impact that jolted through Kate's entire being.

The station wagon shuddered to a halt.

For an instant, Kate sat frozen, staring in horror at the body sprawled across the hood and onto the windshield. The wipers continued their steady sweep—left, right, left—obscenely oblivious to the arm in their path.

An arm that didn't move.

Kate threw the gearshift into park and scrambled from behind the wheel. The wind tore at her anorak, driving rain into every opening. Ignoring it, she reached across the station wagon's hood, groping for a pulse. Her fingers slipped on the cold, rain-slicked skin of the man's neck. Nothing. She pressed harder, just to the left of his windpipe.

There. Weak, but there.

Tha-dump. Tha-dump.

She sagged against the fender, relief flooding her veins. He was alive. She hadn't killed him. Yet. But who knew what his internal injuries might be? Or how long he'd been out in this weather? At the very least, his chances of dying of hypothermia increased with every passing second. Every raindrop. She needed help here. Fast.

"Hang in there, buddy," she muttered to the unmoving form, tugging the cell phone from her jeans pocket. Her heart plummeted down to her toes at the *No Service* displayed in the top corner of the screen. Hell. She'd hoped she hadn't entered the dead cell zone just yet—a zone that stretched for miles, included her parents' farm, and made calling for help impossible.

Pocketing the cell phone again, she squinted into the night against the wind-driven rain. Eight kilometers east to the farm, fifteen in the opposite direction to Graves Corners, and between the two, nothing but the occasional dilapidated storage barn. She was going to have to drive to get help, and that meant moving her victim off the car. And if she had to move him, she had to take him with her, too, because she couldn't just leave him injured in the rain at the side of the road.

As if to underscore her thoughts, lightning streaked again through the dark, and thunder rumbled ominously close. Trees groaned under a fresh onslaught of wind, and a branch sailed out of the dark to land on the station wagon's roof. Kate flinched. Hell.

She wiped a trickle of rainwater from the tip of her nose as she considered the problem of how to wrestle two hundred pounds of dead weight off the car hood and into the back seat. Then she grimaced. Perhaps *dead weight* might not be the best description under the circumstances.

She slid through the mud to the passenger side and tugged on boot-clad feet, grunting as she dragged her victim toward her. If he did have internal injuries, this wasn't going to help matters, but she really didn't have a choice. And if her injury had objected to driving and moving boxes, it really wasn't going to like this next part.

The man's legs slid off the hood, and the rest of him followed, too fast. Kate grappled his arm across her shoulders, only just managing to keep him upright. White heat flared through her collarbone, searing down her left arm to set her fingertips ablaze. She squeezed her eyes shut against the wave of nausea and waited it out.

The pain receded to an angry throb. Grimly, Kate forced her knees straight and adjusted her estimate of her victim's size. The man stood at least six-four, and she'd put his weight at a good two-twenty. She'd be lucky if he didn't squash her own not-inconsequential five-foot-eight frame before she got him loaded into the car.

Keeping her victim wedged between her and the vehicle, she inched along the station wagon's side until she could prop him against the rear panel. Fingers numb with cold, she opened the back door and, with way more determination than finesse, wrestled him into the back seat. Then, fire-hot teeth sinking into her shoulder and fresh nausea roiling in her belly, she collapsed across him.

Freaking hell, that hurt. By the time she got this guy to a hospital, she'd need medical attention herself. Gritting her teeth, she waited for her breathing to slow and her heart to stop behaving like a sledgehammer. Then she levered herself upright, sidestepped the legs hanging out of the car, and slogged around to pull open the other door.

The wind pushed back her hood in another wet gust as she reached in with her uninjured arm to grasp a fistful of wet T-shirt. Lightning flared again. She blinked against the flare and flinched at the crack of thunder that followed overhead. That storm was scarily close.

Bracing a knee against the doorframe, Kate tugged grimly at her unwieldy passenger. Centimeter by centimeter, the man slid into the vehicle. Then, when she could pull no more, she slammed the door, returned to the other side, and tucked her victim's feet out of the door's way. She brushed the sopping hair from her eyes as she straightened again—and froze.

Her fingers weren't just wet; they were sticky.

Rainwater wasn't sticky.

She reached into the station wagon and held her hand under the dim interior light. Dark, viscous fluid covered her fingers. Her heart kicked against her ribs.

Blood.

Lots of blood.

Muttering curses under her breath, Kate maneuvered around to the front passenger door and opened it to rummage through the glove box. She located a flashlight amid the years of accumulated papers and oddities. Weak light glowed when she switched it on—not much, but better than nothing.

She returned to the back seat and leaned in to tug the man's black T-shirt from the waistband of his jeans. Directing the flashlight's beam onto pale skin, she saw what she'd missed before in the dark. Crimson, seeping from a neat hole in the flesh below his left ribcage. A bullet hole. He'd been shot.

Kate sucked in a quick, shocked breath, but didn't doubt her observation for so much as a nanosecond. She'd seen too many gunshot wounds in her thirteen years with the RCMP to mistake this for anything else— and she still had the vivid memory of her own wound, too.

She lifted her head and scanned the surroundings as she ran through the possibilities. Hunting accident? Wrong time of year, and this guy wasn't dressed for the bush. Domestic dispute? Unlikely. There wasn't another farm around for miles, and she didn't think he could have walked far like this. The wound didn't look self-inflicted, either.

Which left the possibility that someone had deliberately brought him out to the middle of nowhere and left him for dead. It was an unsettling possibility at best, and she, for one, didn't care to be here if they came back to check on his well-being.

Mouth drawing tight, Kate slammed the door shut and skidded around to the driver's seat. First things first. Between hypothermia and blood loss, not to mention whatever damage she'd done with the car, this guy needed a hospital *now*. She'd call the local constabulary from there.

Her mind raced as she fumbled with half-frozen fingers for the key in the ignition. Grave's Crossing didn't have so much as a doctor, but once she got cell service again, she could call 911 and then keep driving to meet the ambulance. With luck—

Lightning turned the night daylight bright, and a simultaneous boom of thunder shook the station wagon. Kate ducked. Freaking hell, that was close.

A new, ominous groan threaded through the receding thunder, underlined by snapping and crackling, followed by a crash that sent another vibration through the vehicle. Kate's heart dropped to her toes. If that was what she thought it was...

She retrieved the flashlight from the passenger seat, opened her door, and forced her way out into the storm again. The flashlight beam didn't do more than highlight the pounding rain, but the nonstop flickers of lightning confirmed her worst fears. A massive tree lay across the road a few meters behind the car, blocking her only access to help.

She stared at it. Stared down the road into the dark. Wiped the water from her face. And made the only decision she could.

Her parents' farm it would be.

TWO

The drive took forever and required every ounce of skill and concentration Kate possessed. She nosed the vehicle into the rain at a painfully slow pace, fingers gripping the steering wheel until they ached. Entire sections of the gravel road were all but washed out, and she sent up a silent prayer of thanks each time the old car crept across yet another stretch of gushing water.

A groan sounded from the back seat as the tires jolted over a pothole, a sign that her passenger still lived. Her gaze flashed to the rearview mirror, but she saw only darkness. If the man had regained consciousness, he was at least still prone. She returned her attention to the treacherous road.

"Hang on," she said. "We'll be there in a couple of minutes."

"Where—?" The question hung behind her, half-formed, slurred and faint.

"You're hurt. I'm taking you to get help."

"No."

Another groan as the car jittered over washboard. Kate's shoulder throbbed anew under the unrelenting tension. She gritted her teeth.

"No." The voice from the back sounded stronger, but still slurred. "No help. No hospital."

Kate scowled. An objection like that raised a hundred questions in her cop's mind, but she stilled the urge to interrogate him on the spot. Priorities. First she had to make sure he'd live long enough to answer her questions.

"No hospital," she agreed, "but only because there isn't one near here. Or a doctor. The best I can do in a hurry is my house. If we're lucky, my sister will still be there. She's a nurse, and she handles most of the town's emergencies. You okay with that?"

Another glance in the mirror showed the ghostly reflection of her passenger struggling to pull himself up, his face lit by the glow from the dashboard. Kate tensed, all too aware of her vulnerability if he made a move. But he only closed his eyes and didn't reply.

At last a light glimmered through the trees on the left, and Kate slowed the vehicle to a crawl. The road here dead-ended in a pond, and many an unwary driver had missed the sharp turn into the farm's driveway. She banked left, made the corner without issue, and saw Laura's car parked in a pool of light in front of the barn. Relief washed over her.

"We're here," she told her passenger. "Just hang on."

She pulled up in front of the porch and gave a long blast of the car horn. A light came on outside the door. Laura had been watching for her. Kate switched off the engine, gave another honk, and clambered out. Rain beating against her back and seeping through the anorak to chill her skin, she rounded the vehicle to pull open the rear passenger door. Thunder snarled overhead.

"Right," she said. "We have to get you into the house. Do you think you can help me?"

The man's eyes opened halfway. She couldn't make out their color, but between the dim light from the overhead dome and the floodlight switched on by their arrival, she could see their glaze of pain. She touched his shoulder gently.

"We have to get you inside," she repeated, softening her voice. "Can you help?"

The man nodded. Kate slid her fingers under the waistband of his jeans and pulled. Damn, his skin was cold. A presence loomed behind her, and she looked over her shoulder to find her sister peering into the back of the car, holding up an umbrella that threatened to turn inside out at any second.

"What'd you do, run over something?" Laura asked, squinting into the interior. "Dog?"

"Man," Kate grunted, giving another tug.

"What?" Laura took a startled step backward as the man stumbled from the car, but when he began a slow collapse onto the ground in spite of Kate's best efforts, she leapt forward again and helped prop him upright. Her umbrella disappeared into the storm.

Laura's fingers went to the man's throat. "Thready," she said. "And his skin's like ice. When did it happen? And why the hell didn't you call an ambulance instead of bringing him here?"

"Twenty minutes ago, give or take. And no cell service." Kate adjusted her grip on the man, trying to ease the strain on her shoulder. He slipped sideways. She swore under her breath. "Look, can we continue this inside before you have both of us on the ground?"

Contrition flashed in Laura's expression. "Your shoulder. I forgot. Here, let me take the weight."

She hoisted the stranger's arm over her shoulder, and

together they half-carried, half-dragged their guest up the stairs onto the porch. Kate turned the doorknob and kicked open the door, and they staggered sideways into the house with their load.

"Back bedroom," Kate gasped. Alternately bouncing off walls and tripping over the man's feet, they hauled him down the narrow hallway of the old farmhouse and deposited him on the bed. There, Laura turned professional.

"Tell me exactly what happened," she said, running her hands over her patient's legs.

"He was standing in the middle of the road when I came around a corner. I wasn't going fast—hell, I wasn't going much more than a crawl." Kate massaged her aching shoulder. "I didn't even hit him hard enough to knock him down. He just kind of collapsed across the hood."

Laura flashed her a glance. "He's in awfully rough shape for something that minor."

Kate hesitated, then heaved a sigh. Laura wouldn't like it, but she'd find out anyway. She met her sister's questioning gray gaze.

"There's more," she admitted. "He's been shot. Left side, below the rib cage."

Laura sucked in a quick, startled breath. Her hands stilled in their task of unbuttoning the man's jeans.

"You're serious."

Kate nodded.

"Then we need to get him to a hospital, Kate. The phone's out, but I can stabilize him, we can get him back into the car and—"

"There's a tree down across the road."

"Hell." Laura stared down at her patient and ran a

hand over her short-cropped dark hair. "Hell, hell, *hell*." She bit her bottom lip and then sighed. "All right, I'm going to need some help. Is your shoulder up to it?"

Absolutely not.

Kate nodded. "Of course."

"My bag is in my car. I'll need it and some towels." Laura stripped off her dripping raincoat as she spoke. She draped it over the back of the chair at the desk their mother had used for sewing, then pulled open a drawer and took out a pair of scissors. "And blankets. Lots of them. We need to get him warmed up."

Kate turned on her heel and went in search of the requested supplies. She returned a few minutes later to find that her sister had already stripped the man of his T-shirt and boots, and was peeling back the jeans she'd sliced open. Kate stopped dead in her tracks.

Holy hell, this guy was built. He had it all: heavily muscled shoulders, broad chest, six...no, eight-pack, powerful thighs—his was one of the most impressive physiques she'd ever encountered. Which made the cop in her sound all kinds of alarms.

Someone in his physical condition, roaming the back-country roads in the dark and in a storm, with a gunshot wound...

Her gaze settled on the spider web tattoo on the side of his neck, just below his right ear. A prison tat? The hair on the back of her neck prickled.

Laura cleared her throat. "When you're quite through drooling, I could use a hand over here."

Kate opened her mouth to object, but snapped it shut again. Better Laura drew that conclusion rather than know Kate's real line of thought.

"Sorry," she said, moving forward to set Laura's medical bag and a stack of towels on the night table her sister had cleared off. She dropped the blankets at the foot of the single bed and went around to the other side. A quick glance at their patient's slack features assured her he was unconscious again.

Laura nodded at the oozing hole Kate had seen earlier. "You were right. He's been shot. Twice."

Kate's gaze followed her sister's pointing finger to a second wound in the man's left thigh—this one bleeding more profusely, staining the bedspread beneath him a deep crimson.

"How bad?"

"Both bullets went clean through, thank God." Laura took a pressure dressing from her kit and placed it over the leg. "Hold that."

Kate did as directed, applying a firm pressure to the dressing. She turned her gaze away while Laura removed the man's underwear and spread a towel discreetly over his groin, focusing her attention instead on the man's hand nearest her. She turned it over to see the back.

Nothing. She let the hand drop and reached across to his other.

"If you're looking for gunshot residue, there is none." Laura snapped the second glove into place. "At least, none that survived the rain."

It wasn't what Kate had been looking for, but she nodded anyway, even as she stared at the five tattooed dots on the soft flesh of the man's hand between thumb and forefinger.

The spider web hadn't been conclusive evidence, but this...this was unmistakable. Four dots forming a square to represent prison walls, a fifth in the center representing an inmate.

This man had done time.

Cold trickled down Kate's spine. Bloody hell. Just who—and what—had she brought into the house with her sister?

THREE

Kate's mind raced through an entire gamut of scenarios as Laura tilted the bedside lamp to shine its light on the bullet hole in the man's torso.

What was he involved in? Drugs? Weapons? Human trafficking? Endless possibilities, none of them good. All of them requiring her to get in touch with the local police sooner rather than later.

And to be hyper-alert until she reached them.

She thought of the handgun she'd brought with her from Ottawa. Was it serendipity that she'd driven straight down after work on Monday and hadn't stopped to secure it in her apartment? Perhaps. Though it wouldn't do her much good locked in its box at the back of her childhood bedroom closet upstairs. She'd have to figure out a way to retrieve it without alerting Laura.

"He's lucky," Laura said. "The shot was far enough over to have missed any organs. It just needs cleaning and dressing."

"And the leg?"

"Clean. Missed the bone. Good thing he's still out, though. Even with the local I gave him, this is going to hurt like mad."

Kate studied the man on the bed as her sister flushed the torso wound with saline solution. Thick, dark lashes lay unmoving against high cheekbones, and black hair fell in damp waves over a forehead smeared with mud and blood. Prominent nose, stubborn chin; his was a strong face, nothing delicate about it. It went well with his powerful body...

Kate blinked, startled at the direction in which her thoughts had veered. Giving herself a mental shake, she lifted the edge of the pressure bandage and peered at the hole beneath it. Good. The bleeding had almost stopped.

"How long to clean him up?" she asked her sister.

"Another few minutes. Why?"

"I want to try the phone again. I need to report this to the OPP and get someone out—" Strong fingers closed over her wrist, cutting her off. Her gaze darted up to the man's angular face. Across the bed, Laura gave a sharp inhale, and her hands stilled.

Blue, Kate thought as a tingle ran up her arm. *His eyes are blue.*

The brightest, clearest, most startling blue she'd ever seen. And above them, sweat beaded on his forehead. So. He hadn't been unconscious after all.

"No cops," he grated. His gaze held hers, intense and obstinate. She made herself remain relaxed under his grip.

Calm. Casual. Don't let him know you know. Not until Laura's safe. Not until you have your gun.

"You've been shot," she said. "You need to tell the police."

"No," he muttered. "Just get me patched up and I'll be on my way. No questions. No trouble."

"I can't do that." Kate shook her head, and his gaze turned belligerent.

"You don't understand," he grated. "I need to leave. Now."

"I hate to be the bearer of bad news," Laura's voice intruded, "but you won't be going anywhere for a while. Both bullets passed through you, but you've lost a lot of blood. You'll need at least a couple days of rest before you're mobile."

Beneath Kate's fingers, thigh muscles clenched. Anticipating his attempt to rise, she put her free hand on the mud-spattered forehead, holding him in place.

"Don't," she said. "You'll start the bleeding again."

He stared at her, defeat shadowing his expression. His eyelids drifted shut. Somehow, against the crisp white of the pillow against which he lay, he looked more vulnerable than defiant, and Kate found herself warding off an unnerving surge of compassion.

"Kate?"

Laura's voice drew her attention, and Kate looked over. Her sister's gaze flicked toward their patient and then back again, flashing a warning.

"I'm going to have to mix more saline," she said, her voice studiedly casual. "The distilled water you found under the bathroom sink yesterday..."

"Still there."

Her sister nodded. "Good. While I'm doing that, you should get out of those wet clothes. The last thing we need right now is you catching a chill."

Sibling-speak for *meet me in the hallway, we need to talk.*

Kate cast a last glance at the man on the bed and the pain etched into the lines around his mouth and closed eyes. She withdrew her wrist from his grasp. His hand tightened briefly, convulsively, and then dropped to his side. Laura shook out a blanket and spread it over him, then touched his shoulder with the gentleness that made her such a beloved nurse in the region.

"We'll be back in a few minutes," she said. "And then I'll give you something for the pain."

Tight-lipped, Kate followed her sister from the room.

Jonas Burke waited until the door clicked shut, then slammed a fisted hand against the mattress. Pain clawed through his side. He seized on it, needing it to feed the fury. The fear. Needing it to spur him to action when all he wanted to do was crawl into a hole somewhere and die.

Pain twisted again at his torso wound. Christ almighty, how the hell was he going to get out of this one? Of all the binds he'd been in over the years, this had to be the all-time winner. Shot and dumped out in the middle of nowhere, a wounded animal just waiting to be found...

The blond woman was probably on the phone with the cops right now. Depending on how remote this place was, he'd give himself less than a half hour before they got here. Cops tended to move fast for a gunshot wound. Assuming his ID had been cleaned out, it would take them a day to identify him, plus another for Ramirez and Lewis to drive up to get him and finish what they'd started. Unless...

He flexed his leg experimentally, hissing as white-hot agony washed over him, stealing his breath and churning through his belly. His jaw clenched until his teeth ached.

Slowly, the pain receded to more manageable, dull excruciation. Jonas's fists unclenched, and he stared up at the ceiling from an unfamiliar place of defeat. He'd lived life on the edge for so long, he hadn't bothered worrying about what it might be like to stare death in the face.

He'd always figured the end would come so fast, he wouldn't have time to reflect on it.

He would have preferred it that way.

He lifted his hand to rub his eyes, pausing when his fingers found instead the spot where the golden-haired woman's fingers had touched his forehead. Kate, the other woman had called her. He massaged his temple thoughtfully, a tiny hope flickering in his chest. He could have sworn he'd seen a flash of sympathy in her eyes. If the phone was still out, if she hadn't been able to call the cops yet, maybe he could talk to her. Convince her to hold off until he'd been stitched up and could get out of here. As long as he didn't move too fast—

Reality gusted back, callously snuffing out the hope. And if he did get away? What then? He'd recognized the OPP Kate had mentioned as an abbreviation for the Ontario Provincial Police, which put him in Canada. Wounded, most likely without ID, and on the run. No matter how he played it, he was screwed six ways to Sunday.

A sudden chill rattled through him, and his teeth chattered. Jonas raised his head from the pillow to gaze at the other blankets piled on the dresser across the room. So close, he thought, dropping back again as fatigue swamped him, and yet so very far. Kind of like his grasp on consciousness right now.

Damn.

Out in the hallway, Laura stripped off her latex gloves and glared up at Kate. "Spill," she ordered.

"I don't know what you mean," Kate hedged, tucking a bedraggled lock of hair behind her ear.

"You're worried about something."

"Aside from having run over a gunshot victim?"

"Aside from that, yes. You're my sister, Katie. I know when you're trying to hide something from me." Concerned gray eyes studied her. "What is it?"

"It's noth—" Kate broke off in the face of her sister's scowl. She sighed. "He's served time."

"The tattoos?"

"How did you—"

"I watch television like everyone else." Laura's gaze slid toward the bedroom they'd left. "Is he dangerous?"

"Given the tats and the bullet holes, I'm going to assume yes. At the very least, he's mixed up with dangerous people."

"Who may still be looking for him."

"Maybe."

"What do we do?"

"Keep trying the OPP. Don't let him know we recognized the tats. Stay calm. I don't suppose you can knock him out with something, can you?"

"Sorry." Laura shook her head. "The strongest thing I carry is codeine. It'll make him drowsy, but that's about it. For what it's worth, though, I really don't think he'll try anything—at least, not tonight. I wasn't kidding when I said he'd lost a lot of blood."

"All right," Kate said, eyeing the closed door. What she wouldn't give for a pair of handcuffs right now. Or at least a headboard on the bed that she could tie him to. "You make the saline you need, and I'll try calling the OPP after I change." She indicated her soaked, blood-stained jeans with a grimace.

She turned to head up the staircase to the second floor of the old farmhouse. Laura's voice stopped her on the third step.

"Your shoulder. How bad is it?"

Bad. But if Kate admitted as much, Laura would insist on codeine for her, too, and Kate had no intention of letting drugs cloud her capacity to act if she needed to. She flashed her sister a reassuring smile.

"Surprisingly good," she lied, resuming her climb toward dry clothing and her service pistol.

FOUR

The sound of the bedroom door opening penetrated Jonas's semi-conscious state. He forced open his eyes as the woman named Kate stepped into the room.

"Well?" he mumbled. "Are the cops on their way?"

Kate came to stand by the bedside, and her watchful eyes met his, their color somewhere between amber and golden. Much like a cat's.

He did a mental double-take at the fanciful thought. Damn. He had to be in worse shape than he'd thought, if he was waxing poetic.

Kate shook her head. "Not yet. The phone line's still down."

"No cell reception?"

"We don't have it out here at the best of times, never mind in weather like this."

"Where exactly *is* here?"

He watched her weigh her response, calculating how much to tell him.

"My parents' farmhouse," she said.

"In Ontario."

A nod.

"Where—?"

"My turn," she interrupted.

Shit. He braced himself.

"Most people who've been shot would want the cops involved. Why not you?"

Double shit.

He closed his eyes. "I know what you're thinking, but I'm not a criminal, and I haven't escaped custody."

"I saw the prison tat on your hand."

"It still isn't what you think."

"I'm listening."

"But I'm not telling." He glared at her. "So let it go."

"Fine." She scowled back. "The OPP can handle it."

Jonas ratcheted back his frustration, striving for calm. Reason. She'd shown sympathy before. He just had to find it in her again. He softened his voice.

"I meant what I said earlier. I'm not looking for trouble. If you can just get me patched up enough—"

"Not happening."

His gaze flicked toward the open door. There was no sign of the other woman yet. He took a deep, careful breath around the knife-edge of pain below his ribs. One chance. That might be all he got.

"I promise you I'm not dangerous," he said, injecting as much sincerity and reassurance into his voice as he could muster, "but the people who did this to me are. Right now, they think I'm dead. If they find out otherwise, they'll come after me."

A blond eyebrow rose. "All the more reason to call the cops, don't you think?"

His mouth twisted. "Actually, all the more reason *not* to." Footsteps sounded down the hallway. Desperation crawled through him, speeding up his words. He might have seen a hint of compassion in Kate, but he had no illusions about the other woman feeling the same way. "I know this doesn't make sense, but the people who are after me...they have connections. More connections than

you can imagine. I can't trust the police, do you understand? Please. If you call the OPP, I'm as good as dead."

Shock clouded her eyes. Suspicion and disbelief
narrowed them. The footsteps drew closer. Jonas reached
out to grasp her slender fingers.

"Damn it, Kate, *please*."

"Everything okay in here?" the other woman's voice
asked.

Kate's golden-hued gaze held his for the span of
several heartbeats, and then she tugged free and turned
to the newcomer in the doorway behind her.

"Everything's fine, thanks, Laura," she said. "What can
I do to help?"

The woman named Laura paused, then took up her
place on the other side of the bed again. Avoiding Jonas's
eyes, she pushed back the blanket to expose his leg.

"Hold his leg steady," she said. "The local's going to be
wearing off, and I don't have more. This is going to hurt."

A strong hand settled on his knee. A second hand
closed around his fingers and lightly squeezed. *I'm here,*
it seemed to say. *Hang in there.*

Jonas flashed a glance upward, looking for more.
Hoping against hope for understanding, or even hesitation. But despite her gentleness, Kate was as unsmiling as
her sister, and just as determined to avoid his eyes. His
words hadn't convinced her. Hadn't even moved her. She
would turn him in as soon as she could, and he couldn't
blame her. Anyone in her shoes would do the same thing.

Laura began flushing saline into the hole in his leg,
and a massive wave of agony slammed into him. He met
it head on, letting it carry him on its crest and then pitch
him into the blackness that waited.

* * *

Please. The word wouldn't leave Kate alone, whispering itself into her ear over and over again as she watched Laura work. She didn't think it was a word he used often, this powerful man laid low. That made its impact all the greater. All the more difficult to ignore. She sighed.

"You doing okay?" Laura flashed her a quick look. "You're not going to pass out on me or anything, are you?"

Kate snorted. "Not likely. I've seen way worse than this."

Laura sent another wash of saline over the wound she treated. "You never talk about any of it. Your job, I mean. I don't think I know what it is you even do. Or how you got that." She jutted her chin toward Kate's shoulder.

"Do you really want to know?" Kate asked dryly.

Laura grimaced. "Maybe not about that. But other stuff. You know, when you've had a hard day, or something's gone wrong."

How about when I have a gun tucked against my spine because I'm worried that I've put you in danger?

Kate shifted to relieve the pressure at her back, rethinking having left her shoulder holster upstairs. Tucking the pistol into her jeans might have been more discreet, but it was damned uncomfortable.

"You're a little too far away for me to be dropping in for coffee at the end of a shift," she pointed out.

"I suppose. But still. You know you can call, right? If you need to. Anytime. Especially now that..."

Laura trailed off, but the unspoken end to her sentence hung in the air between them just the same. The empty air, devoid of the presences that had always been a part of this house.

Now that Mom and Dad are gone.

Kate studied her sister's bent head, knowing Laura's words had little to do with a sudden interest in her career. Laura had always been closer to their parents than she had. Choosing a profession they considered suitable, marrying, bearing them two perfect grandchildren, staying close. She'd been everything to them that Kate had failed at, and the hole in Laura's life left by their deaths would be so much greater.

Kate lifted her hand from the muscled thigh and reached across the bed to touch her sister's shoulder. "I know," she said. "And I will. In fact, I'll call once a week, how's that? On Sunday nights, after the kids are in bed."

Laura sniffled and took a long, shaky breath. She nodded. "Good. So. Change of topic. You looked pretty intense when I came back in here. What were you two talking about?"

As she spoke, she lifted the unconscious man's leg and tugged the sodden towels from under it. They landed in a heap on the floor beside the jeans and T-shirt she'd cut from him earlier, and Kate made a mental note to bag the clothes for evidence when they were done. She could check for ID while she was at it, seeing as how she'd somehow overlooked asking him for a name.

Stellar police work, that.

Laura raised an eyebrow. "Kate? What were you talking about?"

"Whether or not I should call the OPP."

Her sister's hands stilled in their unraveling of a length of gauze. She stared at Kate. "I'm sorry, but how is that even a question? You're not actually considering *not* calling, are you?"

Strong fingers twitched in Kate's grasp, and she shot a look at their patient's face. A sliver of unflinching blue looked back at her from beneath not-quite closed eyelids. They stared at one another, each silently challenging the other, and then she turned her attention back to Laura.

"Of course not," she said. "I'll call as soon as the phone lines are back up."

The hand beneath hers curled into a fist. Then, with no more warning than that, their patient swung his legs over the edge of the bed toward her and lurched to his feet. Laura's startled shriek was drowned out by a groan that sounded like it had been ripped from the depths of his soul. His legs collapsed beneath him.

Without thinking, Kate caught him around the waist, straining to hold him upright. A knife edge of pain screamed through her shoulder. Her own legs gave way beneath the two of them, and with a grunt, she lurched forward.

FIVE

"**O**h God! Katie, are you all right? Kate? Talk to me, damn it! Oh, please don't tell me you've passed out, too!"

It took Kate a second to realize she'd managed to land them on the bed. Another second for Laura's frantic voice to penetrate the haze of pain radiating from her shoulder. And several more to become fully aware of the awkward-ness—no, the sheer *wrongness*—of her current position on the bed.

Their incapacitated guest was lying atop her. His nose was smooshed against the curve of her right breast, his nude body pressed against her length, and one of his legs had found its way between hers so that her thigh cush-ioned his...

Well.

Kate's face flamed.

"I'm fine," she growled at her sister, fighting her way out from under the weight holding her against the mattress.

"Stop!" Laura squealed.

Kate froze in mid shove. "*What?*"

Their patient began sliding off the edge of the bed. Kate gritted her teeth and clutched him close.

"You're going to start the bleeding again," her sister said. "Just wait a second."

Laura grasped fistfuls of the bedspread and pulled it taut. "All right. Ease out from under him, but try to keep him from sliding any more. I'll pull him back onto the bed."

When their patient was secure once more, Kate picked herself up from the floor and rubbed her throbbing shoulder. A few more times rescuing this guy and the desk duty she'd been temporarily assigned to would become permanent. She glowered at the man on the bed. He was out cold. Or was he?

"Idiot," she muttered.

Not so much as a flinch rippled over his skin at the insult. Yup. Out cold, all right, because he was way too volatile not to react to that. She watched her sister fuss over the wounds that had started oozing again, careful to keep her attention on Laura's dark, bent head and not certain exposed anatomical features.

"Will he live?" she asked. As discreetly as she could, she reached back to shift her handgun over an inch or two in her jeans waistband, trying not to wince. Great. Now she was going to have a massively sore shoulder *and* a gun-shaped bruise in the small of her back.

Laura regarded her. "You sound as if you'd rather he didn't."

Kate sighed. "Of course not. I'm just pissed at him right now. I thought you said he wouldn't be able to get up."

"I didn't think he could." Laura turned her attention back to the torso hole, taping a bandage over it. "He has to be some determined to get out of here."

Please.

Kate shoved away the memory of his plea. She grimaced down at her shirt, streaked with dried mud and fresh blood. Her shoulder throbbed with a steady, teeth-on-edge ache.

"How bad is it?" Laura asked.

She didn't pretend not to understand. "On a scale of one to ten? About a twenty."

"I'm not surprised, after that wrestling match. I'll give you some of what I'm giving him when he wakes up. It'll help you sleep."

"Thanks, but no." Kate held up a hand to forestall the frown gathering on her sister's forehead. "I can't be out of commission tonight, Laura. Not with him in the house."

"You really think he's that much of a threat?"

"Honestly, no."

"Then who—" Laura broke off and swallowed. "The people who shot him."

Silence followed Kate's nod. Laura swallowed again, her gaze flicking to the window that overlooked the darkened barnyard beyond. Kate rounded the bed to give her a one-armed hug.

"I'm just being cautious," she said. "Besides, there's a tree blocking the only road, remember? No one's coming through tonight."

Laura's tense body didn't relax. Kate grinned and gave her a sisterly nudge with her good shoulder.

"Plus," she added, "there's a cop in the house."

An indrawn hiss of breath sounded from the bed. Kate looked over to find the man struggling to sit up, one hand clutching his side, the blanket Laura had pulled over him falling away from the spectacular chest once again. So he hadn't been unconscious after all. Damn, but this guy was good at playing dead.

Laura made to move toward him, but his outstretched

hand stopped her. Glittering, cold blue eyes fastened on Kate.

"How did you know?" he snarled.

Kate frowned. "How did I know what?"

"How did you know I—" He stopped, his expression giving way to sudden comprehension.

Down the hall in the kitchen, the phone rang.

For a moment, no one moved. Or spoke.

Kate stared at the furious man on the bed. Tension radiated from him, reminding her of a cornered animal. A cornered but still lethal animal.

The phone shrilled again.

Beside her, Laura shifted her feet. "I should..."

Her voice trailed off.

Another ring.

Without taking her eyes from the man, Kate stepped out of her sister's way.

"Go," she said, tipping her head toward the doorway.

The man's jaw clenched, whitening the lines around his mouth. His gaze darted from Kate and Laura to the doorway, then back again, measuring. Calculating. His mouth twisted. His shoulders slumped. Defeat replaced defiance as the phone rang a fourth and then a fifth time. Laura shoved the roll of gauze and scissors into Kate's hands and started for the doorway.

"Laura."

Kate's sister turned to her.

Please.

"Whoever it is, don't say anything about our guest."

"What? But—"

"Not yet."

Laura studied the man, then looked at Kate again. "You're sure?"

"I want to talk to him first."

Slowly, reluctantly, Laura nodded. After a last, lingering glance at the bed, she hurried down the hallway. A few seconds later, the murmur of her voice floated back to the room, and Kate turned her full attention to the man.

He'd pulled himself up in the bed to a half-sitting position, propped against the smooth wooden headboard. A sheen of sweat covered his torso from the effort, and his breathing sounded ragged. They stared at one another for a moment. He looked away.

"Thank you," he said.

"I wouldn't be too grateful just yet," Kate replied. "I'm a heartbeat away from changing my mind unless I get some answers. How did I know what?"

Blue swiveled back to her. Damn, but those eyes of his were intense. Especially when he glowered like that.

"How did you know where to find me? Did they send you?" he growled. He waved off her response before she could form one, and added in a mutter, "No. That doesn't make sense. If they'd sent you, you wouldn't have tried to save my life."

Tried to save his life? She was pretty sure she'd succeeded, given his level of combativeness, and what in hell was he rambling on about, anyway? Kate crossed her arms and took a deep breath, only to exhale again as footsteps in the hall heralded her sister's return.

Laura came into the room, her gaze going between them before settling on Kate. "That was Matt," she said. "Lainie Peterson tore open her forearm on some barbed wire when their cows got loose. The ambulance is already on a call, and it'll take hours to get another. I'm going to have to see her."

"What about the downed tree?"

"They've sent a crew out to open the road for me.

They were going to come here to pick me up, but the storm is easing up, and I said it would be faster if I drove. I wasn't sure—" Laura's gaze slid toward the bed.

"Good thinking," Kate said, although she almost wished her sister had done otherwise. At least then the decision about whether to keep her guest a secret would have been taken out of her hands. "Thank you."

Laura pursed her lips, doubt clouding her eyes, but she nodded and turned away to pack her bag, issuing a set of instructions as she did. "You'll need to finish bandaging his leg, and you'll have to change both dressings tomorrow morning. A little redness and swelling is normal, but—"

"Laura."

Her sister stopped. Looked at her. Sighed. "Of course. You know what to do."

She set a vial on the nightstand. "Painkillers. With codeine. There's enough for twenty-four hours for both of you. That's more than long enough to get him to the hospital he needs to be in."

Kate smiled. "Point taken."

"I hope so." Bag in hand, Laura faced her. "See me out?"

The words may have been framed as a request, but they carried the full force of an elder sister pulling rank. Kate paused only to shoot their patient a dark look.

"Stay," she said. "Because if you try getting up again, you'll be spending the night on that floor."

SIX

L aura led the way to the farmhouse's front door in silence. There, she held out her bag for Kate to hold while she put on her coat and rubber boots. Also in silence.

At last, lips pulled into a thin line and arms crossed, she turned. "Please tell me you know what you're doing."

Kate heaved a sigh. "I wish I could."

"You're not instilling me with confidence here. How am I supposed to leave you alone here with—with"—Laura waved a hand at the door down the hallway—"some criminal whose name I don't even know? What if he murders you in your sleep? I won't know who to blame!"

Kate's lips twitched, and her sister's scowl deepened.

"Don't you dare laugh at me, Katherine Anne Dexter! It's not funny, and I'm worried sick about you."

Handing back Laura's bag with one hand, Kate drew her in for a hug with the other.

"I'm sorry, and you're right. It's not funny. But I'll be fine, I promise. And I'm not saying I won't call the OPP. I'm just saying I want to hear what he has to say first."

"Shouldn't he be telling it to the police?"

Kate grinned. Laura swatted her arm.

"You know what I mean. Do you even have jurisdiction here?"

"Ish."

Her sister's eyebrows shot up. "Ish? What kind of answer is *ish*?"

"The simple version of the complex one."

Kate's sister regarded her for a long moment. Then she sighed. "You're not going to back down on this, are you?"

"Is he in danger of dying if he stays here?"

"No. I've cleaned the wounds and given him a shot of antibiotics. He just needs rest right now. He's strong."

I've noticed.

"Then no, I'm not backing down. I want to know his story before I hand him over."

"Fine." Laura tugged open the front door and stepped out onto the porch. "Have it your way. But keep in mind he's not worth risking your life for. *Or* your career. All right?"

Please. The single word whispered again through Kate's mind, even as she nodded. She didn't think her life was in danger, but she had to admit Laura made a good point about not jeopardizing her career because of a few sketchy details and a man with *dangerous* written all over him.

In neon.

"I'll remember," she said. "Drive carefully, sis, and watch the corner at the end of the drive. It was getting slippery when I came in."

"You have until morning before I call the cops," Laura replied over her shoulder as she descended the stairs. "You know...the ones who are *supposed* to be dealing with this." She pulled open the door of her Jeep, shoved her bag inside, and climbed into the driver's seat. "And for God's sake," she added, "ask the man his name!"

Kate waved her off, watching until the taillights disappeared down the drive and around the corner onto the road. Then she closed the door and turned to lean on it. Twenty feet away, the bedroom and its occupant waited. With a sigh, she pushed upright, adjusted the handgun at her back, and strode down the hall. Time for answers, whether her guest wanted to give them or not.

Staring at the ceiling, Jonas listened to the murmur of female voices floating through the door as he tried to regroup his thoughts. He'd damn near slipped up just now. Come within a heartbeat of letting on he was a cop, only to realize at the last instant that Kate had been speaking of herself.

There's a cop in the house.

Curly-haired, amber-eyed Kate was a cop.

A part of him actually wanted to laugh at the revelation, because what were the odds that Ramirez and Lewis would drop him in the backwoods of Canada somewhere and leave him for dead, and his rescuer would be a bloody *cop*? Jonas shifted his weight on the bed. Fire seared through his side. The leg wasn't so bad. More of a deep, mind-dulling ache than actual pain, as long as he didn't move it.

Except not moving it wasn't an option, because the idea that his would-be murderers might come back to check on their handiwork just wouldn't go away. And if they did, and he wasn't where they'd left him, they wouldn't leave so much as a blade of grass unturned until they found him.

And if they found him here, with Kate—

Jonas shuddered as an image sprang to mind of lifeless golden eyes in a waxen complexion. No. He wouldn't let that happen. If they had to catch up with him, fine. But they wouldn't catch up with him here.

Inch by inch, he fought his way upright through the swaths of agony until he sat on the edge of the bed, injured leg on fire and extended before him, sheet pulled across his midsection. He took a moment to catch his breath, then grabbed two of the tablets Laura had left behind on the nightstand. Downing them, he reached with trembling fingers to snag his soiled T-shirt from the floor.

The bedroom door opened.

"Seriously?" Kate marched across the room and snatched away the T-shirt. "I told you to—damn it, you're bleeding again!"

"Nothing I can't survive," he said. But the rawness of his voice belied his words, even to his own ears.

"Bullshit. Now do us both a favor and lie down, will you? I meant it when I said I can't pick you up off the floor again if you get into trouble."

Jonas caught Kate's hand in mid-air as it aimed for his shoulder. He held her wrist just tight enough to warn her not to try to break his grip, hoping she wouldn't feel the slight tremor in his touch. Wanting only to collapse onto his back again.

"Listen to me," he said. "I know you mean well, but you don't know these people. If they come after me, if they find me here—" He took a deep breath, trying to offset the weird spaciness claiming his brain. He forced himself to continue. "I don't want you to get hurt, Kate, and I can't protect you. Not like this."

Something in the golden gaze softened for a second, but it vanished again quickly.

"You heard the part about me being a cop, right? Believe me, I can look after myself."

That meant she was armed, or at least had a weapon in the house. His gaze skimmed the loose fit of her plaid shirt over jeans, but he detected no outline of a handgun beneath it. He gripped the slender wrist a little tighter, measuring her resistance. Wondering how far he'd get if he tried to overpower her. He could tie her up, maybe. Take her car keys...

"Wanna bet you wouldn't make it as far as the front door?"

"What?"

Gentle fingers pried his hand from her wrist with a demoralizing lack of effort.

"You're thinking of making a run for it. I'm advising you not to." Kate stooped to lift his leg and ease it back onto the bed, giving him no choice but to subside against the pillows. She placed a fresh bandage over his leg wound. "Here. You may as well give in gracefully and hold this."

"I don't do graceful," he muttered, but he put his hand over the bandage anyway, his fingers brushing hers.

"I noticed." She lifted the vial of pills from the night-stand. "Now, how many of these things do you want?"

"Enough to put me out of my misery?" he suggested. Irritably, he waved his free hand at her. "I already took two. I should probably quit at that."

Without comment, Kate set down the pills again and reached for a roll of first aid tape. She unrolled a strip as long as her forearm and clipped it off.

"You don't have to do that," he said. "I'm sure I can manage."

Her skeptical look made words unnecessary. Jonas flinched as she settled the tape along one edge of the bandage he held. Her touch set off an excruciating rever-beration in the otherwise steady throb of pain. He closed his eyes to mere slits, hiding his weakness from her. Kate wrapped the tape around the leg and smoothed it into place. A tingle ran down his thigh that had nothing to do with pain. His eyes shot open again.

Well. That certainly distracted from the discomfort.

Kate snipped off another piece of tape and laid it against his skin. He waited—half in dread, half in anticipation—for the touch of her fingers to follow.

"So," she said. "Do I get a name?"

She moved his hand away from the bandage.

"I'll make it easier," she said when he didn't answer. "I'm Kate Dexter."

He jerked his attention away from the fingers stroking the tape onto his thigh. Swallowed. "Burke," he said, his voice somewhat strangled. "Jonas Burke."

She regarded him. "Actual or alias?" she asked at last.

"Actual."

She nodded, then regarded her handiwork with a grimace. "Hardly as professional as Laura's work, but it should stay on. At least for the night."

"Thanks," he said.

"You're welcome." Kate placed the tape back on the desk. "Now then, Jonas Burke, I'm going to get a bowl of water and a washcloth to clean you up a bit. Can I trust you to stay put this time?"

He knew what she was doing. It was a classic interrogation technique. Build rapport. Do something nice for the interviewee. Get them thinking you're on their side. That you're there to help them.

He knew it, but with the codeine kicking in and the memory of those hands trailing across his thigh, he didn't seem to be able to care as much as he should. He sighed.

"I'll be here."

SEVEN

When Kate returned to the room, Jonas Burke remained where she'd left him on the bed. In fact, from the way he startled when she opened the door, he appeared to have dozed off in her absence. Good. Between blood loss and painkillers, maybe he'd pass out for the night and not make any more boneheaded attempts to leave.

Because between exhaustion and a throbbing shoulder that demanded painkillers of its own, she was no longer sure she could stay awake to stop him.

She set the bowl of warm, soapy water on the nightstand as Jonas struggled upright against the pillows. He took the washcloth she offered and, in silence, rubbed it over his face, leaving streaks of mud in its wake. His gaze drifted in and out of focus as he blinked at her warily.

"I know better than to think you've given up on the questions," he said at last. "What gives?"

Kate gave a short, mirthless laugh. "To be honest? I don't think I'm up to an interrogation any more than you are tonight. We'll leave it until morning."

He swiped randomly at his chest. "And if I leave in the meantime?"

She frowned at the tremble in his hand, her mouth

tightening. Even when he managed to make a connection between cloth and skin, all he did was rearrange the dirt.

"Here," she said. "Let me."

She took the cloth from him, rinsed it, and began sponging the crusted mud from his face. He stiffened for an instant, then his eyes closed and he subsided with a sigh. Kate moved from forehead to cheeks, nose, mouth, chin. His warm breath caressed the back of her hand. She swirled the dirty cloth through the warm water again. Then she hesitated, surveying the broad shoulders and muscled chest that came next. Remembered that moment of feminine interest when she'd walked into the room to find Laura had stripped him naked. Swallowed.

His eyes opened. "Is something wrong?"

Kate's cheeks warmed. "No. Of course not."

She tore her gaze from his and scrubbed at his left shoulder.

"Easy does it," he muttered. "I don't think you're supposed to remove the skin."

Teeth gritted, she eased up on the pressure and coached herself through the steps. *One shoulder done. Rinse the cloth. Wash the other. Rinse again. Chest next.*

Crisp, dark hairs tickled her fingers.

Hell.

Despite her best efforts, her gaze flicked up to his. Glittering blue eyes watching her from beneath half-closed lids, their slow smolder unmistakable. She scowled in return and bit down on the inside of her bottom lip to distract her brain.

Rigidly, methodically, she rinsed the cloth and jabbed it at his eight-pack, trying without success to keep her fingers from brushing the hairs that traveled in a narrow line out of sight under the comforter. Trying with even less success not to notice that this hair was softer than it was on his chest.

Silkier.

She slopped the cloth back into the bowl. Dear lord, what was the matter with her? This was insanity. Despite his assurances to the contrary, he was still a potential threat, and she had no business getting adolescent kicks out of sponging him down. Gritting her teeth, she wrung out the washcloth. She could handle this. She just had his legs left to do, and then—

Strong, tanned fingers closed around her wrist.

"Maybe you should leave the rest," Jonas suggested, his voice husky.

Kate's eyes dropped involuntarily to the sheet covering his lower anatomy. Heat crawled up from beneath her collarbone to scorch her cheeks. *Damn.*

It appeared that painkillers and blood loss hadn't put him entirely out of commission.

She jerked her gaze away and grabbed the bowl, sloshing water over nightstand and floor alike. Ignoring the puddles and shoving aside the melty female part of her, she drew on the tough-as-nails cop she knew herself to be...even if she still couldn't make herself meet his eyes.

"I'll leave your door open," she said briskly. "If you need anything, shout. I'll be on the couch for the night."

"Which is between me and the front door, I'm guessing."

"Close enough that I'll hear you, yes."

"Or anyone who tries to come in?" His eyes drifted closed as shock, exhaustion, and medication took their toll.

"That, too." She moved the vial of pills to within his reach, debating the wisdom of helping herself to them as well, then deciding against it. She'd get by on ibuprofen. Just in case.

"I'll leave the painkillers here in case you need them," she said. "You decide how many you need, but try not to overdo it. I don't think Laura would look kindly on having to come back here for a drug overdose."

"I don't think your sister looks kindly on me at all," he mumbled.

A smile tugged at the corner of Kate's mouth. She turned away. "Get some sleep. You need it."

She made it as far as the door when his voice stopped her. Exhaustion still slurred his words, but there was no mistaking the edge to them.

"Kate, I wasn't kidding about them being dangerous."

She hesitated. *Who?* she wanted to ask him. *Tell me.* But his breathing was already deepening, becoming rhythmic. Her questions would have to wait until morning.

She stood for a moment, watching him sleep, remembering the quiet desperation in his blue eyes. Whoever he was, whatever he was hiding from her, that desperation had been real. She'd stake her career on it. Hell, by not calling the OPP right this instant, she *was* staking her career on it.

"You'd better have one hell of a good story, Jonas Burke," she growled under her breath.

Then she flicked off the light switch and left the room.

Kate roused groggily to a serious crick in her neck and sunshine streaming through the living room window. She frowned about both, then about the hard lump digging into the small of her back. Wincing at the stiffness of her shoulder, she wiggled her fingers between herself and the cushions, her frown deepening to a scowl when she found her pistol there. Why on earth was she on the couch with her—

She bounded upright as the events of the night before flooded back. The accident. Jonas. Bullet holes. Questions. So many questions. She'd meant to stay awake, to make sure no one came looking for him—and that he didn't walk out on her. Had he...?

She listened to the farmhouse, but it sat silent. Too silent?

Rubbing at the deep, unhappy ache in her shoulder, she forced her brain into gear. How soundly had she slept? Could Jonas have slipped by her? The door...had she turned the deadbolt?

A half-dozen strides carried her into the cramped front entry. The deadbolt sat in its locked position, a quiet assurance that no one had left the house—and that no one had come in. At least not through this entrance. Kate turned her head to look over her shoulder. The bedroom door at the end of the hall sat open at the same angle she'd left it last night.

So. He was still in there, was he? The man with prison tats and two gunshot wounds, who wanted her to believe his life was in danger from her own colleagues. In the cold light of day, her indecision of the previous night seemed ludicrous at best. What had she been thinking? Not reporting Jonas to the OPP constituted interference with another police force. At the very least, her actions—or lack thereof—would net her a serious reprimand on her file if they were discovered. And the longer she waited, the worse it would get.

She scowled at the door.

Her feet remained rooted to the floor.

If the phone in the kitchen hadn't rung just then, she

might have remained there all morning. As it was, she managed to grab the receiver from the cradle in the middle of its second ring, easing the swinging kitchen door closed behind her.

"Hello?"

"Oh, thank God! You're still alive."

Kate grinned at the heartfelt relief in her sister's voice. "You were expecting otherwise?"

"I didn't know what to expect under the circumstances," Laura grumbled. "Did he behave himself?"

Heat flared in Kate's cheeks, and her jaw dropped. How had Laura known—

She realized her sister referred to Jonas's attempts to get out of bed, and not the sponge bath incident. She put her free hand up to cover her eyes, shoving away the images of broad shoulders, powerful arms, and a trail of downy hair disappearing under the sheets. Good lord, what had gotten into her?

"Kate?" Laura prompted.

"Of course," she croaked. "Everything is fine. Jonas took the painkillers after you left, and he's still sleeping."

"Jonas—that's his name? Did you find out anything else?"

"Not yet."

"Damn it, this is dragging on too long, Katie. You should have called the police last night. The longer you wait—"

"I *know*, Laura."

Silence. Guilt stabbed at Kate.

"I'm sorry. I shouldn't have snapped like that."

"I'm worried about you, Katie. Blurring the lines like this—it's not like you. I may not know much about your job, but I do know you take it seriously enough to be professional about it."

"I know. I just—" Kate broke off. She just what? Got sidelined by a pair of shocking blue eyes and a rugged physique? No. That wasn't it at all. Understanding slithered through her and settled in her belly, its presence cold and sobering.

It wasn't Jonas's blue eyes at all, but what she'd seen in them. The shocked vulnerability of someone who'd come face to face with his own mortality. She knew the look. Had faced it in the mirror herself, along with the inherent terror that underlined it. And because almost dying once was freaking bad enough, she wanted to make bloody sure she wasn't responsible for someone taking another crack at him.

"I'll call them," she said. "As soon as I've spoken to him. I promise."

If I think it's safe.

"Kate—"

"Let me do this my way, Laura. Please."

Please. Jonas's voice echoed in her head. She pinched the bridge of her nose and closed her eyes.

"Fine," Laura huffed. "Look, I have to run. Erin has soccer practice this morning, if the field isn't under a foot of water. Call me later, okay? After the cops pick him up."

Kate said goodbye to her sister, then replaced the receiver in its cradle. She turned to lean her back against the familiar, ivy-papered wall, studying the farm kitchen. It looked exactly as it always had. Unchanged. Unchanging. The one part of home she'd always relied on to be there for her with its soft, south-facing light, its bottomless pot of coffee, and its endless supply of cookies that had awaited her and Laura when they'd trooped in from school.

Even in her later years—the ones where home hadn't felt like home anymore because of the constant friction between her and her parents—the kitchen had somehow been there for her until she'd finally stopped coming back.

And now...now it stood empty. Devoid of her parents. Devoid of any lingering warmth she remembered. Devoid of everything except...that.

Her gaze fell on the mud- and blood-encrusted pile of clothing on the counter by the sink, starkly out of place in the immaculate room. Her mouth pulled tight. If her mother were still alive, she'd tear a strip three feet wide off Kate's hide for sullying her domain in such a way. The kitchen had been the one place on the farm where dirt had simply not been tolerated.

Rain, snow, or shine, hands were washed at the tap in the barn and boots came off in the enclosed back porch, and woe betide the child—or man—who claimed to have forgotten. A half-smile formed at the memory of her mother tying into her father the time he'd dared bring a piglet, the runt of the litter, into the kitchen for extra care. He'd never repeated the mistake. And her mother had spent the next three nights in the enclosed back porch with a space heater, bottle-feeding the piglet every two hours until it gained enough strength to be returned to its litter.

Guilt prodded Kate into detaching from the wall. She retrieved a paper grocery bag from the space between counter and fridge. Her mother had eschewed all things plastic at the farm, and the clothes had been too wet to bag in paper last night, but they should have dried a bit by now. She shook the bag open and picked up Jonas's T-shirt, grimacing at the clammy feel. After the deluge he'd been through, it was unlikely forensics would find much in the way of evidence on anything, but holding onto them would be expected.

Of course, so would notifying the OPP.

Jonas Burke's story had better be worth the fallout she risked from this. She sighed and shoved the T-shirt into the bag, then lifted the blue jeans Laura had sliced away from their injured guest. A wadded-up paper dropped from the folds onto the counter.

EIGHT

Well. How interesting.

Kate studied the paper she'd coaxed open. It was wrinkled and damp, and the blue ink was smeared, but the phone number was still legible. And it wasn't a local one.

She shot a glance at the kitchen door, then crossed the room and picked up the phone's receiver from its wall cradle again. Given Jonas's reticence the night before, she wasn't expecting much in the way of cooperation from him this morning, either. If she could find out who was at the other end of this number before she spoke to him, however, it might shake a few answers loose.

She jabbed the star button followed by the code needed to block her caller ID, then punched in the phone number from the paper.

A clipped male voice answered on the second ring. "Yeah."

Hardly an informative beginning.

"Can you tell me if I've reached the right number?" Kate rattled off the number she'd just dialed. She walked across the room to the windows overlooking the drive-way, phone cord stretched taut.

"That's it. Who's this?"

Give her name to a possible murderer? Not.

"I'd like to know who I've reached first, please." She toyed with the damp paper, not really expecting an answer, debating how she could officially-slash-unofficially have the number traced. If only her parents had believed in the Internet. Or computers. Or technology of any—

"How did you get this number?" the voice at the other end demanded. A flurry of activity sounded in the background, followed a click as someone else came on the line.

"Who—" Kate broke off as the kitchen door crashed open behind her.

Furious blue eyes glittered from a face stark with pain. Clad only in a towel wrapped around his waist and swaying on his feet, Jonas ground out, "Hang up."

Kate dropped the paper and reached behind her. Her fingers closed over the pistol grip. Then she gaped at the phone—at what the voice at the other end had just said. Or what she thought it had said.

"What?" she asked. "Could you repeat that, please?"

"I said you've reached the ATF, lady, and this is no time for goddamn games. I want to know how you got this number."

"ATF," she echoed. "As in the Bureau of Alcohol, Tobacco, Firearms and—"

"Hang up, damn it!" Jonas roared. "Now!"

He lurched toward her, staggered against the edge of the table, almost fell. Reflexively, Kate took her hand from the pistol and leapt forward to steady him, but Jonas shoved her aside and levered himself upright again. He ripped the telephone away from her and put the receiver to his ear, muffling the unintelligible shouting emanating from it. His flint-like gaze didn't so much as flicker when Kate leveled her gun at him.

"Go to hell, Lewis," he snarled into the receiver, and then he slammed the receiver into its cradle.

Kate's heartbeat hammered in her ears and the pistol grip bit into her hand as she stared at him. Breathing harshly, he stared back. The yellow, teapot-shaped clock on the ivy wall ticked off the seconds.

What the *hell* had that been?

Her guest's face paled to a ghastly shade of gray, verging on linen-white. He put a hand out to the wall for support. Kate hardened herself against the sympathy that threatened once more to overcome her good sense. She had to draw the line somewhere, and her parents' kitchen seemed a good place to start.

Jonas pointed at the paper she'd dropped. The towel wrapped around his waist slipped a fraction. "You found that in my clothes?"

She nodded.

"Figures. They'd want to know when my body surfaced."

She shook her head, trying to make sense of his words. Failing. "That number is for the ATF."

"I know."

"You said you weren't a criminal."

"I'm not."

"An informant, then?" she hazarded.

"No." He reached to pull a chair out from the table, nodding at the gun trained on him. "You may as well put that away. I think I've used up my quota of fast moves for a while."

He sank with a grimace onto the sturdy maple, letting out a soft hiss of air. Kate hesitated, then lowered her weapon, accepting the truth of his words. The man looked like he might pass out any second. Size and conditioning aside, he posed no immediate threat, and they both knew it. But she kept the gun out anyway, setting it on the table and resting her hand atop it as she sat across from him.

She regarded him in silence, rolling her shoulder to ease the ache in it. Jonas wasn't the only one who'd used up his quota of fast moves for a while. The object of her thoughts jutted his chin toward her.

"You do that a lot," he said. "Injury?"

Kate stiffened, disinclined to reveal any weakness to this man. "It's nothing," she said. "I pulled it getting you into the car last night, that's all." Abruptly, she changed the subject. "So if you're not a criminal, and you're not an informant, who are you? And what the hell is your connection to the ATF?"

"You're not going to let this go, are you?" he growled. "No matter how dangerous I tell you it is."

"Not a chance."

Jonas rested his elbows on the polished wood surface and dropped his head into his hands. Fingers raked through thick, dark hair. Bare, muscled shoulders sagged.

"Bloody hell," he muttered.

She waited.

"Bloody, bloody hell." He lifted his face from his hands. Haggard eyes met hers. "My name is *Agent* Jonas Burke, Kate, and that was my office you just called."

Kate blinked at him, uncomprehending. She hadn't known what to expect, but this? This was so far from the realm of any possibility she might have imagined that she couldn't even wrap her head around it.

"Did you hear me?"

She tightened her grip on the gun, giving herself a mental shake. He was lying. Of course he was lying.

"I heard you. I just don't believe you. If you're with the ATF, then why would those guys"—she nodded toward the phone on the wall behind him—"want to know when your body surfaced?"

The blue gaze turned flat. "You know why."

She shook her head. "You've got to be kidding. You really expect me to believe—"

The crunch of tires on gravel sounded outside the kitchen window. Jonas went the color of the bandage taped below his ribs, and Kate's heart took up residence in her throat. Gun in hand, she thrust back from the table and hurried to the window. Holding aside the flowered curtain panel, she looked out into the yard as an OPP cruiser pulled up between her sedan and the family station wagon.

Everything in her froze.

From behind her came the scrape of a chair against the floor.

"Who is it?" Jonas demanded.

She watched the cruiser without answering. No one had stepped out yet. Why? Were they here for Jonas? Her? Had they traced the call she'd made already? No. They couldn't have. Then how—

Laura. It had to have been Laura. Hell.

"Damn it, Kate, *who is it?*"

She hesitated, torn. Jonas was lying. He had to be lying. But what if he wasn't? She dropped the curtain into place and tucked the gun into the back of her waistband again.

"It's the OPP," she said curtly, striding across the room toward the door to the hallway. "I'll be back in a minute."

Jonas let her pass, but his voice stopped her halfway into the hall. "Kate."

She didn't look back.

"I'm telling the truth," he said.

The damp chill of the post-storm morning crawled

under her shirt as she stepped out onto the front porch and closed the front door behind her. She shivered and crossed her arms. Hesitated. Should she wait for whoever was in the cruiser to get out and come to her, or was it better to go to him/her? The pistol in the small of her back felt conspicuously huge. If it was noticed, there would be raised eyebrows. Questions.

But better that than leaving it in the house with the man who'd just made those outrageous claims.

Surreptitiously, she wiped sweaty palms against her jeans.

Pull it together, Dexter.

Relaxing her face into what, with luck, would pass for something resembling a smile, she walked down the stairs and crossed the drive to the police car. Was Jonas watching from the kitchen window? If whoever was in the cruiser looked that way, would they see him? Did she want them to?

A gust of wind lifted the back of her shirt, snagging it on the grip of her pistol. She tugged it back into place. A sandy-haired, square-jawed man watched her from behind the steering wheel of the police car as she approached, grinning through the open passenger window. Recognition sparked in Kate.

"Well, I'll be. Scott Dunham," Kate said. "It's been what, ten years? What are you doing way out here? I thought you were posted on the other side of White-haven." She braced her hands against the car door and leaned down as if she hadn't a care in the world.

Or a possible felon in the house behind her.

"I'm filling in for someone for a couple of weeks. Heard you were in the area, so I thought I'd swing by and say hello." Her high school classmate reached over to place his hand over hers, squeezing gently. "I was sorry to hear about your folks, Kate. I know you weren't close, but I'm sure it's still tough."

"Thanks." Kate patted his hand in return, trying to appear suitably solemn even as relief gusted through her. Laura hadn't given her away after all. Thank heaven. "I think it's harder on Laura because she used to see them almost every day."

"I can imagine. Anything I can do to help?"

Leave! Kate's inner voice screamed at him. She shook her head. "Not really, but thank you for the offer."

To her relief, Scott changed the topic. "You going to be staying much longer? We should get together for dinner one night. Get caught up. Swap war stories."

Kate chuckled. "As tempting as that sounds, I'm heading back to Ottawa tomorrow. But Laura and I are nowhere near done clearing up the house, so I'll probably be back down in a couple of weeks. Can I take a rain check?"

"Of course. Give me a shout when you're back, and we'll set something up." He turned down the volume on his police radio as another car called in a traffic stop to dispatch. "I'd invite myself in for coffee, but I need to get back on the road. Just so you know, we're looking for a guy in the area right now, possibly armed and dangerous. Keep an eye out and be careful, all right?"

"Oh? Who is he?" Kate kept her voice casual, no small feat given her racing heart and constricted breathing.

"Jonas Burke. Six-two, two-twenty, thirty-four years old, dark hair, blue eyes."

"What's he wanted for?"

"Get this, the guy's a rogue agent from the ATF. He killed one of their targets and made off with one point five million a few days ago. We had a 'be on lookout' issued in the region yesterday, and I just got word that he called one of their offices from our area code this morning. They're running a trace, but he blocked the number, so it could take a while."

Shock held Kate's mind immobile for an instant as Scott rambled on to comment first about the nerve of the guy, then about dirty cops in general. Then the questions started forming, coming at her as fast as her brain could jump from one possibility to another.

Jonas had told the truth. He really was with the ATF. But theft...and murder? As jaded as her cop brain was, he didn't seem the type. And how had he gotten shot? His colleagues, as he claimed? By why? Unless he really had gone rogue. Maybe they'd caught him in the act...but no, Scott would have said something about him being wounded.

Maybe Jonas had a partner in crime and there had been a falling out. But if he had so much to hide, why give her his real name?

And why hadn't the ATF told the locals about the female who had made that call in the first place?

Suddenly, her brain zeroed back in on Scott's words.

"—agents up to help with the search," he said.

"Pardon?" Her voice was sharper than intended, and Scott raised a brow. She gave him an apologetic smile. "Sorry, I didn't hear that last bit."

"I said the ATF's sending a couple of agents up to help with the search." He rolled his eyes. "Even with all the roadblocks we've got going, apparently they don't trust us rural types to do our job."

Kate's blood chilled in her veins, and she flicked a glance down the drive, half expecting to see another cruiser—or, worse yet, a nondescript sedan—turning in from the road. Any relief at finding the driveway empty was tempered by a nagging urgency.

Something wasn't right. U.S. agents to help with a search in Canada? No. That didn't happen. Not unless Jonas had told her more of the truth than she'd wanted to hear.

She dropped her hands and stepped back from Scott's cruiser. "I won't keep you," she said. The sensation of being watched prickled over the back of her neck. *Don't look at the house. Don't give him away.* "Take care of yourself, and I'll call you a couple of days before I head back down this way."

"Sounds good." Scott put his vehicle into gear. "Safe drive home tomorrow."

NINE

K ate held herself still, willing herself not to bolt for the stairs as Scott did a three-point turn around the back end of the station wagon and, with an excruciating lack of hurry, drove down the driveway. He braked at the corner by the pond and waved a hand out the window, then—finally—disappeared behind the trees lining the road.

Kate's knees sagged. She wrapped her arms around herself and thought about the man hiding in the house. About how she'd just committed a full-blown crime by not telling Scott he was there. About how she might have just pulled the plug on a rather stellar thirteen-year career.

And for what? A hunch? A stranger's plea?

Turning, she stared at the kitchen window. At the flowered curtain panel held ever so slightly to one side. Slow seconds ticked by. The curtain dropped back into place. Kate exhaled slowly and walked across the driveway and up the stairs, her booted feet thudding hollowly against the wood. She pushed into the house and came nose-to-chin with a waiting Jonas.

"Well?" he demanded. "Was he here looking for me?"

She tried to sidestep around the still mostly naked man, but instead stumbled over a pair of shoes and rammed the side of her head into a coat hook. Rubbing the lump, she favored him with a sour look. Had the front entry always felt this small? And couldn't he have wrapped up in a blanket rather than a towel?

"Unless you have a six-foot-two, two-hundred-and-twenty-pound, dark-haired, blue-eyed twin wandering around the countryside," she retorted, "then yes. I'm pretty sure he was here looking for you."

Which still felt all shades of wrong, because there was no way Jonas Burke could have done what they'd accused him of. She'd been a cop for thirteen years. Interrogated dozens of suspects. Surely she would know if something was hinky here. Surely her instincts would be at least *hinting* that he couldn't be trusted.

Because if Jonas wasn't lying...

Jonas's eyes turned bleak in a face made pasty by pain. He swayed on his feet and rested a hand against the wall to steady himself. Bulging bicep and corded forearm alike quivered with the effort.

"Why didn't you turn me in?"

If he was telling the truth...

God. Her brain hurt just considering the possibility. She scowled at him. "Where's the money?"

He narrowed his eyes. "What money?"

"Don't play games with me, Burke. You're in no position."

His gaze didn't waver. "No games," he replied. "You have my word. What money?"

Kate stared at him for a long moment, her gut churning in sympathy with her thoughts. It would have been so much easier if she didn't believe him. Easier yet if she hadn't made that damned phone call in the first place.

But she did.

And she had.

And now she'd landed herself in the middle of a mess she didn't know how to begin solving. All she knew was that here and now weren't the place and time to figure it out. Not where they could be interrupted at any second and she'd have to start doing some interesting explaining. Not when her personal opinions regarding Jonas's guilt or innocence would mean squat to the powers that be.

Because she very much doubted those powers would make it past the aiding and abetting part.

"I'll find you something to wear," she said. She pushed past Jonas, gritting her teeth against the heated brush of bare skin that burned through her sleeve and imprinted on her arm.

"And then?" he called after her as she stomped up the stairs toward her parents' bedroom and the bags of clothes waiting to be donated.

She didn't answer.

She didn't have an answer.

Fifteen minutes later, dressed in a shirt that strained across his chest and sweatpants that left his ankles feeling distinctly drafty, Jonas stared at the car trunk Kate had lined with blankets—her answer to getting him through the roadblocks she'd told him about. He shook his head.

"I can't ask you to do this."

"You didn't."

"If they search the vehicle—"

"I'll flash my ID. Once they know I'm a cop, they won't search."

"And if they have a dog?"

Kate's lips tightened. Her hands became fists, one resting on a hip, the other on her sidearm in the holster she'd donned. She said nothing.

Jonas made no move to get in with the blankets. "I won't put your career in jeopardy. I'll find another way."

"How?" she snapped. "By sprouting wings?"

Frustration gnawed at his belly, right alongside the fire of his wound. She was right. He'd never make it through the roadblocks on his own, and he wasn't equipped—or in any condition—to strike out by himself in the woods at this time of year. Like it or not, he was at the mercy of this not-altogether-merciful fellow cop.

Kate flipped unruly blond curls over one shoulder. "Whether or not I'm here when they trace that number, I'm screwed. So the way I see it, we have two possible courses of action here. One, I can give you the benefit of the doubt and get you past those roadblocks before your friends come looking for you. Or two, I can drive away and leave you to fend for yourself. What's it going to be?"

Jonas stared into the trunk. So much at stake. So few alternatives. Such a goddamn *mess*.

A hand settled on his arm. He looked down and side-ways into a golden gaze that was equal parts worried and determined.

"If you're telling the truth and you stay," Kate said, "you're a dead man. Let's at least get you out of here so we can figure out your next move."

If you're telling the truth. Jonas tamped down a surge of disappointment at her words, twisting it into irritation instead. Whether Kate Dexter believed him or not didn't matter, because there was no *we*. There had never been a *we* in his entire life, and there never would be, especially if it came with this overwhelming sense of responsibility for someone.

"I'll let you get me past the roadblocks," he said at last, "but that's it. Your involvement ends there, and I go my own way. Even if they trace the number here, you'll still have plausible deniability. You were out at the barn, asleep, in the shower...I don't care what you tell them. All that matters is that you didn't hear me come into the house or make the call. You never saw me, understand?"

One fair eyebrow arched high. "You're kidding me."

He shifted his stance to hide his increasing unsteadiness. Damn. If he didn't sit down soon, he'd fall down. "I don't follow."

Kate didn't immediately respond. Instead, she went around to the car's back seat and pulled out another blanket. When she returned, her face was set and her eyes implacable.

"First of all, I spoke to whoever was on the other end myself, remember? And second of all, not turning you in makes me responsible for whatever happens next, Agent Burke. So until I know exactly what's going on, there is no way in hell I am turning you loose on your own. And because I have no intention of standing around debating the issue, I suggest you get your butt in there"—she pointed at the open trunk—"so we can leave. Unless, of course, you have any better ideas."

Iron-jawed and out of arguments, Jonas folded himself into the barely adequate space of the sedan's trunk. The blanket Kate had retrieved followed him in.

He spread it over himself, then looked up at her. Sunlight framed her head, turning blond curls into a halo at odds with the hardness of her gaze.

"You might want to take another of those painkillers Laura gave you," she said. "There's eleven kilometers of gravel before we hit pavement."

The trunk lid slammed shut.

TEN

I t was a measure of Kate's resentment that she felt no remorse jolting over the potholes left by the previous night's storm. If only Jonas had come clean the night before and told her about being with the ATF, they might have avoided all of—

She sighed and rubbed her shoulder. Who was she trying to kid? They would have avoided nothing, because she wouldn't have believed him, and when she'd found that paper this morning, she still would have made that phone call. Because no matter how much his *please* might have resonated with her, she was still a cop.

For now.

And she still resented the hell out of this whole situation.

But half an hour later, as she sat in a line of cars waiting to go through the roadblock, remorse had not only surfaced, it had blossomed into full-fledged guilt. Tinged with panic. She glanced at her watch for what seemed the hundredth time in the last three minutes. How long could an injured man survive locked in a car trunk, anyway?

Visions of finding an expired Jonas Burke wrapped in blankets danced through her head. If she thought aiding and abetting were bad, try explaining a dead body to her boss. Her gut churned at the idea.

She drummed impatient fingers against the steering wheel. Ahead of her, the OPP roadblock had a van and two semis pulled over for a cursory search. Behind her, a line-up of another dozen cars stretched back. More precious seconds ticked by.

At last the car ahead pulled away, and the OPP constable waved Kate forward in the line. She flipped open her ID and pulled abreast of the female officer, who leaned down to smile at her.

"Good morning, ma'am. Can I ask where you're heading today?"

"Ottawa," Kate replied equably, handing over the ID. "Back to work."

The cop's eyes scanned Kate's badge and ID card. She handed them back. "I have a brother in the RCMP," she said. "He tried to talk me into joining, too, but I wanted to stay closer to home. He ended up posted out in B.C."

Movement at the side of the road ahead caught Kate's attention as a police dog jumped down from the back of one of the semis, followed by its handler. Oh, hell. If they walked back this way...

"That is one of the pitfalls," she agreed, slipping the ID back into her bag on the seat beside her and watching the dog from the corner of her eye. "So, no sign of him yet?"

The best defense, she thought. And the best way to hurry things along, she hoped. The OPP officer looked surprised, and Kate added, "Scott Dunham dropped by my parents' place to let me know what was going on."

"Ah." Implicit trust warmed the other cop's smile, and Kate quashed a wave of guilt. The cop shook her head.

"No, no sign of him yet. They think he may have had an accomplice who helped him get out of the area."

And when they traced the number and paid a visit to the house, there would be no doubt as to who that accomplice was. Shit. Kate's fingers tightened on the steering wheel. Why hadn't she thought to cover her tracks better at the house? To remove the evidence of Jonas's stay there—or at least her part in it.

She scowled. Why? Probably because she wasn't used to being on the evidence-hiding side of the law, that's why. But with luck, she could still make things look different than they had when she'd left the house.

"Well," she said to the OPP officer, "good luck finding him. You have a lot of territory to cover."

"Tell me about it." The cop stepped back from the car. "Have a good day, Constable Dexter, and safe driving."

Palms slick with sweat, Kate nodded and put the sedan into gear. She drove past the vehicles on the shoulder of the road, giving a wide berth to the dog handler as he and his canine waited for the second semi trailer to be opened. And then she and her fugitive were through.

She didn't pull over right away. First, because she needed to find a place secluded enough to let a man out of her trunk without attracting attention. Second, because she wanted some distance between her and her colleagues. And last but far from least, she also had to take care of her little evidence problem at the farm. She switched on the hands-free unit clipped to her visor.

"Call Laura," she instructed when it powered up. She sent repeated glances into the rearview mirror while her sister's cell phone rang. *Pick up, pick up, pick up.*

"Hello?"

"Laura, it's me."

"Katie! Oh, thank God. I've been worried sick about you. I've been calling and calling the farm, and I was just about to phone the OPP and—" Laura broke off. "Wait. You're calling from your cell. You're not at the farm."

"I left an hour ago. Laura, I need—"

"Kate, there are cops crawling all over town. They have roadblocks set up on every road in or out, and—"

"I know. I just came through one." Kate switched on her left signal and pulled into the passing lane to go around a line of vehicles. Laura still hadn't responded when she moved back into the right lane. "Laura? You there?"

"You have him with you, don't you?"

"Yes. And I need you to do something for me."

"Damn it, Kate—"

"Laura," Kate cut her off. "Whatever you've heard about Jonas—"

"Beyond the fact he killed someone?"

"He didn't—" Kate stopped. She didn't actually know that, did she? She'd asked about the money, but not the murder. *Why not the murder, Kate? Why didn't you ask about the murder?*

She took a deep breath. That was a question for another time. After she'd thrown potential pursuers off their trail. "Laura, Jonas Burke is an agent with the ATF."

"He's...what?"

"An agent with the ATF. The Bureau of Alcohol, Tobacco, Firearms and Explosives. In the States." Kate peered again into the rearview mirror. "Scott Dunham stopped by the house this morning. Jonas is a cop."

Long seconds ticked by as she let her sister absorb the news. Another look at the mirror. This time, her gaze zeroed in on the vehicle following. Catching up. Her neck muscles clenched. Was that a light bar sitting on top of it? The car pulled out to pass, near enough for her to make out its roof racks. Kate gritted her teeth. This was going to be a long freaking drive.

"Then why are they looking for him?" Laura asked at last.

Kate massaged her shoulder. "I think he's been framed."

"You *think*—? Katie, listen to yourself. What if you're wrong? Think of the danger you could be in! And even if you're right, you're a cop. You don't get to make calls like this. No. No, you need to turn him over before you get in trouble, Katherine Dexter. *Now*."

Kate pressed her lips together. "I've just helped him get through a roadblock, Laura. Trust me, it's way too late for that."

Her sister sucked in a ragged breath. "Oh, Katie...what are you going to do?"

"Yeah. Still working on that part."

"Can't you just drop him somewhere?"

Kate snorted. How many times had she asked herself that very question in the last hour? She shook her head. "I wish, but no. Not turning him in makes me responsible for him, and..." Kate hesitated. If she shared more, she might be putting Laura at greater risk. And if she didn't, Laura would very likely refuse to help. Or worse, do what she thought was right.

"And...?"

"And if he's telling the truth, there's a chance other cops framed him."

She heard Laura's sharp intake of breath. "Are you serious?"

"Unfortunately." Kate spotted a sign for a picnic rest area coming up in a few kilometers. If it was the one she was thinking of, she could pull behind the buildings, and no one would see her. She focused back on the conversation. "Laura, I need your help."

"Name it."

"I need you to go back to the farmhouse and remove any sign of you having been there. Bandages, saline remains, all that kind of thing. Take it with you. Make sure you wear gloves to do it. Then put Jonas's clothes in the garbage and tear open some of the bags of clothing in Mom and Dad's room. And pull out the contents of the medicine cabinet in the bathroom and scatter them over the counter. Oh, and the kitchen. Leave a mess in the kitchen, too. Can you do all that?"

"You want it to look like he doctored himself up after you left."

"Yes."

"I'll go there now," Laura said.

"Good girl. And there's one other thing." Another sign for the picnic area slipped by on the right. Two kilometers. "When you're done, there's a paper on the kitchen floor with a phone number on it. Call the number, hang up as soon as someone answers, and go home. And Laura, if you're followed or seen, or if the cops come to your door asking questions later, I want you to tell them where I am and what I've done. No hesitation. Promise me?"

"But, Kate—"

"No hesitation, Laura. You have a family to think of, and this is my mess, not yours. Promise me."

"I promise," her sister whispered. "Be careful, Katie. Please."

Kate ended the call and signaled for the turn into the rest stop. She pulled in behind the washroom buildings, coasted to a stop, and killed the engine. Then she took a deep breath and unbuckled her seat belt.

Time to find out if Jonas Burke had survived, or if her walk on the wrong side of the law was about to come to an abrupt end with a body in her trunk.

ELEVEN

Kate's heart twisted as she watched Jonas climb stiffly out of the trunk. She remembered all too well the level of pain during the first few days after a bullet wound, and she couldn't even begin to imagine how much worse it must be after the ride he'd endured.

He staggered, and she reached out a hand to steady him. He shook her off.

"I'm good," he muttered.

The edge in his voice said otherwise, but Kate didn't argue. She doubted she'd be feeling overly friendly after that ride, either. She plucked one of the blankets out of the trunk in case he needed it, then slammed down the lid.

She turned back to find Jonas with his arms stretched overhead, bending from side to side at the waist as far as his injury would allow. "Don't overdo," she warned. "I'd rather you didn't bleed all over my car."

Jonas shot her an oblique look and stretched a little further. Kate pressed her lips together and returned to the driver's seat. A moment later, Jonas slid in beside her. She started the car.

Neither of them spoke as she pulled out of the rest stop and back onto the highway, but when Jonas took out the painkillers and selected two, courtesy demanded she ask, "How bad is it?"

"Bad."

She looked over at him. Maybe he wasn't being taciturn just for the sake of it. Pale face, sweaty brow...

"There's a truck stop about ten kilometers from here. We'll take a break," she said. "Get some coffee."

Talk.

Her stomach rumbled.

"We'll get breakfast, too," she added. "When's the last time you ate?"

"No idea. But I'm fine, and we should keep going. They'll have the trace on your number any time now."

"All taken care of." Kate filled him in on what she'd sent Laura to do. This time, grudging admiration met her sideways glance.

"And because you've already left," he said, "they'll think I'm still in the area."

"That's the idea. When we get to the restaurant, I'll call Scott Dunham—the OPP officer who came to the house—for good measure. Tell him I remembered hearing something last night out near the barn, but I didn't investigate because of the storm."

The blue gaze regarded her for a moment before he murmured, "Not bad, Constable Dexter. You've earned yourself that coffee after all." Then, closing his eyes, he leaned his head back against the seat and said nothing more.

Kate chose a booth at the rear of the truck stop and took the side facing the door.

"I'm sure you'd much rather be sitting where you can see things, but I'm not half-smashed on painkillers," she said, sliding one of the laminated menus across the table to Jonas. "And the fewer people who see your face, the better."

"Good points."

He set the menu aside, and Kate looked askance at him. Surely he must be hungry by—

Understanding dawned. She pushed the menu in front of him again.

"My treat," she said. "Next time I'm down your way, you can buy me dinner."

"You don't even know where my way is."

"I'm a cop. I'll find you." She pointed at the menu. "Eat."

Jonas looked as if he might continue arguing, but then his stomach rumbled. He picked up the menu as a skinny, teenaged waitress arrived at the table. Without so much as a muttered greeting, she filled their cups from the pot of coffee she carried, then sauntered off.

Jonas gazed after her. "I'm assuming she'll return for our order."

Watching the girl rejoin a lanky youth at the counter, Kate grimaced. "I wouldn't hold your breath."

"I won't, believe me. I had quite enough of that while I was riding in the damned trunk. You might want to have your exhaust system checked, by the way. I think it's leaking."

To Kate's surprise, a teasing light danced in his eyes, taking the growl out of the words. The man had a sense of humor after all, did he? She opened her mouth to respond in kind but snapped it shut again as, over Jonas's shoulder, she saw a dark sedan turn into the parking lot.

Her companion's gaze sharpened, and everything about him went still. "Trouble?" he asked.

Barely breathing, Kate watched a man and woman

step out of the vehicle. Then the woman took a baby from the back seat. Kate's shoulders sagged. "It's nothing. A family."

But the intrusion of reality had shattered the tentative lightness of a moment before. Jonas twisted around to lean his back against the window and stretch his injured leg along the bench seat. His eyes darted up from the menu at every movement in the restaurant. Every sound.

Kate studied him over her own battered menu. A dark, heavy shadow covered the strong jaw, and tension coiled through every muscle of his body. He didn't look much more reputable by daylight than he had when covered in dirt and blood last night. He did, however, look every inch a man on the run. A man she was helping to run.

She scowled at the breakfast list. Now that the adrenaline of getting him away from the farm and through the roadblock had dissipated, the reality of her situation had begun to settle in. It wasn't a very pleasant reality.

She was in so much trouble, it made her head spin. Aiding and abetting, interference in an investigation...and a dozen other charges, if she thought about it. Which she wasn't going to, because holy hell, those two alone were bad enough.

And for what? An uncorroborated, wild story from a complete stranger? That, and—

Please.

She stifled a curse, slamming a mental lid on the plea that kept returning to haunt her. The worst possible reason of all.

"I'd offer you a penny if I had one." Jonas's quiet voice broke in on her thoughts.

Kate shook her head. "Even if you had the necessary funds, I don't think you'd want to know."

"That anxious to get rid of me?"

"That transparent?" she countered, surprising a chuckle from him. He had a nice laugh. Rich. And speaking of rich...

She set aside the menu. "We need to talk."

Jonas stayed silent for a moment, toying with the plastic clip that held the daily specials list in place. He studied the woman across the table. From golden cat's eyes and tumbled blond curls to slender shoulders and hands so slim they bordered on delicate, Kate Dexter looked nothing like a cop. At least not one tough or experienced enough to get involved with the shit-storm his life had become. She lacked so much as a hint of the edge that marked a veteran of the job.

Convincing her to disengage, however, wouldn't be easy. Not with that iron core of stubbornness he'd seen. He'd have to tread lightly.

"Fire away," he said.

"It's not just the money," she said. "You've been accused of murder, too."

He let out a hiss. "Son of a—" He caught himself mid-curse and darted a quick glance around them. He lowered his voice to a snarl. "Who?"

"The target they say you stole the money from."

Those bastards.

For a heartbeat, a crimson cloud of pure, unadulter-ated rage clouded Jonas's vision. Ramirez and Lewis had set him up so well, so thoroughly—and he'd walked right into it. *Those absolute bastards.*

He placed the menu on the table. Blinked back the haze. Pushed away the sick sense of betrayal. Then he unlocked his jaw.

"How much?" he asked.

"One point five million."

He stared out the window.

After a moment, Kate cleared her throat. "You need to tell me what went down, Jonas. If I'm going to help you—"

"No."

"Pardon?"

"I said no. You're not going to help me. These people —the ones who set me up for this—they're not going to stop until they find me, Kate. You *cannot* get involved."

"Let me get this straight." Kate leaned back in her seat. "You've been shot, there's an international warrant out for your arrest, you've been accused of *murder,* and I don't know you from Adam, but you think I should just take your word for it that you're innocent and turn you loose? Is that what you'd do if the tables were turned? Really?"

Jonas's gut twisted at the suggestion. At the thought of her bleeding from a bullet wound. In pain. Hunted by her colleagues.

Turn her loose? More like find the pricks who'd hurt her and—

He gave himself a mental shake.

"If I knew as much as I do? Yes," he lied.

"Therein lies the problem, because I don't know as much as you do, because you're not goddamn telling me."

Touché.

And stalemate.

Jonas shifted his weight on the bench seat and eased his leg into a less uncomfortable position. Silently, he cursed the fire that had steadily grown in his side during his stint in Kate's car trunk and the painkillers that weren't doing nearly as good a job as he needed them to.

"Look," he said patiently. "There's nothing you can do. If you go to your higher-ups with my story, they'll demand you turn me in. If you don't turn me in, you'll be charged. If you do, the Canadian authorities have no choice but to hand me over to the ATF. No matter how you come at this, Kate, you can't—"

"All right," she snapped. "I get it." She rested an elbow on the table and ran restless fingers through her hair, chewing absently at her bottom lip. Cat's eyes glared at him. "What about proof? There must be something somewhere."

"New Jersey. If I'm in custody, I'll never get to it."

"What about some*one*? A partner? A friend in the agency?"

Rick Honeyman. Jonas dismissed the name as soon as it whispered through his mind. If his handler started poking through files, Lewis and Ramirez would only go after him as well, and Honeyman didn't stand a chance against them. Not in his condition. Jonas shook his head.

"I won't put anyone else in the line of fire," he said. "This is my battle."

Kate's gaze narrowed, and he saw a thousand and one arguments milling behind it. But for the first time, he also saw a hint of uncertainty. He seized on it.

"Do you believe I did it?" he asked. "Killed someone? Took the money?"

"It doesn't matter what I believe."

"Humor me."

Kate met his gaze evenly, her eyes assessing, considering. Dishes rattled loudly somewhere in the restaurant behind him, and a baby wailed in protest. *You tell 'em, kid.*

He waited for Kate's response.

"No," she said at last. "I don't think you did it."

"Then you need to trust me on this. Get me somewhere safe today, then walk away. Plausible deniability, remember? Go back to your life, Kate. While you still can."

Indecision flickered over her face. He saw the words *I can't* forming on her lips.

"Please," he said wearily. "Just...please."

Kate's mouth snapped shut and the golden eyes turned dark. Abruptly, she slid out of the booth and stood up.

"I have to call Scott," she growled. "If that waitress ever comes back, order me a ham and cheese on brown. No fries."

TWELVE

He'd just had to go and use that word again, hadn't he?

Please.

Kate paced the tiny, badly lit washroom, cell phone clutched against her ear. Damn it to hell and back, what *was* it about Jonas Burke that he could put so much into such a small word? Dozens—no, hundreds—of other people had uttered the same word to her before, and she'd never had a problem refusing them. *Please don't tell my wife. Please don't take me in. Please let me go just this once, and I promise I'll never do it again.* It was all part of the job, and she'd hardened herself against the word years ago.

Until Jonas Burke had come along with his blue eyes and—

"Constable Dexter?" The OPP dispatcher interrupted her thoughts. "You're connected to Constable Dunham now. You can go ahead."

"Kate?" Scott's voice boomed into her ear. "Change your mind about dinner?"

"Sadly not." She forced a laugh, then launched into her rehearsed story, ignoring the guilt that gnawed at her belly. When she'd finished lying to him, her friend and fellow cop thanked her for the information and promised to take another run out to the farm. After a few more pleasantries, their call ended. Kate stared at the cell phone in her hand, then raised her gaze to the mirror. She regarded the indecision in her reflection's eyes. The deep unease. The borderline panic.

Phone still clenched in one hand, she rested her fists against the grimy porcelain sink and bent her head. She thought back twenty-four hours, to when she and Laura had worked shoulder to shoulder, packing up their childhood home. Even with all that had happened in the previous months—her parents' car accident and subsequent funeral, her fateful lack of focus going into that drug bust days later, not seeing the gun until too late, the surgeries that followed—life had still seemed straightforward compared to what it was now. She'd known what to do, what to expect, how to move forward.

Her weekdays had been divided between doing physical therapy, resenting the desk duty she'd been assigned to, and spending every free hour she could find at the gun range, trying to recapture the skills that had made her one of the top sharpshooters on the RCMP's Emergency Response Team. She'd driven down to the farm almost every weekend, helping Laura pack up their parents' home and deal with their loss. Much of it hadn't been pleasant, but it had been predictable. It'd had a rhythm.

And now...now she stood in a filthy truck-stop bathroom, helping a fugitive escape the law she had sworn to uphold and wondering what in hell to do next.

She looked up into her reflection's eyes again and watched the flare of panic deepen. She was in way, way over her head with this. She and Jonas both knew it, and the longer she stayed, the worse it would get.

Bottom line, Kate, she told herself. *Go from there.*

Bottom line, no matter how much she wanted to help him, he was right. Her choices numbered exactly two. She could either turn him in or turn him loose. The choice was hers, and she needed to make it. Now.

Please.

With a groan that came all the way from her toes, she pushed away from the sink, pocketed her cell phone, and flung open the bathroom door.

Well, at least she'd have plausible deniability, right?

Jonas was halfway through a smoked meat on rye—a Canadian favorite he took advantage of whenever he was on this side of the border—when Kate returned to the table.

"Long phone call," he remarked. He bit into his sandwich again, watching her as he chewed.

Kate didn't look at him. She picked up the ham and cheese she'd requested and took a bite.

"Any problem with your OPP friend?" Jonas asked.

She swallowed. "No. And Laura's call to the Bureau worked. They think you're still in the area." She set down the sandwich and pushed away the plate.

Not hungry? he wanted to ask.

Not your concern, he answered himself.

Kate's gaze lifted to his at last. "I've decided you're right. About turning you loose, I mean."

A tiny shaft of disappointment surprised him. He turned his back on it and choked down another bite of sandwich. Odd that it tasted so much like sawdust when he'd expected to be ravenous. That ride in the trunk must have been harder on him than he'd thought. "Thank you," he said at last, because this was what he wanted. What was best. For both of them.

Kate leaned back, hands in her jacket pockets, watching him. The keys in her right pocket jingled as she played with them. "What will you do?" she asked at last.

"Take a couple of days to recover. Find a cash job for a few weeks until I have enough to get me back to the States. Go after Lewis and Ramirez."

He watched her wrestle with the questions he knew she wanted to ask. Then she pressed her lips tight and nodded. "Fine. I'll take you as far as Ottawa. There are a couple of cheap motels—"

"No."

"Jonas—"

"No, Kate. You know I don't have money with me, and I won't take money from you." It had been hard enough accepting lunch from her. "A shelter will be fine."

"And a couple hundred dollars will give you a key and your own bath—"

"I said no," Jonas growled. He pushed away the plate of half-eaten food, unable to stomach any more of it. "Take me to Ottawa. That's it, that's all. I'll find my own way from there."

Her gaze narrowed, turning analytical, seeing more than he wanted her to see. More than he wanted to show. Damned pain, wearing him down like this. He fought down an urge to cross his arms. Kate's head tipped to one side.

"You're not very good at accepting help, are you?"

"I wouldn't know, given that I make it a habit not to accept it."

"Not ever?"

He scowled. She watched him for another few seconds. Then, with an almost imperceptible shake of her head, she stood up from the table and dropped a crumpled twenty beside her plate.

"We still have three hours ahead of us," she said. "We should go."

A green distance sign slid past on the right side of the highway and Kate sighed. Twenty-three kilometers to Ottawa. She rubbed a hand over her eyes and yawned.

God, what a trip.

She shot a look at her sleeping passenger. Now that she'd made the decision, dropping Jonas off downtown would be a relief. For the entire three hours since they'd left the truck stop, her gaze had darted continuously from road to rearview mirror to side mirror and back again, watching for pursuers. Her good shoulder had wound itself into a gnarled mass of knots, and she was no longer on speaking terms with the bad one. She'd never felt so paranoid in her entire life—and that included all of those less-than-savory undercover assignments she'd done early in her career.

She eased her aching neck to one side, then the other. Never mind. Half an hour more and it would be over. Or at least, her part would be. Beside her, Jonas slept on, resting against the passenger-side window.

Kate cleared her throat.

"Jonas? We'll be getting into Ottawa soon."

He didn't stir. With a sigh, she reached out to touch the hand resting on a cotton-clad thigh.

"Jonas, wake up. We're almost—" She broke off, drawing back as if scorched. For-real scorched. Freaking hell, the man felt like he was burning up.

Keeping one hand on the steering wheel and one eye on the road, she leaned across to rest the back of her hand against Jonas's stubbled, fire-hot cheek. His hand came up to push her away, and he mumbled something unintelligible. Kate gripped the wheel with both hands again and stared at the highway unfolding before them.

A fever. He had a fever—and probably an infection to go with it. The question of *now what?* barely brushed across her mind before she dismissed it. Because there was no question. Not anymore.

They'd run out of options, plain and simple.

Freaking, freaking hell.

She put her hand on his arm, wincing at the heat radiating through the shirt fabric. "Jonas, can you hear me? You have a fever. I think it might be an infection. We have to get you to a hospital."

Jonas struggled to sit up straight but sagged against the door again. His head moved—barely—in the negative. "Hospital—cops—can't."

Kate bit back a string of curses. He was right. If she took a gunshot victim to an emergency ward, the hospital would report it. They would have no choice. And then Jonas would be screwed, and she would be screwed, and—

Her gut twisted at the potential outcomes.

"Sister," Jonas muttered. "Call."

His body trembled under her touch, and his teeth chattered. Kate bit her lip, considering his suggestion, hating to involve Laura any more than she already had. She weighed the pros and cons of both alternatives: hospital, cops, and an inevitable visit from the ATF, or her apartment and only a potential visit from the same?

Along with the potential for having Jonas die in her care, of course.

To underline her thoughts, Jonas shivered again. Kate scowled and reached into the back seat for the jacket he'd shed earlier. She spread it over him as best she could with one hand. His fingers clutched at it, drawing it up under his chin. Blue eyes, fever-bright, opened to meet hers.

"Your sister," he mumbled. "Call."

"Fine," she capitulated with a growl. "But only on one condition. If Laura says you need a doctor, that's the end of it, because there's no goddamn way I'll be responsible for you dying, Jonas Burke. Understood?"

Silence met her words, extending so long that she shot another look his way, expecting to find he'd passed out. He hadn't. He just stared back at her, the bitter defeat in his gaze echoed in the lines around a mouth pulled tight.

"Jonas," she began, her voice softening.

He turned his head away and closed his eyes.

THIRTEEN

Somehow, Jonas managed to stagger into Kate's building and then her apartment more or less under his own steam. She intervened once to keep him from careening into the wall as he came off the elevator, and again when he would have fallen over the back of the sofa in her living room.

She steered him down the hall to her bedroom, ignoring his protests as she pushed him onto the down-filled duvet covering her queen-sized bed.

"I won't take your bed," he growled, trying to rise again.

"Right now you will shut up and do as you're told," she retorted, tugging her cell phone from her pocket, "or I'll call the bloody ambulance instead of Laura."

Jonas subsided, visibly shivering. With one hand, Kate hit the call button beside her sister's name on her phone; with the other, she reached to pull the other half of the duvet over him. The phone rang in her ear. Jonas closed his eyes.

Kate's heart skipped a beat. He looked awful. His skin had taken on a pallor that contrasted sharply with the heavy shadow of stubble across his jaw line, and two bright spots of color over his cheeks looked as if they'd been painted on, like a clown's makeup. His entire length shuddered under the duvet.

Laura's phone continued to ring. Jonas's chest rose and fell unevenly, rapidly.

"Come on," Kate muttered at the phone. She stripped off her jacket and draped it over the back of the chair by the dresser. "Answer the damned—Laura?"

Her sister's voice turned instantly sharp. "What's wrong?"

"I'm fine. I promise. But we have another problem." Quickly, Kate described Jonas's condition, ending with, "What do I do?"

"You take him to the hospital like you should have done in the first damned place!" Laura snapped. "He needs medical attention, Kate. Probably antibiotics, possibly even surgery. He needs to see a *doctor*."

As if he'd heard her sister's voice—heaven knew Laura had been loud enough—Jonas's eyes opened and his gaze met Kate's, bright with fever, clouded by denial. Kate hesitated, knowing Laura was right...but knowing, too, that Jonas would never forgive her for not trying.

"I can't." She raked the hair back from her face and closed her eyes. "Trust me, sis. Please."

The same plea Jonas had used. On the other end of the phone, her sister hesitated.

"Please," Kate said again. "Just tell me what to do."

Laura let out an impatient whoosh of air. "All right, fine," she snapped. "But if he dies, Katherine Dexter, it's on *your* head, not mine. Have you looked at the wounds yet?"

"No. Hang on, let me have a look." She tried to tuck the phone between ear and shoulder, but the ache that had been plaguing the latter flared at the suggestion, and she caught her breath.

She switched the cell phone to speaker and set it on her nightstand, then flipped back the duvet. The plaid flannel shirt was too snug to lift, so with teeth gritted, she undid the bottom few buttons and eased the fabric aside, then peeled back the dressing.

"Laura? I have you on speaker. The wound on his side is pretty red. It looks sore."

"Are there any red streaks radiating from it?" Laura's voice asked from the nightstand. "Any kind of a discharge or swelling at the site?"

Kate tilted the bedside lamp to shine on Jonas's torso and leaned closer for a better look. "No. Nothing."

"What about his leg?"

"He's sleeping right now. I don't think I can—" Kate broke off as Jonas's hands went to the waistband of his sweatpants . She swallowed.

"Never mind," she told her sister. "He's awake. Wait a minute while he gets undressed."

Laura muttered something, but Kate missed it, focused as she was on Jonas lifting his hips to slide the sweatpants down over them. On the knowledge that he wore nothing beneath them. On trying to keep her brain focused on the current emergency rather than—

She swallowed again, harder this time, and wrenched her attention back to her sister's voice.

"What?" she asked. "Sorry, I missed that last bit."

"Color me not surprised," Laura muttered. "Just look at the man's leg, Kate."

Jonas had collapsed back on the pillow, the duvet haphazardly covering his nether region and sweatpants still clinging to his thighs. Kate went to the foot of the bed, steeled herself, and tugged the garment the rest of the way off. She removed the second bandage.

"The same. No red lines, no discharge. A bit of swelling, but not much."

"Good. That's good. That means his body is fighting off the infection for now."

"So what do I do?"

"Keep him quiet and hydrated, give him acetaminophen for the fever, and check the wounds every couple of hours. As long as there's no change in the next twenty-four hours, he should be fine, but if you see any signs of red lines or discharge, or if there's any swelling, get him the hell into a hospital, all right? And if the fever hits one-oh-four, or the acetaminophen doesn't take it down, or he's still running a temperature at this time tomorrow, see a doctor."

"Anything else?"

"Yes. It damn near kills me to say this, but he needs somewhere to stay until the holes heal. He can't go wandering off by himself the way he is. If a hospital really isn't an option..."

"Yeah, yeah." Kate didn't want to hear this right now. Didn't want to think about anything beyond not having Jonas Burke die in her bed. "Thanks, Laura. I'll call you again in a couple of days."

"*Tomorrow*," her sister corrected. "You'll call me tomorrow. In the morning. Because if I don't hear from you before breakfast, Katherine Dexter, I will call the ambulance myself. And the cops *you* should have already called. Are we clear?"

"We're clear. And, Laura? Thank you. I owe you for this."

"Yes. You do. And I'll thank you to not get yourself arrested and thrown in jail so that you'll be able to pay me back."

Kate might have chuckled at her sister's tart words if

they hadn't had such a large grain of truth behind them. As it was, she had to dig for a smile and force a note of lightness into her voice. A semblance of reassurance.

"I'll do my best," she promised. She reached out to hit the *end call* button on the cell phone. Jonas's chest rose and fell with deep, even breaths, but even in sleep, he looked truly ill. A string of curses ran through her mind, but none seemed sufficient. She settled for a succinct, heartfelt, "Shit."

It had been one thing to get him through the road-blocks and away from the search for him; it was quite another to keep him squirreled away in her apartment for who knew how many days. The difference between claiming, *"What cookies?"* and being caught with her hand in the damned cookie jar.

Jonas's powerful frame shuddered, and Kate's heart did a guilty little flip-flop in her chest. She'd have time enough to regret her involvement in this later, when he was back on his feet again. For now, he was sick and vulnerable, and far more in need of pity than she was. With a last, deep sigh, she set to work.

As carefully as she could, she eased off his shirt one sleeve at a time. Then she rolled him over until she could pull the garment out from under him, trying—and mostly failing—to keep the duvet tucked around his hips while she did so. Her shoulder gave a twinge of pain, a welcome distraction from hormones that had no business flaring up, no matter how smooth Jonas's skin was. Or how solid the muscles beneath that skin. Or how many of those muscles her hands had to caress as she—

Kate's cheeks flared hot. *Touch,* she scolded herself, balling up the shirt and tossing it onto the chair to join her jacket. *You had to touch him, not caress. And now you're done.*

She pulled up the duvet and tucked it around his shoulders, then looked down at him. Her fingers curled into her palms against a sudden desire to sweep the hair back from his forehead, and her hormones did another little jig along tightened nerve endings. Laura's voice echoed in her mind.

"...he needs somewhere to stay until the holes heal. He can't go wandering off by himself the way he is. If a hospital really isn't an option..."

Freaking hell, this was going to be an interesting few days.

FOURTEEN

Jonas came awake to dark silence and a tangle of damp covers. He lay without moving, listening to the stillness, trying to orient himself. A truck rumbled by outside, its brakes hissing as it rolled to a stop. Faint light crept around the edges of the blind-covered window above his head, just enough to outline the room's features: double sliding closet doors, a long, low dresser with a chair beside it, a nightstand and lamp beside him. Nothing looked familiar.

He frowned. The last thing he remembered was lunch in the truck stop. Kate had agreed to take him to Ottawa, they'd gotten back into the car, he'd dozed off, and then —nothing. Certainly nothing that involved a bed that smelled like...he sniffed. Summer. It smelled like summer, and sunshine, and—

Kate. Where was Kate?

Gingerly, all too aware of the hole in his side, he pushed himself up on one elbow and switched on the lamp. When his eyes adjusted to the glare, he took more thorough stock of his surroundings. Pale blue walls. White furniture. White sheets and lamp. Red chair. Floral duvet sprigged with some kind of red flower. Daisies? The overall effect was cool. Fresh.

Undeniably feminine.

He hadn't expected this side to Constable Kate Dexter. Not that he'd spent much time dwelling on his rescuer's personal tastes. He'd been more interested in getting as far away from her as he could. And he was still interested in that, he told himself firmly. No matter how he'd ended up in Kate's apartment, leaving was his top priority now that he was awake.

Yawning, he scratched absently at his chest. His hand stilled and he raised an eyebrow. He was naked. How in hell had he gotten naked? His gaze snapped back to the chair, taking in the neatly folded jeans and shirt there.

Kate?

A not-unpleasant tension thrummed through him at the thought of her efficient, slender hands stripping him of his clothes, the imagined sensation of her blond curls brushing like fine silk against his skin as she leaned over him. He coughed. What in hell was he thinking? The absolute last thing he needed in his life right now was a distraction like Kate Dexter. The sooner he left here, the better, because...

He frowned at the fog settling over his brain.

Well, because reasons. He was sure he had them, but with fatigue crawling over his limbs like a weighted blanket and that summer scent rising from the sheets beneath him, he couldn't quite remember what they were. He fumbled with the lamp switch and the room plunged back into darkness.

To hell with it. Thinking was going to have to wait. And leaving, too. Just until daylight. It would be rude to wake Kate up right now anyway. Or to leave without saying thank you. He pulled the duvet across him, its cotton crisp and cool against his skin, inhaled deeply of summer, and dropped back into sleep.

* * *

Kate set the tray on the nightstand and glanced at the black shock of wavy hair sticking out from under the duvet, all that she could see of her guest.

"Jonas," she called softly. The black waves didn't stir. She tried again, a little louder. Still nothing. She frowned. Surely he hadn't gotten worse again.

She'd checked on him every hour on the hour until his fever had finally broken at midnight of his second night in her bed, well beyond the deadline Laura had given. She'd sponged his overheated body, changed the duvet cover when it became drenched with his sweat, rolled him from one side of the bed to the other to let the sheet dry beneath him. She'd been a regular Florence Nightingale for thirty-six hours, but what if that hadn't been enough? Unease gelled in the pit of her stomach. Had she relaxed too soon?

She stretched out a hand and eased back the duvet. Jonas's face might have been carved of wood, it was so still. The beginnings of minor panic prickled through her chest, stealing her breath. Freaking hell, now what? Casting aside gentleness, she grabbed his shoulder and shook.

"Jonas, wake—"

The rest of her demand ended in a garbled choke as a strong arm pulled her down onto her back, looped under her arm and around her neck, and braced behind her head in a half nelson. Kate clutched at it, struggling for air, and almost instantly Jonas's hold loosened until his forearm rested across her chest—muscular, hot, heavy.

"God, Kate, I'm sorry," he muttered, his words warm against her ear. "Are you all right?"

Crisp chest hair rasped against a blouse that had just

now become an entirely inadequate garment, and a dozen traitorous sensations made breathing even more difficult than when he'd taken her down. She nodded, not trusting her voice. Her heart thundered against her ribs, and heat scorched her face in the wake of the molten fire flooding her limbs. She pulled against Jonas's arm.

"May I get up, please?"

Surely she only imagined his brief hesitation before he released her—and her answering reluctance to leave his warmth. She clambered off the bed and straightened her shirt, trying not to close her eyes as the fabric slid over sensitive breasts.

"I brought you breakfast." Crap. Was that husky voice really hers? Freaking hormones. She cleared her throat. "You haven't eaten for a while. I thought you might be hungry."

Jonas remained silent for several seconds, his eyes hidden beneath a forearm as he lay back against the pillow.

"I am," he agreed at last, moving his arm to prop himself up in the bed. "And thirsty."

She handed him the glass of orange juice from the tray, careful to keep her fingers clear of his. He drained the contents and gave the glass back to her.

"I don't remember a thing after leaving that truck stop yesterday. What happened?"

"Fever. You wouldn't go to a hospital. And it was the day before yesterday."

He stared at his, blue eyes startled, then scowling. "You should have woken me."

"With what, my magic wand? Your fever didn't even break until last night. You slept because you needed it." Kate grabbed the duvet and held it in place when he tried to fling it back. "You *still* need it."

"What I *need*," he retorted, shaking off her hand and swinging his bare legs out of the bed, "is to get as far away from you as I can."

He pushed himself upright to sit on the edge of the bed, but almost instantly, every ounce of color drained from his face. Without comment, Kate pressed her lips tight, stooped, and lifted his feet back onto the bed. Jonas subsided against the pillow, eyes squeezed shut.

She regarded him with equal amounts of concern and annoyance as he struggled to push back the pain and regain control. Could he not, just for two seconds, make this easier on himself? On her? She pulled the duvet across his nakedness and made a concerted effort not to notice that her breasts hadn't stopped tingling from his touch yet.

"I repeat," she said, "You still need sleep."

Eyes still closed, he shook his head. "I can't. If Lewis and Ramirez connect us and come asking questions—"

"I get it," she interrupted. "I really do. But like it or not, you're going to have to heal before you can go anywhere on your own. Stay here and let me help, Jonas. Just for a few days. Get some rest, focus on healing, decide what your next move is. Please. You know I'm right about this."

He declined to respond. With a sigh, Kate moved the tray closer to him, and then she and her tingling breasts headed for the door. The sound of her name stopped her. She turned back to meet the hard glitter of his gaze.

"I know you mean well," he said, "but *if* I stay—"

Kate pursed her lips at the emphasis on *if.* Jonas either didn't see or chose to ignore it, continuing without pause.

"—this is as involved as you get, is that clear?"

She crossed her arms. "Please tell me you don't think you can give me orders like that."

He scowled. "I mean it, Kate. You don't need this, and I don't need your help."

Leaning her good shoulder against the doorframe, she let her gaze travel the length of his prone figure. "Because you're totally able to look after yourself at the moment, you mean?"

"You know what I mean."

"I know you've been shot," she corrected. "And that you're not very good at accepting help. But you can relax, Burke, because I'm offering you a place to hole up in for a few days. Nothing more, okay? Now eat your breakfast and get some rest. I want you out of here as much as you do. "

Jonas glared at the door long after Kate closed it behind her, leaving her parting words hanging in the air. Damned right, he wasn't good at accepting help. And for good reason, too. He'd been six when he'd gone into his first foster home, already streetwise and carrying a chip on his shoulder, the weight of which would have slowed most men down.

Help back then had consisted of one family after another trying to break him, to make him surrender to their rules. It was never about what mattered, what would have helped *him*. There had been no job for the homeless mother who'd had to give him up, no attempt to keep him with the baby sister he'd so desperately tried to protect.

By the age of eight, he'd learned repeatedly that the kind of help offered by others couldn't be depended on. That he was the only one he could ever really trust. The message had been reinforced repeatedly throughout his teen years and adult life, and oh, look. Ramirez and Lewis had hammered the lesson home yet again just days ago.

With a grunt, Jonas locked away the memories he preferred not to dwell on. He pushed back the covers and levered himself upright, slowly this time, respecting the tight, fiery knots in his gut and leg that could explode without warning if he abused them.

He rubbed a hand over his bristly jaw line, pausing when the scent of vanilla wafted up to his nose and walloped him in the gut. His arm tingled with another memory, this one of Kate's softness beneath it. The tickle of her hair across it. The warmth of her—

Jonas held his arm away and stared at it, horrified at its treachery. Jesus, but he needed to get away from here. Kate's help—and those golden cat's eyes—be damned.

He stood, giving his body time to adjust to the demands being made on it. If he took it slowly enough, this might work. He hobbled across the room to the clothing piled on the chair, telling himself that the knife in his thigh was normal; the pain, within acceptable parameters. Sweat beaded on his brow. Sweatpants and shirt in hand, he returned to sit on the bed. He slid his legs into the pants one at a time, took a deep breath, and stood to pull them on. The too-quick movement knocked him right back down again.

Lying on his back, he stared at the ceiling, coming to terms with the reality he'd been handed. As much as he hated to admit it—and it really did gall him—he wouldn't make it a block like this. He was going to have to take Kate up on her offer, at least for a day or two.

Hell.

FIFTEEN

J onas limped out of the bedroom a few minutes later, almost colliding with Kate as she emerged from the bathroom. The amber gaze swept over him from head to toe, and her lips compressed. He braced for the forthcoming lecture.

Instead, she flicked off the bathroom light switch and said, "I'll pick up more painkillers today. You'll have to make do with extra-strength acetaminophen in the meantime. It's in the kitchen cabinet above the fridge."

Jonas didn't reply, taking in the stocking-covered toes peeping out from beneath charcoal slacks. His gaze traveled upward, noting how the gray fabric flared slightly below her knees but deliciously hugged the rest of her leg; settling on the pale gray blouse clinging to the curves his arm had—

Kate cleared her throat. "Did you hear me?"

"I heard." Jonas ground his teeth. "Kitchen cabinet above the fridge. Got it."

Her cheeks flushed with pink, Kate turned and continued down the hallway, twisting her hair up and clipping it at the nape of her neck as she walked. "The coffee's still fresh if you want some, and I left sandwiches wrapped up in the fridge for your lunch. I'll make spaghetti for dinner when I get home."

"Where are you going?"

Jonas hadn't meant it to sound quite so abrupt, but the sexy sway of her hips leading him into the living room was damned distracting. It threw him off his stride.

"To work."

She sauntered past him to the hall closet. Walked, actually. But focused as he was on those hips, it looked a hell of a lot more like a saunter. He scowled.

"Do you think that's wise?"

She looked over her shoulder at him as she pulled open the closet door. "I think it's what pays my rent."

"What happens if someone starts asking questions?"

"I've already missed one day. Questions are more likely if I miss another."

A valid point, but not one that quelled the vague panic in his gut at the thought of remaining here like a sitting duck, waiting for Ramirez and Lewis to turn up. Or at the idea of Kate being out there on her own, unprotected from them. Kate extracted a heavy metal lockbox from the floor of the closet, opened it, and took out her service weapon. Jonas's mouth twisted. Well, maybe not entirely unprotected.

"You understand how dangerous these people are, right?" he asked abruptly.

She shot a pointed look at his leg. "I think I have a rough idea, yes."

She checked the ammo clip and tucked the weapon into the side holster he hadn't noticed clipped to her belt. Damned sexy hips.

"Stay," he said gruffly. Kate's hands stilled.

Shit. That hadn't come out the way he'd intended.

A silent second passed, followed by three more. Jonas cleared his throat.

"I've been working undercover for almost eight

years," he said, "and Lewis and Ramirez got the drop on me. You—" He gestured vaguely in her direction.

The amber gaze snapped to meet his. Her hands settled on the damned hips. "I what?"

"When is the last time you even pulled that thing, let alone used it?" He jutted his chin toward the gun she'd strapped on.

"In the kitchen at the farmhouse," she retorted. "Remember?"

Touché. But not what he'd meant.

Kate raised an eyebrow. "You don't think I'm capable?"

There was no easy way to say it. "Not when it comes to dealing with this, no. If you were in uniform, working the streets, maybe, but you sit behind a desk, Kate. If they figure out your connection, if they find you, you won't stand a chance. So please. Stay here and lie low where I can keep an eye on you, just for a couple of days. As soon as I can leave town, I'll call Lewis again. It will draw their attention away from you, and then your life can go back to normal."

There. He'd come up with a plan at last. Of sorts.

Kate stared at him for a moment. Then she shrugged into a gray blazer that matched the pants she wore and slipped her feet into a pair of low-heeled black shoes.

"The television remote is on the coffee table," she said, as if he hadn't spoken. "I have satellite and Netflix, so you should be able to keep yourself occupied until I get home. If anything comes up, my office and cell numbers are beside the phone."

"That's it?" Jonas scowled at her. "You're not even going to respond to my suggestion?"

"Is that what you think it was? A suggestion?" Kate picked up a briefcase and pulled open the apartment door. "Funny. To me, it sounded more like an insult. I'll be home at five. Try to get some rest."

Stretched out on the couch, Jonas listened to the sounds of Kate's return home. The key in the lock, the opening of a closet door, the clunk of the heavy gun box returning to the floor after she put away her weapon, the closet door closing again. He couldn't keep up the pretense of sleep forever, but—

A soft, heavy something landed on his chest. He cracked open an eye and stared at the plastic shopping bag. Raised his gaze to the woman beyond.

"Clothes," she said, walking away. A second later, he heard her in the kitchen.

He cleared his throat and raised his voice over the clatter of pots and pans. "You shouldn't have bothered. I'm fine with these."

"You sweated out a fever in those ones," she called back. "Trust me, you need the change."

He plucked at a handful of shirt. Sniffed. Grimaced. She had a point.

"You're welcome," she added loudly. A pot landed in the sink with a metallic bang, and the water came on.

Jonas sighed and moved the bag of clothes off his chest. Gingerly, he swung his feet off the couch and onto the floor. She was right. He should thank her. Not only for the clothes, but for taking him in like this. Saving his life, not turning him in...damn, but he owed her. So much.

The knowledge had been eating away at him all day. He wasn't used to owing anyone for anything. He made a point of avoiding situations that called for indebtedness of any kind. Or thanks. Or apologies, for that matter—which he also owed Kate after this morning. He winced at the slam of a cupboard door and levered himself upright. No time like the present...if only to keep her from knocking the place apart.

He arrived in the doorway as Kate turned off the water and lifted a pot from the sink. "Can I help?" he asked.

Kate jumped, sending water sloshing across her feet. She cursed and set the pot on the counter. Jonas handed her the tea towel looped through the fridge door handle beside him. She took it wordlessly, dried her feet, mopped up the puddle, and tossed the towel into a corner.

He leaned a shoulder against the doorframe and slid the tips of his fingers into the front pockets of his sweatpants. "I didn't mean to startle you."

Kate turned her back on him. "It's fine." She set the pot on the stove and turned it on. "And no, I don't need help."

He watched her take out a jar of spaghetti sauce and a box of pasta from a cupboard, then moved out of her way when she crossed to the fridge and took a bag of meatballs from the freezer.

"Thank you for the clothes," he said when she returned to the counter.

She snorted. "Was that as painful as it sounded?"

She wasn't going to make this easy, was she? Not that he could blame her. He hadn't exactly been a model of appreciation so far.

"Thank you for everything else you've done for me, too," he said. "And I'm sorry for this morning. I didn't mean to insult you. I'm sure you're a perfectly capable cop."

She stared at him over her shoulder. "My goodness, you're just a fountain of good manners all of a sudden, aren't you?"

Jonas flexed his jaw. He supposed he had that coming.

"I haven't had much practice at accepting help," he said. "And I'm not used to having someone else to worry about when I'm in a situation. I'm not very..."

"Well socialized?" Kate suggested tartly, when he trailed off.

A smile tugged at the corner of his mouth. "Not quite the words I was looking for, but no, I suppose I'm not...well socialized. I *am* sorry, though, Kate. And I'm very grateful. So...friends?"

He pulled one hand from its pocket and held it out to her. Pink blossomed in her cheeks as she stared at it, then she turned her back on him again.

"Fine," she muttered. "Apology accepted."

Jonas let his hand drop to his side again. His gaze slid over Kate's slender, ramrod-stiff back. If he didn't know better, he might think he hadn't been the only one affected by this morning's unplanned wrestling session. How intriguing. He coughed to cover his sudden startlement. No. No, not intriguing. Alarming. He had no room in his life for complications right now. Any *more* complications, that was.

Especially ones that came with amber cat's eyes and soft—

"Are you all right?" Kate frowned at him. "You look like you're in pain."

"I'm good," he said. Lied. He took a step backward,

into the hallway. "If you're sure you don't need help, I'll go change."

"I'm sure." She waved him off. "Go. Dinner's in twenty. And I did my best on the jeans, by the way, but I may have erred on the large side, so there's a belt in the bag if you need it."

SIXTEEN

Two days later, Kate pushed back a stray curl that had escaped its French braid and shot an impatient look at the wall clock above the door. It *still* wasn't four o'clock? Was the blasted thing even working? She sighed.

Across the desks that butted against one another, a tall, lanky man looked up, an amused twinkle dancing in his brown eyes. Corporal Dave Jennings had been her handler when she'd worked undercover on a smuggling operation three years ago, and he'd been more than happy to welcome her as his investigative partner for the duration of her recovery. The arrangement suited Kate equally well. She could think of a dozen members in this section alone who would have driven her nuts if she'd had to share an office with them for the past few weeks. Being sidelined by that bullet still wasn't her idea of fun, but at least Dave's sense of humor made it bearable.

"Hot date tonight, Dex?" Dave leaned back in his chair and laced his fingers behind his head. "I thought you had a little more sparkle than usual the last couple of days."

Heat crept into Kate's cheeks. "I don't sparkle."

Dave snorted. "Sure you don't. Just like you haven't started clock-watching the second you park your butt in that chair every morning."

Her gaze slid away. She couldn't argue with that, because she'd noticed the tendency herself. And she still hadn't made up her mind whether said clock-watching—or the accompanying breathlessness—was due to anticipation or dread of quitting time and the return home. To her apartment. To Jonas.

She aimed a dark look at Dave.

"For your information, smartass, the only date I have is with a set of weights." Not a bad idea, now that she mentioned it. She hadn't been to the gym in more than a week, and she was supposed to be doing those exercises the physio assigned for her shoulder at least every third day. Plus, maybe a good workout would wear off some of her frustration.

Fresh heat flared in her face.

Stress, she corrected herself. It would help alleviate some of her stress. Across the desks, Dave smirked.

"Sure," he said. "The thought of working up a sweat makes *me* sparkle, too."

Kate's lips compressed.

"All right, all right." Her partner raised his hands in self-defense, but the smirk remained. "You're not sparkling. And you're as sweet as ever. Now, why don't you take that sunny disposition of yours home early today? I'll get twice the work done without you fidgeting across from me."

Kate made her shoulder muscles unclench through sheer willpower. She achieved an apologetic smile much the same way.

"Maybe you're right." She shot a rueful look at the paperwork on her desk. It didn't seem to have diminished much in the last couple of days, and it probably wouldn't diminish much more before Jonas was out of her life.

Five days he'd been with her now, four of them spent confined to the apartment, where his edginess had increased along with his strength.. If she had to listen to him pace the living room floor one more night, she'd—

She broke off the thought and sighed. She'd what? Go out there and give in to the fantasies that kept her awake as she listened to his steps? Find out what he wore to sleep in the sofa bed he'd insisted on taking? Anything? Nothing?

Heavy warmth unfurled in her belly. Man, oh man, she hoped he was leaving soon. Like tomorrow.

Next week, a little voice inside contradicted.

Today.

Next month.

Maybe he'd already be gone when she got home.

No.

The phone on her desk rang, startling her into knocking over her coffee mug. She sprang to her feet, frantically trying to rescue files and confine the spreading liquid. Dave reached across and snagged the receiver from its cradle.

"Customs and Excise, Constable Dexter's desk." He paused for a second, then asked, "Can I tell her who's calling?"

A slow grin spread across his face. "Hang on a second." He put his hand over the receiver and, with an exaggerated clearing of his throat, held it out to her. "I may be wrong, but I think your weights are calling."

Kate snatched the phone from him. "Dexter," she snapped into the receiver.

"Bad day?" Jonas's rich, deep voice reached through the line to squeeze the breath from her.

She sank into her chair and sighed. "More of a bad

mood," she admitted. "What's up? Do you need something?"

Dave propped an elbow on the desk and rested his chin in one hand, watching her with avid interest. She turned her back on him.

"You been out much today?" Jonas's words and tone were casual. Too casual. Apprehension crawled down Kate's spine.

"No. I've been in the office all day. Why?"

"It's probably nothing, but there's been a gray sedan parked in the parking lot across the street all day. It's the only vehicle that hasn't moved."

"Can you see a plate number?"

"Not from this angle."

"I'll check it out when I get home."

"Good. And Kate—watch yourself, okay?"

Kate's heart did a sideways skitter. *Easy, girl,* she told herself wryly. Concern didn't equal interest, and even if it did, she didn't *want* interest. Not from someone with as much baggage as Jonas carried. Not if she was smart.

"I'll be careful," she said.

Jonas replaced the receiver hard enough to make the phone jangle its protest. He jammed his fingers between the slats of the horizontal blinds and pried open a space wide enough to see the street three stories below. The gray sedan in the parking lot in front of the donut shop still hadn't moved.

It had been there yesterday, too.

And he felt like a goddamned sitting duck.

He let the blinds fall back into place and turned to stare at the living room. His gaze traveled the taupe leather sofa bed that dominated the room, its matching armchair angled nearby. A square, black-lacquered coffee table sat in the middle, devoid of the book of contemporary photography and vase of willow-twigs that Kate had moved to allow easier access to the sofa bed. In the far corner, beside a gas fireplace, hung the television he'd watched way too much of in the last few days.

A single piece of artwork dominated the wall over the fireplace—a rendering of a farm, with weathered-silver barns and sheds tucked in behind a white farmhouse. Two little girls played on a swing under a spreading maple in front of the house, and a litter of puppies gamboled around their feet. It should have been out of keeping with its cool, sophisticated surroundings. But it looked very right.

Very Kate.

Jonas scraped a hand through his hair, ripping his thoughts away from his hostess. Again. If he didn't get out of here soon...*nope. Not finishing that thought. No way.*

He flexed his thigh experimentally, pleased when the resulting twinge didn't even make him wince. The same trial for his gut wasn't as satisfactory, however, and wrested an involuntary grunt from him. One down, one to go. Damn.

He parted the blinds one last time. The car was still there. Still empty. He blew out a long breath and rolled his shoulders to ease their tension. It was probably nothing. Just his paranoia. Served him right for sitting around this apartment watching *Columbo* reruns.

About to turn from the window, he paused as a maroon minivan turned into the parking lot and claimed the space beside the sedan. The two front doors opened and a man and woman got out. They were too far away to make out facial features, but Jonas's insides turned cold nonetheless. What if it was—

The woman removed a denim cap and tossed it into the van, shaking back bright red hair. Jonas released the breath he'd been holding. Carmen Ramirez's hair was black. His shoulders slumped. He needed to get out of here and deal with this so he could stop jumping at shadows.

It wouldn't be easy, and he still didn't have much in the way of a plan, but he wasn't worried. If he could make it to Jersey and his stash, he could disappear into the streets indefinitely while he rounded up the evidence he needed. It'd be like old times, only with higher stakes. Because survival would be a little trickier with the very people he'd worked beside gunning for him—and the law on their side instead of his.

If he could make it to Jersey.

He stalked toward the kitchen, gritting his teeth against the nagging discomfort in his side. One more night's rest. That should be enough. It had to be enough.

He'd leave tomorrow.

SEVENTEEN

Kate pushed open the apartment door to find Jonas waiting on the other side. Her heart skipped a beat. After a small hesitation, she tugged the key from the lock and crossed the threshold, studying him. He stood taller. Stronger. An air of tense watchfulness about him that reminded her of a caged jungle cat contemplating freedom on the other side of its bars. Her heart skipped another beat, but for a whole different reason.

She dropped her keys on the entry table.

He was ready to leave.

"You're home early," he said.

"I had some leave time coming to me. I thought I'd check out that vehicle you mentioned. The plate came back as registered to an Ottawa resident."

"Sorry." His mouth tightened.. "Paranoia on my part."

"Understandable, given the circumstances. You look like you're feeling better."

"Much. I'll be leaving tomorrow." Blue eyes watched her, as if waiting for a reaction.

A sudden hollowness took up residence in her chest. Kate turned away to take off her coat. She hung it in the closet and pulled out her gun box. Jonas cleared his throat.

"Nothing out of the ordinary on the way home?"

She shook her head. "Nothing."

She set her weapon into the box, locked it, and replaced it in the back corner of the closet. Was it just her, or was conversation between them even more stilted than usual? She swallowed a snort at the thought. *Usual.* Jonas had been with her less than a week, two of which he'd been unconscious. He pretended to sleep until after she left the apartment in the mornings; they exchanged surface pleasantries over dinner when she returned home; and she'd taken to hiding in her room as soon as the meal was over, claiming file work as a flimsy excuse that went undisputed. The word *usual* didn't apply to anything in this situation.

"You'll be glad to get me out of your hair," Jonas observed. Despite its neutrality, the deep rumble of his voice set off an answering vibration in Kate's belly.

She took a steadying breath and faced him again. He'd crossed his arms and leaned against the wall, muscled forearms flexed. A thrum of coiled power rolled off him. Oh, he was definitely feeling better, all right. Kate's gaze slid away as a warm flush started at the soles of her feet and worked its way up her body.

"It hasn't been that bad," she said, sidling past on her way to the kitchen. She battled the urge to stop at his side and meet the intensity in those glittering blue eyes she tried so hard to avoid. Needed to avoid, if she wanted not to throw herself at him. The idea of a casual fling might have crossed her mind in the last few days— perhaps even more than once—but one with the kinds of complications Jonas Burke came with?

That, she could do without.

One more night, Kate. You can do this.

"You could have fooled me, the way you disappear into your room at precisely six-thirty every night." Jonas had followed her, taking up a post in the kitchen door-way. His heat tugged at her as she opened the fridge door to take out a pitcher of filtered water.

"I told you, I have—"

He interrupted her with a snort. "No one takes that much paperwork home with them every night, Kate. Not unless they're avoiding something else."

She took a glass down from the cupboard opposite the fridge, still entirely too close to the man in the doorway for peace of mind. Or peace of body.

"It's okay to admit you want me gone," Jonas contin-ued, a growl threading his voice. "We're both adults here, and I'm well aware you didn't ask for any of this."

"That's not—" She stopped herself, but too late. From the corner of her eye, she saw Jonas frown.

"Not the reason?" he finished. "Then what the hell *is* the reason? Why can't you bring yourself to exchange more than half a dozen words with me over dinner, or tolerate my company for more than a few minutes at a time?"

She rounded on him, her temper flaring. "Don't you dare put all this on me. You're just as bad, sitting there glowering over your plate every night, pretending you're asleep when I leave in the morning. You've made it just as obvious that you don't care for *my* company, Agent Burke."

"Touché," he said, folding his arms again. "Except that's not my reason, either."

The scent of magnolia shampoo reached out to Kate, carried by the heat of his body. She'd never dreamed it could smell so...male. Her world tipped a little to the side, and her grip on the pitcher tightened. Shit.

"We should probably talk about this, don't you think?" Jonas said.

She gave up on the idea of water and shoved the pitcher back into the fridge. She forced her gaze to meet his. To remain steady. But she kept the fridge door open as a shield between them, just in case.

"There's nothing to talk about," she said. "You're leaving in the morning, and I'm going back to my life. End of story."

For a moment, she thought he might argue with her. Hell, a part of her *wanted* him to. Wanted him to push the fridge door closed, take a step closer, reach for her...

But then a shadow darkened his eyes and his lips drew tight and the moment passed.

"You're right," he said. "I wasn't thinking."

Kate swallowed a wholly unreasonable pang of disappointment, struggling to regain mental balance. Then she closed the fridge door and scooped back the hair from her forehead, sighing. "Forget it. Look, it's too early for dinner, so I'm going to head downstairs to the gym for a while. You probably shouldn't do much just yet, but there's a sauna there if you'd like a change of scenery."

"I would like that," Jonas agreed, and just like that, things between them went back to normal.

Which ranked right up there with *usual.*

Jonas endured four suffocating intervals of ten minutes each in the cedar sweat box before he emerged into the main gym's cool air for the final time. Saunas had never been his idea of a good time, but when Kate had suggested it, he'd figured it beat the hell out of sitting by himself in the apartment letting his mind go over that little incident between them again and again.

Not that his attempt at avoidance had worked. He

grimaced into the towel as he wiped his dripping face. Whoever said you couldn't run away from your problems must have encountered blond curls and amber eyes at some time in his life.

He swiped the towel over the back of his neck. What he really needed—if it wasn't for the minor detail of two bullet holes—was a good workout. Something to get his blood moving again. Something other than—

Hell. There he went again. It was going to be a long last night at this rate.

To distract himself, he studied the weight room, separated by a wall of windows from the pool area they'd entered through. It was a well-equipped setup, with free weights and mats lined up along one wall, and just about every weight machine possible spread out across the rest of the floor space. A half-dozen people hoisted and grunted their way through various routines, nodding acknowledgment at one another as they swapped equipment. In the pool, four others stroked steadily through the water.

Jonas turned his attention to locating Kate. If she was going to be much longer, maybe he could head back to the apartment ahead of her and get dinner started. Anything to stay—

The thought evaporated as he spotted the familiar blond curls. Kate sat on one of the leg machines, resting between sets. Her eyes were closed and her head was tipped back, and a fine sheen glistened over the skin of her neck and chest. Jonas's throat tightened as his gaze lingered on the steady rise and fall of the latter. Kate took a deep breath and tensed. Her thighs strained together, pulling against the machine's weight. Long, lean muscles stood out beneath soft, supple skin. Her legs moved apart, then together. Apart. Together.

Jonas swallowed on a dry mouth, unable to tear his gaze away. Or to banish the sudden, vivid image of those thighs tangled in sweat-dampened sheets, parting to wrap around—

Someone brushed against him, mumbling an apology, and he jolted back to reality, realizing he blocked more than one person where he stood. He also realized the potential for extreme embarrassment if anyone happened to notice his current physical state. Bloody hell.

He lowered the towel he'd used for mopping his face to a more strategic location, then turned and headed for the change room. Shower time.

The colder the better.

EIGHTEEN

Kate spotted the well-dressed couple as she wiped down the hip adduction machine with her towel. They stood in the pool area, just inside the door, scanning the water, their heads tipped toward one another in discussion. They carried no equipment bags with them, and their demeanor was unmistakably that of cops. Her heart dropped to the floor. Instinctively and without a shadow of doubt, she knew who they were. Knew they'd found Jonas.

And she had about two minutes to make sure they lost him again.

As nonchalantly as she could manage with her heart thundering in her ears and her gut screaming at her to *run*, she strolled toward the changing rooms, wiping her face with a towel to hide it as she kept as many of the machines as possible between her and the windows onto the pool. She hesitated long enough to ensure the couple hadn't yet moved or taken an interest in her, and then she pushed into the men's locker room.

A nude, dripping Jonas looked over his shoulder at her entry and dropped his towel to cover his butt. "Kate! What the—"

She held a warning finger to her lips, then scanned the room, ducking to make sure no one was in any of the toilet stalls. They were alone. Thank God most of the men in the building favored a later evening workout time, leaving the gym to the female occupants at this hour. She motioned for Jonas to join her at the door. He wrapped the towel around himself and strode to her side.

Kate cracked open the door. "See them? The couple by the pool."

Jonas paled. "Bloody hell. Ramirez and Lewis. I saw her get out of a van across the street earlier, but I thought I was wrong. She's dyed her hair. Is there another way out?"

"That's the only door. I'll have to create a distraction, something to draw their attention—"

"Wait." Jonas put a hand on her arm, holding her back. He nodded across the locker room, and she followed his gaze to the long, narrow windows running along the top of the wall, each covered by a wire mesh screen. "We can get out there."

"We?" she echoed as he returned to his clothing on the bench. She had barely enough time to register denim sliding over strong legs and molding itself to tight, muscled buttocks before he swiveled back to her.

"You can't stay behind. If they're here, it means they know who you are." He brushed past her and grabbed his T-shirt out of a locker.

"I'm a cop, Jonas. What are they going to—?" She broke off as he tugged the T-shirt over his head and sent her a sardonic look.

What would they do? How about shoot her, for starters? And leave her for dead? Like they'd done to one of their own.

Like they'd done to Jonas.

Hell. Still hesitating, she cracked the door open for

another look at Ramirez and Lewis. If there had been a uniformed officer with them—someone official—she might have given them the benefit of the doubt. Might have insisted she remain behind to talk to them while Jonas escaped. But there wasn't. Instead, the couple was showing something to a group of swimmers near the diving board, and Kate's next-door neighbor was pointing toward the weight room. She eased the locker room door closed.

Jonas dragged a bench across the ceramic floor toward the windows. She winced at the noise reverberating off the metal lockers as he positioned it parallel to the wall. He glared over his shoulder at her.

"Kate. You have no choice. You have to come with me."

She dragged a hand over her curls, hating that he was right. Then, with a nod of acknowledgment, she grabbed the end of another bench and pulled it over to rest against the door. First things first. They needed to get out of here, at least for now. Needed to buy themselves time so Jonas could figure out his next move and she could figure out how to extricate herself from that move. She placed a second bench end-to-end with the first. When someone opened the door, there would be about six inches of give before the opposite end met the lockers. It wasn't perfect, but it would work.

Jonas flashed a look over his shoulder as she joined him. "Good thinking," he said, handing her the mesh grate he'd pulled from the window. "What's on the other side of this, anyway?"

Kate leaned the grate against the wall. "The back alley, I think. I've never paid that much attention. Never thought I'd be crawling out one of them."

"I doubt very much you ever thought you'd be doing

any of this." He motioned her onto the bench beside him. "Come on. You first."

Kate grabbed the windowsill and, gritting her teeth against the strain in her shoulder, hauled herself up. She had her torso through the opening and was swinging one leg up to follow when there was a sudden commotion outside the room door. Looking back, she saw her makeshift barricade slide forward a few inches before it caught and held. A man peered through the opening, and startled eyes met hers. The face disappeared, and more shouting ensued.

"They'll be coming around," she told Jonas.

"We're good. Just go," he replied. But the tension in his voice belied the calm of his words.

Adrenaline surged through her veins. For a split second, she viewed herself and the situation from a distance, as if watching a movie. Because things like this just didn't happen in real life.

Then Jonas's hand was on her hip, urging her up.

"Go," he said again, and Kate went.

She landed awkwardly in the alley and crouched against the brick wall of the building, massaging her shoulder. Above her, the right side of Jonas's upper body emerged from the window. One of his legs slid through the opening, then the other. He hung for an instant by his hands, then dropped to the ground beside her. Sweat beaded on a brow a shade paler than it had been a few minutes before. Catching her look of concern, he grimaced and shook his head.

"Don't ask," he advised, then scanned the alley behind her. "We need to move. Somewhere with a lot of people is best."

With an effort, Kate mustered her scattered thoughts.

Where did you run when you were the hunted instead of the hunter?

"A mall?" she suggested. Anywhere she could catch her breath and pull herself together again.

"Too bright. What about somewhere downtown? We can look for a pub or something where the lights are low."

"This *is* downtown."

"I thought you said Ottawa was big enough to hide in."

"When you're on the right side of the law, it seems plenty big enough to lose someone. I've never had to look at it from the other perspective." She heaved herself to her feet. "We'll head down to the Market. It's Friday, so there should be enough of a crowd to lose ourselves in for a while."

She hoped. Dear heaven, how she hoped.

There may have been a steady stream of pedestrians along the sidewalks of Ottawa's Byward Market, but Jonas decided *crowd* was a gross exaggeration. He scowled as he followed in Kate's wake, dodging a couple perusing a menu tacked to a board outside a tiny cafe. There certainly weren't enough people here to hide among. Especially not dressed as Kate was, in her gym shorts and a tank top. All along their route, people were looking back as she passed them, smirking and shaking their heads at the nutcase who didn't know how to dress for a rapidly cooling, late October evening. Blend in, she did not.

Kate stopped under the overhang of a questionable-looking restaurant, and Jonas watched her dig through the pouch she wore clipped around her waist. Whatever was in it was all they had between them. Everything else was either in her locker at the gym or in her apartment, neither of which he could let her visit anytime soon.

"Hold out your hand," she ordered. Jonas obliged, and she counted out some small change into his palm. "...eighty-five, ninety-five, four, four twenty-five, four fifty." She grinned at him triumphantly. "Enough for two coffees. This place even offers free refills. Interested?"

Jonas peered into the restaurant, past the signs and menus covering the grimy window. Small. Dim. No matter where they sat, they'd be able to see who came in the door. It was a good place to for them to get their bearings. And to get Kate off the street and out of the wind. Shoving the handful of change into his pocket, he reached for the door handle.

A few minutes later, he curled his fingers around his steaming mug of coffee and waited for the waiter to move to another table. As soon as he was out of hearing range, Kate cleared her throat.

"Well," she said, "this is an interesting turn of events."

Elbow on the table, Jonas rested a fist against his mouth and stared at the shivering, inadequately clad woman across from him. With makeup removed and blond curls scraped up into a haphazard ponytail, she looked about fifteen. He shook his head. He didn't even know where to begin.

"I should've left sooner," he said finally.

Rubbing her hands over her upper arms, Kate shrugged. "They would've still found me."

"But only you. You could have denied any knowledge of me. Told them the same thing you told your OPP friend. They would have had nothing, Kate. They would have left you alone and moved on." He scraped fingers through his hair. "But now..."

Silence met his words. The ones he'd spoken, and the ones he hadn't. *Now they know you're involved. Now you're in it up to your neck. Now they can't let you live because of what you might know. What you might say.*

Kate shivered again.

Jonas nudged her coffee mug closer. "Drink. It'll warm you up."

She sipped at the steaming liquid. Two tables away, a raucous group of teen males burst into laughter. Jonas glanced over and met the bold gaze of one. The boy made a display of studying Kate's long, bare legs, smirked at Jonas, and then disappeared behind his hand to make a remark to his friends. Fresh guffaws filled the tiny restaurant. Jonas scowled. Dressed as she was, Kate was entirely too memorable and would make it all too easy to track them.

"So," Kate said, "what now?"

"We get you as far away from them as we can. Your sister is out of the question—that's the first place they'll watch. Who else can you stay with?" He didn't like how she'd started shaking her head, but he forged on anyway. "I'll move fast to get things wrapped up, so it should only be a few days. Two weeks, tops. I'll call you when it's safe."

Kate shook her head again. "You forget one thing. I'm a cop. Ergo, just about everyone I know is a cop, too. If I turn up on someone's doorstep wanting to hide out for a few days, there'll be some serious questions. And before you ask, a hotel is out of the question unless I can get back to my apartment first. I have no money, no credit cards, no ID, nothing."

Jonas pointed at her waist pack lying on the table by her elbow. "Nothing in there?"

"The change I gave you and my keys. Not my car

keys, mind you"—she grimaced over the rim of the coffee mug—"because that would make things too easy. Just the ones for the apartment and the locker I can't get near, because it's too bulky to carry the others with me at the gym."

Jonas leaned his head back against the wall behind his chair and closed his eyes. Damn, damn, damn. It wasn't just that he wanted Kate out of danger; he wanted her out of his hair, too. He didn't want to be responsible for someone else's life.

Especially not hers.

He cracked his eyelids open enough to study her. Her confidence in her abilities was a good thing overall. Hell, a cop without that kind of confidence couldn't do the job. In this case, however, he suspected it was *over*confidence, because no matter how capable she thought herself, he'd swear on his own life she'd never tangled with the likes of Ramirez or Lewis. Which made the abilities she prided herself on untested. And *that* made her dangerous—to herself and to him.

She would, without doubt, slow him down. Get in the way. Distract him. He closed his eyes again and gritted his teeth until his jaw ached. He'd be second-guessing his every move, his every step, all so he could make sure she stayed safe. Alive.

She was a liability. It was that simple.

Which was why he couldn't take her with him.

But he couldn't leave her behind, either.

NINETEEN

Kate watched a host of emotions play across Jonas's face, none of them nice. The anger and frustration of the man she'd brought in from the storm had resurfaced with a vengeance, and she realized just how little she really knew about him.

How little she wanted to know.

Hell.

She tugged the elastic from her hair and slid it into the pouch at her waist, then ruffled her curls into a semblance of order. In all honesty, her avoidance of Jonas this week hadn't been entirely due to unruly hormones. Part of it had been simple self-preservation. A certainty that she hadn't wanted to learn more about him or his story or the mess he'd landed himself in. And now they were here.

"You'll have to come with me," Jonas announced.

Kate couldn't help but bristle at the peremptory tone. "Excuse me?"

"Just until I can find somewhere safe to stash you," he added, as if she hadn't spoken.

"You're not *stashing* me anywhere."

He scowled back. "Well, I'm sure as hell not taking you with me. It's too—"

"Dangerous," she interrupted. "Yes, you've told me.

And I've told you: I'm not some fragile piece of pottery that needs to be wrapped up and stored away somewhere. I'm a cop, Jonas, and a damned good one at that."

Refusal darkened his expression—as if it needed darkening—and she sighed, waving away the words she saw forming on his lips.

"Enough," she said. "I get that you don't want help. Hell, I don't particularly want to *give* you help. But if you're right about me being a target now that your friends have shown up, then I'm up to my ass in this—whether either of us likes it or not—and that changes things."

She caught the waiter's eye and held up her mug for a refill. He headed in their direction. She turned her attention back to a tight-lipped, simmering Jonas.

"You don't know what you're getting into," he hedged.

"Then tell me."

"Damn it, Kate…" He trailed off, cradling his head in his hands, elbows resting on the table.

The waiter refilled both their mugs and departed. Kate regarded Jonas's bent head. Was it really *that* hard for this man to accept help? As if he heard the thought, he raised his head and met her gaze, his own diamond hard.

"Fine," he said. "You want the story? Here it is. Six months ago, I was assigned to infiltrate a weapons ring in New Jersey. We'd received intel that a small-time arms dealer, Joseph Quinlan, had a new client in the works, someone with a lot of money, and that his business would be growing exponentially as a result. My usual handler had been sidelined with an injury, so Lewis and Ramirez were assigned to work with me. Once I had Quinlan cold, they were responsible for—"

"I know how a takedown works."

"Right. Well, when it came time for the buy, the only ones who showed were Quinlan, me and my two partners." Jonas's mouth twisted. "There was no buyer, no money, and no backup. Just us. Lewis and Ramirez shot Quinlan first, then me."

"What about the money they said you took?"

"As fictional as the buyer, I'm guessing."

"Wait." Kate frowned. "You think Lewis and Ramirez set up both you *and* Quinlan? But why?"

"My guess? Me, because I was nosing around too much. Quinlan, because he was bad for business."

Her jaw dropped. Cops on the take was one thing, but what Jonas suggested? Holy shit. "You think they're dealing," she said. "Agents in the ATF."

"Yes. And not just them." Jonas took a swig of coffee and set down the mug again, staring into it. "About eight months ago, I started digging into some old files at the Bureau in my spare time. One of my deals had gone sour at the last minute a few weeks before—something I thought I'd tied up tight. Not only did the perp come out squeaky clean at the takedown, but the shipment never surfaced again. Anywhere. It was the third time it had happened since I transferred to the New Jersey bureau."

His gaze returned to hers. "I'm not a careless man, Kate. Before Jersey—in fourteen years with the Bureau— I'd screwed up exactly once. I found it hard to believe I'd become that sloppy almost overnight. Then, when I started digging, I found a lot of deals in Jersey had a tendency to go bad."

"Hell," she breathed. "You think someone higher up is involved?"

"I think it's possible. That's why I haven't called in. I don't know who I *can* call."

Kate sat back, digesting the impact of his words. Their enormity. Her brain churned. Somewhere in the back of her mind, she realized, she'd been considering the possibility that Jonas would turn himself in to the RCMP after all. She'd been prepared to guarantee his safety if he did, certain she could ensure he was handed over to the custody of someone other than Lewis and Ramirez. Someone who could carry out an investigation, who would make sure Jonas stayed alive for a fair trial. But this...this changed everything.

Regardless of Jonas's story, the force would have no choice but to turn him over to the ATF, because refusal to do so would do untold damage to the working relationship between the two agencies—not to mention cause serious political waves. And if Jonas was right about having stumbled into a whole nest of dirty cops, then it wouldn't matter which agents took actual custody of him. It would just be a matter of time before some kind of "accident" resulted in his death. Guaranteed.

And if *he* died, any loose ends would die with him.

Kate tucked her hands under the table, clenching them in her lap. Hell, hell, *hell*. There really was no way to extricate herself from this, was there? For better or worse, until this whole mess was sorted out, her future had just become inextricably linked with Jonas Burke's.

And her career was about to be shot all to hell in the process.

God. Laura was going to kill her for this. If Kate lived long enough.

She swallowed against the lump in her chest and tried to think past the paralysis of panic. They needed a plan. They. Jonas and her. Together for the foreseeable future. She forced herself to take a long, slow, controlled breath.

"All right, then," she said. "I guess we'd better figure

out what we're doing. I assume you have proof of all this?"

"Not here, I don't."

Of course. Any evidence that existed would be in New Jersey, which was about as accessible as the Antarctic at the moment, given that Jonas had no passport or ID with which to make it past the border guards. Kate drummed fingertips on the tabletop. There was no way around it. They were going to have to bring someone else in on this. Someone they could trust. Someone who would trust *them*.

Jonas so wasn't going to like this.

She stood abruptly and held out a hand across the table, palm up. "I need a quarter."

Blue eyes narrowed. "Why?"

"So I can get us across the border."

"How—"

"Please don't ask," she said, "because I really don't want to fight with you. Just...trust me."

His expression went flat. Unreadable. She suspected it had been a very long time since he'd trusted anyone. Was he even capable? She waited.

The bell over the door of the restaurant tinkled. A second later, a cold draft hit the back of Kate's legs and her bare arms. The hand she'd extended wobbled as she shivered, and a shadow crossed Jonas's eyes. His jaw like concrete, he dug out one of the coins she'd given him earlier from his pocket and placed it, warm from the heat of his body, in her palm. His fingers closed over hers.

"I'm sorry," he said. "I'm sorry you've gotten messed up in this, and I'm sorry I don't know how to get you out of it."

"Me, too," she said. "But let's remember that it's not your fault, shall we? I could have turned you in anywhere along the line, Jonas, including now. *My* decisions put me here, not yours."

She tugged her fingers free of his, resisted—only just—the urge to smooth away the scowl between his brows, and headed for the pay phone at the back of the restaurant.

TWENTY

Jonas followed Kate through the poster-papered doorway and up a set of uneven stairs lit by a single dim bulb at the top. He made himself focus on the rhythmic beat of music filtering through the wall to their left, rather than the equally rhythmic sway of the female rump ascending at eye level in front of him. Another time and place, maybe, but for now, if he and Kate were going to be spending time together, he couldn't afford to let himself be distracted.

Neither of them could afford it.

His fingers brushed against something sticky on the handrail, and he grimaced, rubbing his hand against his jeans. Kate looked over her shoulder.

"It's a bit loud in here," she said, her voice raised over the thud of drums, "but the clientele tends toward the closed-mouth side if someone starts asking questions. It's a good place not to be noticed."

She reached the top and pulled open a heavy metal door, and the music volume increased by a factor of about a thousand. Jonas winced and put his mouth close to her ear.

"A *little* loud?" he yelled.

She grinned at him and stepped into the bar. Jonas followed. Standing behind the still too-scantily clad Kate, he scanned the interior, taking in the mostly brick and rough wood construction, the tables crowded together, the lights focused on a corner of the room he couldn't see over the heads of the patrons. The place was packed. That was good. And there were two additional exit signs that he could see. Also good.

Kate tugged at his sleeve. "This way," she bellowed.

With little other choice, Jonas followed as she threaded her way between tables, stools, and people, heading toward what turned out to be a nook tucked around a corner at the back. Kate had refused to tell him what she was up to, and he found himself studying everyone in his path with a jaundiced eye. *Trust me*, she'd said. She had no idea what she asked.

Kate ducked under a rope that cordoned off the nook. Jonas scowled and did likewise. Again he took stock. It was marginally quieter away from the speakers and subwoofers, and all the tables but one were empty. There were no other exits here. Kate stopped beside the occupied table. A tall, lanky man rose to his feet, gaze focused not on Kate, but on Jonas.

His gaze was not friendly.

Dressed from head to toe in leather studded with enough metal to weigh down an elephant, his entire air was one of menace. Jonas's hands curled at his sides. What in hell was Kate planning? To have Hells Angels accompany them across the border? He shot her a hard look.

Oblivious, she stood on tiptoe to speak into the other man's ear. His gaze remained locked on Jonas. His expression didn't change. Kate dropped back down to her heels and motioned Jonas forward. Not without second thoughts, he stepped away from his only escape route. Out in the main bar, the music hit a discordant, jangling series of notes that signaled the end of a song, and then a woman's voice informed the audience the band would be taking a half-hour break. Canned music took over at a slightly lower decibel level.

"Much better," Kate said. "I wasn't sure my voice would hold out past introductions."

She paused and cleared her throat. Her gaze skittered away from Jonas's. He scowled, unease growling through his gut.

"Kate?"

Reluctant amber eyes met his. "I trust him, Jonas. Remember that."

What in hell—?

She took a deep breath. "Jonas, this is my partner, Corporal Dave Jennings. Dave, Agent Jonas Burke of the ATF."

Her *partner*? But Jonas had no time to process the announcement—or the discrepancy between this man's appearance and Kate's usual office attire—before the other man's stance shifted to aggressive.

"What the hell, Dex. There's a—"

"There's a warrant out for him," Kate interrupted. "I know. But it's not what you think. I can explain."

"You—" Her partner stared at her. "You're kidding me. You're *harboring* him? Are you out of your goddamn mind?"

Jonas glanced toward the exit. This was such a bad idea, he didn't even know where to begin. If only Kate had said something, told him what she planned, he could have—

Warm fingers settled onto his knotted forearm. Squeezed gently.

"Sit," Kate urged. "Dave's okay."

Jonas looked again at the leather- and metal-clad man

towering behind her. At the menace etched into every watchful line of Dave Jennings's body. Like hell he was okay.

"You should have told me," he muttered, for her ears only.

"You wouldn't have come with me if I had," she whispered back. "We need help, Jonas, and I trust Dave. Please. Give him a chance."

"Dex?" Jennings asked. "Everything all right?"

Amber eyes met Jonas's, communicating reassurance. "Give *me* a chance," she said.

"Five minutes," he growled. "And then I'm out of here, with or without you."

The three of them sat at the table, Jonas carefully positioning himself with clear access to and an unobstructed view of the only doorway. Jennings's narrowed eyes assured him the other man had noticed. They both waited for Kate to begin. The music from the bar vibrated through the floor beneath their feet.

She took a deep breath. "We've worked together a long time, Dave. You know I wouldn't lie to you."

"I'm listening."

"Jonas was framed, but we have to get him back to the States if we're going to prove it."

Kate's partner scowled. "*We?*"

In a few, rapid words, Kate filled him in on how she'd found Jonas and all that had happened since, ending with, "They tracked us to my apartment this evening. They don't want Jonas arrested. They want him dead. And they can't afford to leave any loose ends. I need—"

"Are you out of your mind?" Jennings demanded for the second time, staring at her. "There is no way in hell I'm helping you go underground, Kate. Turn him in.

Now. Like you should have done at the beginning. Let the force sort things out. If what he says is true—"

"The force won't sort out anything, and you know it. They'll turn him over to the ATF. They'll have no choice. And if they do, he's as good as dead."

"But *you'll* be alive."

"Maybe. Maybe not. And even if they don't come after me, I'll have Jonas's death on my conscience."

"Then lie low. Find somewhere to hole up. Hell, you can stay with—"

Kate cut him off. "No. You have a family, Dave."

Dave Jennings studied his partner for a long time, his expression fierce and his lips pressed tight. Then he thrust a hand through his hair. "Freaking hell, Dexter. You're killing me here. You're absolutely certain he's clean?"

Kate's eyes flickered over Jonas, and the trust he saw in the brief look warmed him to the center of his jaded soul. She really did believe in him, he realized with slow shock. He couldn't remember the last time anyone else had. She turned back to her partner.

"I'm certain."

Jennings regarded her for another moment. Then he nodded. "All right. What do you need?"

Not until the words were uttered and the tension left his shoulders did Jonas realize how wire-taut he'd been strung. He slumped back in the chair, ignoring the question niggling at the back of his brain: Just how close did a partnership have to be to foster the kind of trust Jennings had in Kate? Not that it mattered, because it was none of his business.

No distractions.

"Whatever you can give us," Kate was saying. "A vehicle, if you can, and some cash. I'd ask you to go back to the apartment for my keys and wallet, but if they're watching..."

"Will a thousand do?"

"I don't have that much in my account, and even if I did, I can't repay you until—"

"We'll worry about it when you get back." Jennings took out his wallet and handed a bank card to her. "The code is the same as my extension at the office. Do you have your badge with you?"

"I have nothing. No driver's license, no badge. Nothing."

Shrugging out of the studded leather jacket he wore, Jennings handed it across the table to Kate. "My spare piece is in the left hand pocket." He reached down to retrieve a brown paper bag from the floor and handed that to her as well.

"Are you sure? If anyone finds out—"

"It would just be one more item on a growing list of transgressions where this situation is concerned," her partner pointed out. "Take the piece, Kate."

"Thank you." Kate stood and glanced at Jonas. "I'll be back in a minute. Dave brought some jeans and a shirt for me to change into."

Jonas watched Kate make her way out into the noisy, crowded main bar area, heading for the ladies' room. When he was sure she was out of earshot, he turned to Jennings.

"You can't let her come with me," he said.

"Excuse me?"

"I said, you can't—"

Jennings waved him silent. "I heard you. That wasn't a request for you to repeat yourself, it was my expression of incredulity. You heard her. She'd never risk someone else's safety for her own."

Frustration drove Jonas out of his chair to pace the floor between tables. The bullet holes in his side and thigh tugged uncomfortably, irritated by his climb out the gym window, reminding him he wasn't quite there yet. Wasn't in top form. Maybe wasn't capable of looking after Kate if things went sideways.

"And I'm not willing to risk *her* safety," he growled. "There must be some way to convince her to lie low, damn it. We both know she's not up to handling a situation like this."

"Because of her shoulder, you mean?"

Her shoulder? Right. The one she rubbed at all the time. He'd never gotten around to asking her about it. He shook his head. "The shoulder only compounds matters."

"Then what?"

Jonas snorted. He had to spell it out? "She's behind a desk all day. When was the last time she was even out in the field? Has she *ever* been out?"

Jennings shook his head. "I'm confused. What exactly did Kate tell you she does?"

"She didn't have to tell me. I've seen how she dresses for work, and I know what the streets look like on a cop. She doesn't have it."

Surprise glinted in Jennings's eyes. "Wait. You've decided she's a pencil pusher?" He snorted. "I'm guessing you haven't told her that."

"You're telling me she's not?"

Jennings laced fingers behind his head and tipped back in his chair. He regarded Jonas for a long moment without responding. Then a corner of his mouth quirked upward. "I'm telling you that I might not like her decision to help you out, but I trust her to look after herself. She's a good cop, Agent Burke. Excellent, even. If I were you, I'd worry less about her and more about how to deal with your little problem when she gets you where you're going. I'd also ask her about the shoulder some time."

Before Jonas could absorb the other man's words—or the new information they carried—Kate came through the opening from the bar again, brown paper bag in one hand and Jennings' leather jacket in the other. She'd changed into jeans and a moss-green sweatshirt, under which Jonas's trained gaze could make out the faint bulge of the weapon Jennings had given her.

A determined amber gaze locked with his, and he knew he'd lost the battle.

Like it or not, Kate was coming with him.

TWENTY-ONE

Kate reached the table where Dave still sat and held out the bag that now contained her gym clothes. "Thank you."

"You're sure this is the only way?" he asked.

"I'm sure."

Dave climbed to his feet and took the paper bag from her. "Then forget the thanks," he said gruffly, looping an arm around her shoulders, "and just promise me you'll come back in one piece."

"I promise." She returned her partner's hug, met Jonas's grim expression over his shoulder, and stepped back. "We should get going. I want to make the bridge as soon as possible, before your friends decide to file paperwork on me as well."

For a second, she thought Jonas might object yet again to her continued presence, but instead he glanced at Dave, paused, and then gave a single, cryptic nod.

"Ready when you are."

"Johnstown?" Dave asked.

Kate nodded. "The border guards there don't ask me for ID anymore." Liaising with them was a major part of her job working with Dave, and she'd come to know most of them as friends. Most of them. "I'll tell them I left my wallet in Ottawa."

"You really think they'll let you through?" Dave looked skeptical.

"I think it's our best chance. Our only other option is to try a river crossing somewhere, and that will take too long."

"What about after you cross?"

She looked askance at Jonas.

"New Jersey. Newark." Jonas replied. "I have resources there."

Dave nodded. He held out a set of keys to Kate. "All right. There's another grand in my savings account if you run short. Take what you need. The SUV is parked on Dalhousie. Insurance and registration are in the glove box."

Kate took the keys from him. "What will you tell Julie?"

"That I loaned it to a friend whose vehicle broke down. She buses to work, so I can use hers. What do you want me to tell the office?"

"Play dumb. You haven't seen me or heard from me. There's no point in you going down with me."

Her partner nodded again, and his somber gaze met hers. "Be careful out there, Dexter. No more hospital visits, understand?"

Kate glanced at the glowing blue numbers on the dashboard clock. Ten forty-nine. The deeper dark of the countryside had settled about them after they left the city, dotted with lights from homes and farms set back from the highway. Above the shadowed trees, a full moon had begun its ascent, a bright, shining disk hanging in the sky. Jonas's presence loomed in the passenger seat beside her. He hadn't said *boo* to her since they'd left Dave at the bar, and the hour's drive to the U.S. bridge had begun to feel like a lifetime.

She didn't even want to think about the days to come.

Lips pressed tight, she adjusted the rearview mirror, noting a set of headlights about a half kilometer back. She supposed Jonas was having some issues coming to terms with their unplanned partnership. Frankly, she was having issues, too, now that they'd managed to escape the immediate threat and the accompanying adrenaline rush. How in the name of sanity had she managed to convince herself that taking up Jonas Burke's cause was a good idea? A man who claimed to have no friends and more than his share of enemies. Who even now maintained a taut, stubborn silence that seethed with his disapproval at her involvement.

And, last but far from least, whose every shift against seat leather made her libido do a sinuous shimmy from the roots of her hair to the soles of her feet.

She exhaled in a gust that drew a glance from Jonas. Not that she could see him look her way in the dark, but she could sure as hell feel it.

Her toes curled inside her running shoes. She glanced again into the rearview mirror. The headlights were still there. Still the same distance back. She eased her pressure on the gas pedal, and Dave's SUV slowed fractionally. If the lights caught up and passed them, all was good. If they maintained their distance, however...

Jonas cleared his throat, startling her into a small swerve over the center line.

"Seeing as how I can't get rid of you and we have some time to kill," he said lazily, "I suppose you might as well tell me about yourself."

She raised an eyebrow. "Small talk, Agent Burke? Are you sure you can handle that?"

"It's going to be a long few days if we're not speaking."

"True." Kate rested an arm along the base of the driver's window and flexed her one-handed grip on the steering wheel. "Fine. What would you like to know?"

"You could start by telling me about your shoulder."

From silent to blunt. There didn't seem to be a happy medium where conversation with this man was concerned.

"Jennings said I should ask," he added.

Kate frowned. Dave knew she didn't like to talk about the shooting. Why—?

"He seemed to think I was operating under a misapprehension where your policing skills were concerned."

Ah. A smile tugged at Kate's lips. "Maybe a little," she agreed.

"So—the shoulder?"

"I was shot. Drug raid."

A cough. Then, "You. In a drug raid."

She glanced sideways at his shadowy form. "You did catch the part about me being a cop, right?"

"You just didn't strike me as that experienced. I stand corrected. How long did you work narcotics?"

"I didn't."

"Uniformed backup?"

"Third through the door, actually. Tactical."

The hair prickled along the nape of her neck. Those headlights in the mirror weren't any closer. Damn. She eased off the gas another fraction.

"No wonder Jennings found me so amusing," Jonas muttered. "You should have told me."

"You didn't ask, and it didn't seem—"

"Worth the effort?" he interrupted.

"Important," she said, her brows drawing together at

the bitterness underlying his words. "You were going to be leaving, and I was going back to my life, remember? The...incident...it isn't something I talk about."

Jonas went quiet again. It didn't last.

"Were you at your parents' house to recover?"

"No. To help my sister with their estate. They were killed in a car accident a few months ago."

"I'm sorry."

"Don't be. We weren't very close."

"Your job?" he hazarded. "Your sister mentioned that she didn't even know what it was you did. I'm guessing your career choice wasn't a popular one?"

Kate thought back to their time at the farmhouse. She frowned. "I thought you were out cold when we were talking about that."

"I'm good at playing dead," he said without apology, as she tried to remember what else he might have over-heard. "Your job?" he prodded.

She stared through the windshield into the night. "No, my career choice wasn't popular."

Understatement of the century. There had been a chance of forgiveness once, when she'd brought a man home to meet them a few years after joining the force. Grant Douglas had been ultra polite, conservative, and business-suited—much more in line with what her parents had wanted for her. What they'd expected from her. Especially when, at Grant's urging, she'd introduced him as a special envoy to the U.S. embassy rather than a fellow cop, and the status he'd bestowed on her by asso-ciation had almost made up for her uniform and gun.

Until she'd broken off the engagement a year later.

Her father had never spoken to her again. And because her mother had never been very good at standing up to him, Kate hadn't exchanged more than a few words with her mom after that, either. Which made it all the more ironic that she and her ex-fiancé had remained on such good terms.

Her gaze flicked to the mirror again and lingered there. The headlights were still there. Her neck hairs prickled again, and she tapped a finger against the steering wheel.

"Kate?" prompted Jonas's deep voice.

"Hm?" She realized he was waiting for a response to something. "Sorry, I wasn't listening."

"I said it's a good thing your sister doesn't seem to share their..." He trailed off and twisted in his seat to look over his shoulder. "Trouble?" he asked.

"I'm not sure. It's been there since we got onto the highway."

"That's why you slowed down."

She nodded. "But it hasn't gotten any closer."

"Right." Jonas swung around to face forward again. "There's an exit coming up. Take it."

She switched on her turn signal and, a second later, slowed as she moved into the right-hand exit lane. They drove onto the ramp, their headlights highlighting the curve of the road, the safety barriers, the trees on both sides. The car that had been following them whizzed past on the highway.

Swallowing hard, Kate gripped the steering wheel with both hands. She continued right on the road at the top of the ramp, then made a U-turn and doubled back to the entrance onto the highway. As if by some unspoken, mutual agreement, neither she nor Jonas attempted to return to the conversation, signaling an end to their attempt at small talk. But not to their tension.

A couple of kilometers down the road, Jonas leaned forward to turn on the radio, his arm passing near enough to Kate's that she felt a brush of air against her skin. The loss of his heat when he withdrew again. She shifted away from him, leaning against her door as a woman's throaty croon joined the thrum of the engine in the space between them, singing the lyrics from an old-time song about being vexed, perplexed, and oversexed.

Kate's gaze swung to the radio. Seriously?

From the seat beside her came the unmistakable sound of a muffled snort. She froze, and her entire body flushed hot, putting her instantly back in her kitchen, with Jonas inches away and the fridge door between them.

"We should probably talk about this, don't you think?" Jonas had asked.

And she had replied, ever so blithely, *"There's nothing to talk about. You're leaving in the morning, and I'm going back to my life. End of story."*

Except now it wasn't.

"Bewitched, bothered, and bewildered am I," crooned the voice.

TWENTY-TWO

Kate slowed to the posted speed limit as they approached the border crossing. On the left, the CBSA—Canadian Border Services—slid past, lit up by enough lumen power to highlight its every detail: the long, low brick buildings; the parking area empty of all but a handful of vehicles that included an RCMP cruiser; the lanes with their barriers, two of the four closed at this hour.

Ahead, the two lanes of the bypass curved past the duty-free shop, then merged into one before becoming part of a road again. Beyond that, the bridge across the St. Lawrence.

The knot in Kate's stomach sent out tentacles to wrap around her lungs.

Two and a half kilometers of bridge, followed by an attempt to enter the United States of America without ID.

Without her badge.

Illegally.

Freaking hell.

She wiped a sweat-slicked palm against one thigh. Warm, strong fingers closed over hers.

"You don't have to do this," Jonas said. "We can find another way."

"I'm fine." She tugged her hand free of the comfort she

didn't want to need and wrapped it around the steering wheel again. "And this really is the fastest way. We've been working on a joint file with your customs guys for the last three months. I've been down so often they haven't bothered asking me for ID the last two times. We've even started going for coffee together."

"But you've never gone through with a passenger at nearly midnight on a Friday night."

No. No, she hadn't.

"It'll work," she said. *It has to work.* "You pretend you're asleep. I'll tell them you're a colleague or something. As long as they don't ask for your ID, it'll work."

"Or something?" Jonas echoed. "I hope you have a better idea than that by the time we get there."

A high-pitched trill cut off any retort Kate might have made. Her eyes locked onto the lighted display of a cell phone on the console between the seats—a cheap burner she'd bought when they fueled up before leaving the city. She'd called Dave with the number. No one else had it. The phone rang again. She picked it up, eschewing the customary *hello*.

"What's up?"

"Where are you?" her partner demanded, his voice tight.

Beneath the tires, the asphalt road gave way to the bridge's deck, and the high-pitched hum of rubber against metal filled the vehicle. Pole-mounted lights passed by overhead, illuminating the interior in flashes.

"We just hit the bridge."

"Turn around. Now."

She peered out the windshield at the bridge framework slipping by on both sides. "There are cameras. If I pull a U-turn, they'll—"

"There's a warrant out, Kate. For you. The border crossings know."

A hiss of air beside her told her Jonas had heard. The knot and all its tentacles turned to ice. Kate struggled to breathe. "What? But how—?"

"I don't know. It doesn't matter. Just *turn around*."

She lifted her foot from the gas. The vehicle began to slow. They passed under the first of the suspension bridge's two towers. "They'll come after us."

A tiny pause. "Yes."

They passed under the second tower. Ahead, a sign announced the U.S. border. She had no time for hesitation. She needed to make a decision. Now.

She dropped the phone onto the console, slammed on the brakes, and wrenched the steering wheel hard left. The SUV swerved into the oncoming lane, coming to a stop with its nose a foot from the rail. A minivan screeched to a halt inches from Jonas's door. A cacophony of horns blared.

"Kate?" Jonas's voice was tight.

She shook her head, slammed the gearshift into reverse, and stomped on the accelerator. To the chorus of more horns, she slewed backward into the second point of a three-point turn. Braked. Threw the gearshift into drive. Wrenched again on the steering wheel. Jammed the gas pedal to the floor.

The SUV shot forward with a roar, headed back across the dark river toward Canadian soil. The howl of tires against metal rose in pitch as the speedometer climbed. A hundred kilometers an hour. One twenty. One thirty. The lights of CBSA came into sight at the end of the bridge. Headlights in the other lane streamed by in a blur. Beneath the vehicle, the bridge deck gave way to pavement.

Kate did a rapid calculation in her head. The SUV could take out one of the barriers without a problem, but the armed CBSA officers were another story altogether—and they'd have had more than enough time to get into position. Even if she and Jonas didn't get shot, chances were good that their vehicle would take a hit. And if that happened...

Jonas's hand closed on her arm, warm and strong. "Don't," he said gruffly. "Whatever you're thinking, don't. Stop now, Kate. I'll tell them I took you hostage. That I forced you to drive me here."

She flashed him the briefest of looks. "And what, you let me go to work every day until now?"

His grip tightened.

"We'll think of something else. But you have to stop. Running from Lewis and Ramirez is one thing, but running from your own colleagues? I won't let you do that."

Kate stayed focused on the road ahead, and then she saw it. The fork, where the road that had brought them here looped around the Canadian border facility. The way in to the bridge and the U.S. and, in the current circumstances, their only way out. She tugged her arm away from Jonas's grip.

"Too late," she said. "And I'd hang on if I were you. Things could get a little hairy."

She veered to the left, into the one-way, oncoming traffic. A sedan swerved to miss her, its sole occupant leaning on the horn and gesticulating madly.

"*Jesus!*" Jonas muttered. From the corner of her eye, she saw him cinch his seat belt tighter. She thought about doing the same, but didn't dare take either hand from the wheel.

The road widened to two lanes, giving her more room

to maneuver, but not much. Cars sped by, dodging left and right as she barreled toward them. The SUV's speed climbed to a hundred and forty as they blew past the CBSA building, the parking lots, and a lone figure racing for the police cruiser parked under a lamppost. A directional sign blinked past: left to the 401, right to County Road 2, which was little more than a meandering two-lane road that followed the river. Hell. Which one? She'd been in her fair share of high-speed chases before, but never on this side of the fence.

Focus, Dexter.

They could go faster on the 401, but once they hit the divided four-lane freeway there was no way off until the next exit—and every likelihood that exit would be blocked by the time they reached it. A county road, on the other hand, would have side roads. Places to lie low until the heat died down. If she could stay far enough ahead that long.

She raised her voice over the engine noise. "I'm going to take the secondary road!" She slammed on the brakes long enough to negotiate the sharp right turn, then opened up the gas again as they once more headed past the CBSA toward the river, this time on the opposite side. "There are more places to hide."

"Good," Jonas said tightly. "Then I suggest you find one. We've got company."

Kate glanced at the flashing blue and red lights in the side mirror. The RCMP cruiser. Freaking hell. Adrenaline surged through her veins as she approached the intersection for County Road 2, desperately trying to remember the lay of the land in these parts. She'd driven this area a handful of times, tops, and never at insane speeds in the dark.

The T-intersection had only one stop sign—hers. She

ignored it, took the corner on two wheels and a prayer, and bounced off the curb, narrowly missing a hydro pole and a second police cruiser, this one belonging to the OPP. The SUV settled onto all four tires again, and she exhaled in a gust. In the rearview mirror, she saw the police cruiser's dome lights come on. The vehicle pulled a sharp U-turn and got in line behind the RCMP car.

And then there were two.

Shit.

"You're doing great," Jonas said. "Ignore them. Stay focused. Where to from here?"

His voice held the level of calm reserved for discussing dinner plans, and Kate swallowed a burble of hysterical laughter as they shot through the sleepy riverside township. *Later, Dexter. You can lose it later.*

But not now. Definitely not now. Because *where to?* She didn't have a freaking clue.

Sirens screaming in their wake, they rocketed past houses and along the river shoreline. Lights grew fewer, the night darker. The road curved inland again, running through trees and between farm fields. The flashing red and blue in the mirror grew brighter. Ahead, the taillights of a semi-truck and trailer loomed in their path. Beyond, the headlights of another truck headed toward them.

A plan formed.

Perhaps not the smartest plan, but a plan nonetheless. One that would give them the distance they needed if they were going to have a hope in hell of losing the cruisers. They hurtled toward the semi ahead of them, and then, before she lost her nerve, Kate swerved around it into the other lane—and the path of the other truck. Hot on her tail, both cruisers followed.

The oncoming truck flashed its headlights at them,

and the semi alongside them sounded its air horn in long, frantic blasts. With her foot pressing the gas pedal to the floor, Kate willed the SUV to greater speed, but the heavy vehicle was already moving flat out.

Jonas cursed.

Kate prayed for a miracle.

Behind them, the police cruisers careened back in behind the semi as blinding white filled the windshield. Kate waited another heartbeat and then, with the shriek of brakes filling her ears, yanked the steering wheel to the right and swerved back into her own lane in front of the semi she'd passed.

Close.

Too close.

Way too close.

Shaking and hollow with shock, Kate looked into the rearview mirror at the truck jack-knifed across the road and the lights of one cruiser sitting too low to still be on the road. She wanted nothing more than to pull over and puke her guts out, but instead she swallowed the bile rising in her chest, resolutely kept the accelerator glued to the floorboards, and sped on into the darkness.

TWENTY-THREE

J onas watched the police car's lights in the side mirror. Kate's driving stunt might not have thrown off their pursuers altogether, but it had at least gained them some distance. Their only issue now was how to keep it. He glanced at the tightly wound woman gripping the steering wheel.

He cleared his throat. "Talk to me," he said. *Keep me in the loop.*

She shook her head, her eyes darting to the rearview mirror. Jonas's heart sank. She had nothing to say. No ideas. And the flashing lights were slowly gaining.

Then, "The owner's manual," she said. "It should be in the glove box. Find out which fuse is for the headlights in this thing."

"Can't you just turn them off?"

She reached out and hit a switch. The lights illuminating the road in front of the vehicle remained on. She shrugged as she met his gaze. "Daytime running lights," she said. "They're required by law in Canada."

A safety feature that would, ironically, be the death of them both if they didn't disable it.

Jonas felt for the glove compartment release. It dropped open, its interior lit by a small bulb. The owner's manual sat front and center, on top of a plastic folder.

Dave Jennings was an organized man. Jonas tugged the book free and slammed the compartment closed. He switched on the overhead dome, raising an eyebrow at Kate.

"Can I ask how you plan to see where you're going without headlights?"

"Moonlight and blind luck," she replied. "Unless, of course, you have any other ideas?"

The tension underlying her voice told him she thought the idea as bad as he did, but no, he had nothing else to offer. Driving blind through the dark it would be. He flipped to the index at the back of the manual.

In the side mirror, the cruiser behind continued to gain on them.

"Now is a good time," Kate said through clenched teeth. "This thing won't go any faster."

"Hang on," Jonas growled back. "Okay, I've found the schematic."

He studied the page for a moment, running a finger down the list of fuses at the side, matching them to their numbers on the diagram. Then he flipped back a page, searching for the fuse box location itself. His gaze locked onto another diagram. Flicked to Kate. Went back to the drawing.

They had to be joking.

"Damn it, Burke!" Panic laced Kate's voice.

He unclipped his seatbelt. "Fine, but just remember this was *your* idea," he muttered.

"What do you mean?"

"The panel's under the dash on your side."

Ignoring her mumbled, "Are you freaking *kidding* me?" he slid down in his seat and lay sideways across the console between them. His head came to rest on Kate's thigh. Their speed faltered for an instant. Then she pushed down on the accelerator again, a bunched tension replacing the softness beneath Jonas's cheek. He swallowed. Hard.

Hell. If impure thoughts hadn't already crossed his mind where Kate Dexter was concerned, that reaction would have made damned sure they did.

Clenching the owner's manual between his teeth, he fumbled for the fuse panel cover, located under the dashboard just above the accelerator. Kate's leg shifted under his cheek. He bit down harder on the book, fighting to hold onto the urgency of their situation. To ignore the body heat warming his stubbled jawline and the overwhelmingly female scent electrifying his senses.

God, even her kneecaps smelled delicious.

The panel cover parted from its catches without warning. Jonas grabbed for it but drew back when his hand connected instead with a fine-boned ankle. He extracted the manual from between his teeth.

"Sorry," he muttered. Kate said nothing. He peered at the myriad tiny fuses and the maze of wires sprouting from the panel. Great. In his present state he should figure out which one to pull by next Christmas. He held the manual at an angle to catch the light, searching for some kind of similarity—any similarity—between the diagram and the real thing.

Reaching through the wires, he tugged at one of the fuses. The heater fan died. Kate moved again, her firm, jeans-clad thigh rubbing against his head.

Jonas closed his eyes. *Give me strength*, he pleaded silently. *And failing that, a really cold shower would be nice about now.*

He opened his eyes and replaced the fuse. The SUV cornered sharply, and he flung out an arm to keep from sliding to the floor as his face mashed into supple denim.

The vehicle straightened out again. He turned his nose and mouth away from Kate's leg, breathed, and reached for another fuse.

"That's the radio. The clock just went off," Kate said from above him.

"Thanks." Back in with that one. A third one out.

"That's it." Her voice was filled with relief. The SUV slowed as she adjusted her speed to navigate by moonlight alone.

Now the cruiser would really be gaining on them.

Jonas squinted at the book again, tracing a finger over the schematic and studying the accompanying list. He peered at the panel under the dash. He'd just removed the third from the bottom in the second row, and that had been—

"You can come up now, Burke," Kate snapped.

Funny how she called him Burke instead of Jonas whenever things got a little tense between them. He tipped his head back and shot her a grin.

"Actually, I can't. The headlights are on a different fuse from the taillights."

She stared straight ahead.

"And the brake lights are on another altogether."

Her lips compressed, but he was wise enough to swallow the chuckle that threatened. Antagonize her enough and she might slam on the brakes just to dump his butt on the floor, and they didn't have that kind of time to spare. He returned his attention to the manual, found the fuse he thought he needed, and yanked the real-life one from the panel. Then he pushed himself upright and glanced at the side mirror. No flashing lights for the moment, but he doubted they were far behind.

"Try the brakes," he ordered.

The vehicle lurched. Jonas saw no corresponding glow at the back of the vehicle.

"Got them," he said with satisfaction. Only the dome light remained to give them away. He switched it off and snapped his seatbelt back into place.

"Good," said Kate. "Then hang on."

The four-by-four slewed violently to the right, fish-tailed twice, then spun left and came to a shuddering halt at the rear of an unlit, deserted service station. They waited in silence, both twisted in their seats to stare through the back window down the highway. The flashing lights came into view around the corner on the county road they'd left, then disappeared on the other side of the abandoned service station. Jonas and Kate turned to the windshield. They waited some more.

The cruiser's lights speared through the trees on the other side of the building. Its speed was unchecked. Jonas expelled a long breath. They'd done it. They'd lost him. *Kate* had lost him. And Jonas didn't know whether to kiss her or tear a strip off her a mile wide for the stunt she'd pulled to get them here. He cleared his throat.

"Do me a favor?" he asked.

"What?" Her voice sounded as shaky as his guts felt in the aftermath of their run.

"That truck thing you did back there? Please don't get any more adventurous than that with me in the vehicle."

She looked at him. He looked at her. A tiny giggle escaped her. He reciprocated with a snort. Suddenly, the floodgates of tension thrown wide, they both roared with laughter. They sat in the dark, two cops wanted by the law on both sides of the border, running for their lives, and collapsed in waves of hilarity.

At last their laughter died away and Kate restarted the vehicle and put it in gear. "We'll head closer to Cornwall," she said. "There are a couple of motels on the outskirts. We'll find one where we can hole up until morning. The local force won't have a lot of cars on the road at this hour, so we should be okay."

And just like that, their shared moment of amusement was done. With a sigh tinged with more regret than he'd admit to, Jonas settled back in his seat and returned to watching over the dark side mirror as Kate navigated through the countryside by moonlight.

TWENTY-FOUR

J onas stood in front of the service station, staring across the road at the long, low motel opposite. Specifically, at the chipped, faded door with the crooked number fourteen tacked to it. A string of flatbed trucks lumbered along the road, laden with construction materials and equipment, cutting off his view. He waited for them to crawl by, tapping the folded map against his thigh. Wondering if Kate had woken yet.

He wanted out of this "partnership" so badly he could taste it, dry and bitter on his tongue. Out of the partnership, out of the responsibility that came with it, and—most of all—out of the slow suffocation that came with having to rely on another human being. Even if that being was Kate.

He scuffed at the gravel shoulder. A spray of pebbles scattered across the pavement and disappeared under one of the flatbeds. Christ, he hadn't partnered with anyone in so long, he couldn't even remember how. Reported to, yes. Protocol had required him to check in regularly with Honeyman, his handler, but that was it. A discreet phone call, a brief meeting at a coffee counter, a text-messaged update. Short points of contact to reassure the agency that he still lived, or to pass on information he'd garnered. Undercover work suited him that way.

Jonas's mouth twisted. Given his reputation, he suspected it suited the agency, too. As good as he might be at his job, he knew full well he wasn't particularly popular among his colleagues. The few partners he'd had in the beginning had never lasted long, and he suspected putting him in undercover work had been his superiors' last-ditch effort to avoid more complaints about him. Fortunately, the arrangement had worked out in every-one's favor.

Until now.

The last truck passed by in a swirl of dust, and Jonas stared again at the tired door of room number fourteen. He squared his shoulders. Right. If he couldn't get out of this, they'd just have to set some ground rules up front. Kate might be a more experienced cop than he'd first thought, but the sooner they established who was in charge, the faster they'd be able to solve this mess and go their separate ways again. Alone.

The way his life was supposed to be lived.

He strode across the road.

Kate woke to the sound of pounding on a door. For a moment, she considered burrowing deeper under the covers to escape it. Then memories from the night before flooded back…with panic hot on their heels.

They'd been found.

She bolted upright in the motel bed. Motel. Because that's where she and Jonas had ended up last night. In a shared room. For safety, Jonas had said, and she'd been too exhausted to argue.

"Jonas!" she hissed at the lump on the other bed, separated from hers by the width of a nightstand. The lump didn't move. She tried again. "Jonas! Wake up—we've got company."

The pounding at the door came again. The lump still didn't respond. Kate slid out of bed and reached out to shake Jonas, but her hand met with no resistance under the mound of covers. Freaking hell...he wouldn't have. Would he?

Her gaze flicked toward the bathroom, but the door stood open, the room within dark. Cold slivered through her belly. Jonas was gone. She didn't want to believe it, but the cold covers and empty room spoke for themselves. He'd left. Taken off the first chance he'd had, just as he'd wanted to do all along, without so much as a word to her.

She wondered what had finally triggered him to run: that abhorrence of help he seemed to have, or the overzealous sense of responsibility that had him believing she'd be better off without him?

More pounding. Whoever was out there wasn't giving up. Panic born of sleep deprivation welled in Kate's chest. She took a deep breath, counted to three, and re-engaged her brain. Right, so there were two possibilities here. One, it was the local police at the door, in which case, she'd be okay. Probably going to prison, but at least she'd be alive.

The second possibility was that it was Jonas's pursuers out there, in which case...panic welled again. Freaking hell, she was going to have to hold them off until the locals came.

Whatever reasons Jonas had decided he might have, he'd chosen a lousy time to bolt.

Grimly, Kate picked up Dave's gun from the night table and checked its clip. Light glinted off the bullets nestled within. She shoved the clip back into place and then, on silent feet, padded across the carpet to the door. If there'd ever been the slightest question about her taking up a life of crime, this time with Jonas would have made her decide unequivocally against the possibility. Her nerves wouldn't stand the pressure.

Except she'd already taken up that life, hadn't she?

Hell.

Holding her breath, she put her eye to the peephole on the door. A distorted image of Jonas filled her view, his fist raised. Kate's jaw dropped, and she wrenched open the door as his hand descended.

"Will you be quiet!" she growled. "You're making enough noise to wake the dead!"

Jonas lowered his hand. "I forgot my key."

She waffled between annoyance and sheer, overwhelming relief that he hadn't deserted her after all. Before she could decide on a reaction, his gaze dropped to the sweatshirt she wore, making her suddenly and acutely aware that the bottom of the garment barely brushed the tops of her thighs. Heat climbed into her cheeks.

Jonas's gaze returned to hers. "Sorry," he said.

For what? Forgetting the key? Or staring at her like that and waking the unwanted fire in her belly again? Kate turned and stalked across the room to the jeans she'd left on a chair. She set down the gun and, with her back to Jonas, slid one leg at a time into the garment, ignoring the click of the door. The overhead light came on, dispelling the room's dimness.

"I thought you might have decided to take off," she said.

He didn't answer, and Kate's lips tightened. So. He'd considered it again, had he? Color her unsurprised.

"Where did you go?" she tried again as she did up the

zipper and snap. "And what happened to safety in numbers?"

"You were sleeping." He'd closed the door and leaned against it. His powerful, navy T-shirt-clad shoulders lifted in a shrug.

"You could have woken me."

"I needed to think."

"We stick together, Jonas. That's the deal." She held aside a curtain and peered out at the parking lot. If he'd been spotted—

"No one's there," Jonas said. "I made sure."

She let the curtain drop into place and reached for her socks. "So what were you thinking about?"

"What's next. Where we go from here."

"That's something we should discuss togeth—"

"No," he cut her off. "It's not."

Balanced on one foot, Kate raised an eyebrow, studying him. The grim jawline, the rigid shoulders, the crossed arms with hands fisted. "You have some kind of bee in your bonnet this morning. What's going on?"

His jawline took on an even more belligerent set. "I don't work well with a partner, so—"

"No shit," she muttered. Socks on, she straightened up.

Jonas's scowl deepened. "*So*," he repeated, "we need to set some ground rules before we go any further."

This time, both of Kate's eyebrows rose. "Ground rules. Such as…?"

"Such as who's in charge."

She didn't even try to hold back the snort. "You seem a little unclear on the concept of *partners*, Agent Burke. We're in this together, remember?"

"And it's my intention to get you safely *out* of it."

"Oh, for—" She broke off, rolling her eyes. "You can't

seriously still think I'm not capable of holding my own. Not after yesterday."

His gaze flicked away from hers. "You're more experienced than I thought," he allowed, "but—"

"But what? Finding us transportation and getting us safely out of a high-speed chase wasn't enough to convince you I'm up to the challenge?"

"That's not the point." The blue eyes snapped back to glare at her. "I know the people we're up against, Kate. You don't. When it comes down to it, I need to know you'll do what I say when I say it. Without argument. I need to know you trust me."

"And I need to know you trust *me*." She returned his glower. "See? Already we're thinking alike. Because *partners*."

"Damn it, Kate, it's not that I won't consider your input, but we're going to be in *my* territory, gunning for people *I* work with. I need to be the one calling the shots."

Consider her input? He had to be kidding.

"Fine," she snapped. "Then let's start with how you plan to get us out of the country into *your* territory to begin with."

"I don't know yet. I'm still considering the options. We'll have to be..." He trailed off as she crossed her arms, pursed her lips, and curled her sock-footed toes into the carpet. "Let me guess. You have an answer, don't you?"

"I might."

"Well? Are you planning to share it or not?"

"Partners, Jonas."

Thunder settled over the dark brow. Kate met his stare without flinching—and, she hoped, without revealing the turmoil in her gut. Was she pushing too hard? Too fast? Jonas wasn't the kind of man to tolerate being cornered like this. What if he—

"Fine," he growled. "You win. Partners. *For now.*"

Kate swallowed a tart observation about how much it must have hurt for him to give in. That really *would* be pushing her luck. "Good," she said, keeping her tone mild.

"Good," he echoed, not quite as mildly. "There's a restaurant next door to the motel office. You can tell me your idea over breakfast."

Turning his back on their fledgling agreement, he pulled open the door and stalked outside. Kate sighed, slid her feet into her running shoes, scanned the room a final time to be sure she had everything, and slipped Dave's gun into the waistband of her jeans under her sweatshirt. Then she followed in Jonas's wake.

Baby steps, she told herself as she locked the door and pocketed the key. It was at least a start.

TWENTY-FIVE

Jonas held open the door of the coffee shop for Kate to precede him. She hesitated on the threshold, scanning the interior even as he did, proving anew the experience she claimed to possess. Knowing that didn't make it any easier to have her around, any more than having this *partnership* forced on him.

Or having her breast brush against his arm as she slipped past him.

Grinding his teeth together, he stared past her, focusing on the eating establishment. It was bigger than he'd expected, and busier, given the motel's location on the outskirts of what wasn't a big town to begin with. That was a good thing, making it less likely anyone would pay attention to them.

A scattered few tables sat empty, including one near the back with access to the kitchen—and an emergency exit, should they need it. Jonas opened his mouth to direct Kate to it, but she'd already started in that direction, and he clamped his lips together again as he followed.

To his surprise, Kate left the seat facing the restaurant's entrance for him, taking the one opposite. He stood beside the empty chair.

"You should take this one. You're the one carrying the

—" he broke off, glancing at their surroundings. Not the best place to be discussing weapons, if one wanted to keep a low profile.

"And you're the one who knows who to watch for." She plucked a plastic-coated menu from beside the napkin holder and sent him what he could only term a sardonic look. "This is what partnership looks like, in case you were wondering."

"I know what—" He jerked the chair out from the table as the waitress stopped by with a coffee pot. He slid his mug across the table to be filled. "What's fastest?" he asked the waitress.

"That would be the morning special, hon." The frizzy-haired woman, who appeared to be the sole waitress in the place, slopped coffee into first his cup, then Kate's. "Bacon, ham, or sausage. Your choice of eggs. Toast. Home fries."

"Bacon," he said. "Over easy. Whole wheat."

Kate tucked the menu back into its holder by the napkins. "I'll have the same."

The waitress set the coffee pot on the table and tugged an order pad from her apron pocket. After noting their orders in a scrawl decipherable only to her—and, hopefully, the cook—she retrieved the coffee, slanted Jonas a smile, and departed.

"I think she likes you," Kate murmured.

Still smarting from his lost battle and in no mood for humor, Jonas ignored the remark and reached across the table for the sugar and two creamers. He dumped them into his coffee and stirred, watching Kate massage her shoulder.

"Sore?" he asked grudgingly.

Her hand stilled, and she glanced at it as if surprised

to see it there. Then she dropped it into her lap. "A little, I suppose. I hadn't really thought about it."

"You gave it quite the workout with that driving stunt last night." He set the spoon on the table. Kate shrugged.

"It is what it is at this point. At least it's usable."

Jonas felt certain there was more to it than that, but he reminded himself—for the four thousandth time—that he didn't want to know. Didn't want to care. And sure as hell didn't want to be any more involved than he already was.

He looked past her, studying the other patrons without seeing them, mentally testing and discarding a dozen different topics of conversation as the silence stretched between them—again. Impatience threaded through him. He might not be the world's greatest conversationalist, but something about Kate seemed to shine a spotlight on that particular shortcoming. He shot her an irritated look, then clenched his fists to keep from reaching out to smooth the tumble of blond curls.

And *that* wasn't helping.

"You need a hairbrush," he growled.

Kate put a hand to her hair, grimacing. "That bad?"

No. That good. That sexy. That damned unsettling.

He shoved aside his libido's response. "Too memorable," he said instead. "We don't want to attract attention."

Nimble fingers raked through curls, dividing them into three sections, and a few seconds later, a not-quite-tidy but far more discreet braid hung over one shoulder. Kate patted at first one, then the other of her jeans pockets. She made a face.

"No elastic, but it should hold for a while."

Jonas set his jaw and went back to staring over her shoulder, abandoning any attempt at small talk.

If the wait for breakfast had been strained, the meal itself was even more so. Kate made a handful of attempts at conversation, but by the time Jonas mopped up the liquid yolk from his plate with the last of his toast, she'd given up and was ignoring him as studiously as he tried—and failed—to ignore her. Jonas shoved the toast into his mouth, chewed without tasting, and swallowed.

A bloody fine partnership this was going to be.

Across the table, Kate's slender hands spread strawberry jam over the last of her own toast. Even white teeth bit into the morsel. The tip of her tongue emerged to flick a crumb from her lip.

Jonas dropped his fork onto the empty plate with an unnecessarily loud clatter, and she looked up, one brow raised. Jonas shook his head in response, taking a swig of coffee that threatened to choke him. Beneath the table, his free hand clenched into a fist on an equally tense thigh.

Christ. If he intended to survive the next few days, he really, really needed to stop noticing Kate Dexter the way he did. Even if there was some kind of attraction going between them—which he wasn't admitting to—he had no room for someone like her in his life. And she had less room in hers for someone like him. The sooner they were done with this whole mess, the better.

Jonas pushed aside his plate and looked around for the waitress and her coffee pot. With breakfast out of the way, it was time to hear Kate's idea on how to—

He glanced across to find Kate watching him, her golden eyes narrowed. He bit back a groan. Hell, he was beginning to recognize that look of hers. She had more questions. He headed them off with one of his own. Or tried to.

"So about this plan of yours—"

"How did you get to where you are?" Kate interrupted.

"With the Bureau, you mean?" When she nodded, he shrugged. "I just sort of fell into it. They were looking for people at the same time I was looking for work."

"When did you join?"

"Fifteen years ago, right out of college."

Kate traced a fingertip around a spoon on the table, but her gaze didn't leave his. "The ATF doesn't just go looking for people. Someone must have pointed you their way. Your dad?"

Jonas snorted at the suggestion. "He would have been the last person to refer me to a life of law enforcement, believe me. Last I heard, he was doing time somewhere in California. I haven't seen him since I was three."

He watched her bite her lip. Knew she held back an *I'm sorry*. He opened his mouth to divert her from the topic, but she wasn't done yet.

"Who, then?" she asked.

Jonas sighed, knowing she wouldn't be sidetracked until she had the full story. "A Chicago cop who got tired of busting my butt when I was a kid," he replied. "I think he figured the best way to keep me out of trouble was to get me on his side."

"What about your mother?"

"Damned if I know." Jonas shrugged again. "She ditched me and my sister when I was six and Lizzie was four. We went into foster care, separate families."

Kate's frown deepened, tugging at her brows. "Not together? No aunts or uncles?"

None that wanted us. "No."

"Did they at least keep the two of you connected?"

With the ease of long practice, Jonas detached himself from the memories. "Lizzie stayed with the same family until she graduated from high school. I was a pretty angry kid, and her family didn't consider me a good influence. I don't blame them. I got bounced around a lot, then spent a year on the streets before Mike Callahan straightened me out."

Distress clouded the golden eyes. "That must have been hard for you, losing your sister as well as your mother."

"It was a long time ago. I survived."

The gentle gaze didn't waver, however. If anything, it intensified. "I know," she replied. "And I know you're not looking for sympathy, Jonas, but that doesn't stop my heart from breaking for the little boy you used to be."

For a long moment, Jonas said nothing. Could think of nothing to say. Hell, couldn't think, period. He stared at the butter knife his fingers had curled around. Kate's words echoed in his skull, battering at the shell he'd so carefully constructed around himself over the years.

He knew his background had left its mark on him. He never denied that it had made him who he was and shaped how he'd chosen to live. He'd never kidded himself about any of that. He'd just always thought himself satisfied with it. Until now.

Until his own heart ached at the thought of the little boy he'd once been—and hollowed in the face of a life that suddenly stretched out so emptily before him. His gut twisted. Damn it. One way or another, this partner-ship with Kate was going to be the death of him.

He shoved his plate to one side and unfolded the map he'd purchased earlier, spreading it across the table between them.

"You said you knew how to get us out of here," he said. "Show me."

TWENTY-SIX

Kate studied Jonas's dark head as he leaned over the map between them, grumbling about her proposed idea for getting them across the river to the States. A shock of black hair had fallen across his forehead, and her fingers itched to push it back. To smooth the furrow from his brow that remained in the wake of their exchange. She held back a sigh.

She might have a cop's instinct down pat, but would she ever learn to heed her feminine one? The one that had tried so hard to tell her to mind her own business? To warn her that she didn't want to know anything more about this brooding man? She was treading on increasingly thin ice where Jonas was concerned, and she needed to back away now, while she still could.

He jabbed his finger at a spot on the map and looked up.

"I still don't like the idea, but—" he broke off, and his dark brows pulled together in an angry slash as she tried to rearrange her expression into something that didn't reflect the mooning she knew she'd been doing. "Damn it, Kate—"

She cut him off with a wave of one hand, mustering a smile she hoped looked only half as forced as it felt. "It'll work," she said. "The plan, I mean."

Jonas's scowl deepened, and she stood up from the table, trying to deflect the lecture she saw forming behind his eyes. She reached for the bill beside her plate and made her voice light. "Ready to go?"

Strong fingers closed over her wrist, warm and vise-like around the slender bones. Her pulse leapt, and she hoped against hope Jonas wouldn't feel it beneath his fingertips. He looked up at her.

"We need to talk," he said, his electric blue gaze threatening to hold her as captive as the hand around her wrist. She blinked and turned her head to watch the restaurant's front door swing closed behind a pair of men. Truckers, most likely.

"There's nothing to talk about," she said. "We have a plan, and now we should get moving. We don't want to stay anywhere very long."

"We're not going anywhere," Jonas replied grimly, "until you come clean with me."

His hand slid from her wrist to her hand, and her heart skipped several beats. She wished to God he would let go before common sense caved to the desire to twine her fingers with his. "About what?"

"About all of this. Why you're here. Why you're doing this. Why you didn't hole up back in Ottawa when you could. You're a cop, Kate. A good one, from what I've seen."

A tiny thrill of pleasure ran through her at his words. She quashed it, making herself stay focused as he continued, "Why involve yourself? And don't tell me you had no choice, because we both know you did. You could have turned me in before things got this out of hand. Or you could have just turned me loose. So why? Why are you here?"

A wariness in Jonas's eyes, as much as the rigid set of

his powerful shoulders, told Kate he needed a straight answer.

But he wasn't going to like it.

She took a deep breath. "Because you need the help. And because I couldn't live with myself if I turned away and something happened to you."

Blue eyes turned hard.

"I've managed on my own my entire life," he snarled. "I *don't* need help, and I won't let you be responsible for what happens to me. Are we clear?"

He glared up at her, a hardened, proud, and bitter man who truly believed what he said. He didn't need anyone. He didn't need her. When their job was done, he would walk out of her life, and she wouldn't be able to stop him.

Even if she wanted to.

And she did, she realized. Oh God, how she did.

So much for backing away.

Somewhere beyond their table someone dropped a dish, but the sound of shattering glass came from another world, an alternate reality. This world—her world—centered around Jonas, around the grip on her hand that tightened to painful, around the crystalline eyes that stared back at her, rejecting every revelation she'd just undergone.

"Don't," he said.

Don't what? she wanted to ask, but she already knew.

Don't care about me, that one word said, hanging heavy in the air between them. *Don't ask me to care in return. Don't see a future in me.*

Don't.

The angry word denied a connection between them. Denied a connection between Jonas and anyone at all. Whatever he had lived through had built impenetrable walls around him, setting him apart from the rest of the world.

When she'd told him earlier that her heart broke only for the little boy he had once been, that hadn't been entirely accurate. Her heart broke too for the man who'd had to bury that little boy so many years ago. But he wouldn't appreciate the sentiment, and so she kept silent, her hand still held captive in his, until he slowly released her and turned his head to stare out the window.

"Don't think I haven't considered the idea, Kate," he said, a rawness in his voice underlining his words. "You're what every man would give his right arm for. You're honest, warm, giving—not to mention sexy as hell. A long time ago, I dreamed of meeting someone like you, you know. Thought I could settle down like other people, normal people. I thought I could buy a house, have the requisite dog and kid, go camping on the weekends, coach Little League. But it's just not in me. I've been alone too long, had to fight for too much. I don't have anything to give someone like you. I'd suck you dry and destroy you without even meaning to."

Kate could think of nothing to say. She rubbed absently at the marks he'd left on her wrist.

"If you want to drop out of this mess, I'll understand, believe me," he added, turning to look at her with what she could only describe as challenge.

Because he expected her to do just that, she realized. He expected her to leave, because it was what everyone in his life had always done.

More than likely because he'd driven them to it.

Kate lifted her chin.

"No way, Burke," she said. "I'm not letting you make me into another disappointment in your life, so stop feeling sorry for yourself, and let's go find out if my contact is still around. If we're lucky, we might make it out of here tonight."

Kate was at the cash register before her words registered in Jonas's mind, and at the glass front door before he caught up with her, still trying to come up with a response.

He'd really hoped he'd given her reason to bail out of the whole damned mess this time, before she got any more involved. Before she got hurt, and not just physically. He flinched at the memory of that raw pain in her expression when he'd rejected her help. Rejected her. It had taken everything in him not to stand and reach for her, to—

He locked his hands behind his head, flexing his shoulders in a stretch as he trailed a ramrod-stiff Kate toward the motel office. Hell, who was he trying to kid? The idea of hurting Kate didn't bother him nearly as much as the fact that he was beginning to *care* whether she got hurt. Because he'd meant every word he'd said to her: He had no room in his life for a relationship. Any capacity for love had been snuffed out over a lot of ugly, painful years until all that remained was an instinct for survival that ensured he'd lead a very long life. Alone, the way he was meant to be.

And someone like Kate deserved one hell of a lot better than that. He just needed her to understand that.

Kate stopped in her tracks on the sidewalk running the length of the motel, and he veered sideways to avoid knocking her over. She rounded on him with a fierce glare.

"Will you please give it a rest?" she demanded.

Impatient. She had the nerve to be impatient with

him, when *she* was the one creating complications. He opened his mouth to object, but she overrode him.

"I refuse to pretend I don't like you, Jonas, because I do. I may not like how you do things, but that's my problem, not yours. You, I like. I like your sense of humor, I like how easy you are to talk to—when you're not sulking, that is—and I like your honesty. So yes, I care about what happens to you. Last time I checked, that wasn't a crime."

Amber eyes flashing with annoyance dared him to disagree. He did so, but with great caution. "I'm just afraid it's gone beyond friendly caring."

"My problem. Not yours," she said again.

No. No, it's definitely my problem, too.

"It's not that simple—"

She cut him off. "It's exactly that simple. I don't want to see you get killed, and I don't want to see *me* get killed. We have a better chance of coming out of this alive if we work together."

"And afterward? What do we do when all this"—he waved an encompassing hand—"is over? What then, Kate Dexter?"

The question hung between them for a long moment. Kate looked away, too late to hide the return of the raw pain he'd seen before. Something twisted deep inside Jonas's gut.

"Then," she said, her voice flat, "you pay up your tab and I go home."

"Home to what? If you keep this up, you're not even going to have a job when you get back."

"I'm pretty sure I already don't have a job. Not after last night. At least let me have a good reason for losing it."

He stared down at her for a long moment, wanting to

believe she could pull this off. That he could. Sunlight broke through the clouds, sparking off her hair.

"Do you really think they'll fire you?" he asked at last. "Even if we prove I'm right, and I vouch for you?"

"I don't know. Maybe. Given the number of laws I've broken, probably." Kate shrugged. "On the other hand, Dave's father-in-law is an assistant commissioner. If I'm lucky—and if Dave can manage to pull a few strings with him—they'll just ship me off to Tuktoyaktuk or some such for a few years."

She offered him a lopsided grin along with the attempt at reassurance, the pain he'd glimpsed in her eyes hidden behind that unsinkable humor she seemed to possess. A little of the tension uncoiled from Jonas's shoulders. Maybe she could do this after all. Maybe they could part as friends when this was over. He cleared his throat and, even as he hated himself for his cowardice, joined her in the spirit of denial.

"Is that bad?" he asked.

"No idea. Mostly cold, I think," Kate replied.

As Jonas followed her into the motel office, he was almost convinced that her cheerfulness was real.

Almost.

TWENTY-SEVEN

Kate paused inside the door of the bar, her nose wrinkling at the sour odor permeating the air—a mix of stale beer, sweat, and old vomit, if she judged correctly. A steady thud of music vibrated through the floorboards as she scanned the gloomy interior. The place was already half full, even though it was only eleven-thirty in the morning. Her gaze passed over the scattered tables, most occupied by single males, and settled on the stage at their center. A blond, skinny woman gyrated there, clad only in a G-string and a feather boa—neither of which provided enough coverage to count as clothing.

Kate held back a shudder of distaste. The place hadn't changed one iota in the three years since she'd last set foot in it. She just hoped that held true where James Lazarus was concerned.

She looked around as Jonas's shoulder brushed against hers. He stared over her head, brows drawn together, jawline flexing.

"Nice company your informant keeps," he muttered.

She raised an eyebrow at the thread of a snarl running through his voice. "Yours hang out in better places, do they?"

His gaze flicked to hers and away again, and his glower deepened. Kate held back a sigh. His mood had steadily worsened since breakfast, and she suspected he'd been going over their conversation in his mind again. And again and again and again, making more out of it each time he did so. She'd done her best to ignore his ill humor, hoping that if she behaved normally, he would follow suit, but he hadn't, and her patience was beginning to wear thin.

"Why don't you wait—" she began.

"No." His flat gaze returned to her. "No way am I leaving you on your own in here."

She didn't even try to hold back the eye roll. "Oh, for —" she broke off, biting back an epithet that wanted to follow. She debated having—again—the conversation about how she was a cop, but decided it would do no good. Not with Jonas in his current frame of mind.

Gritting her teeth, she turned her back on him and threaded her way through the tables toward a darkened corner, ignoring the assessing male gazes that followed her. She paused to let a waitress pass by to set a drink on a nearby table. The leering man seated there ran his hand suggestively over the woman's mini-skirt-clad backside, and Kate's skin crawled in silent empathy. God, how she remembered those looks and touches. Hell, even some of the clientele themselves looked familiar from her days of working undercover here. One hundred and sixty-seven days, to be exact. She'd counted them.

"How long did you say you worked here?" Jonas growled in her ear.

"Six months, give or take," she replied. She saw him level a glare at the man trying to feel up the waitress, and a spark of mischief made her add, "but only as a waitress, not a dancer."

Jonas's expression darkened even further, but she felt no remorse. Served him right for being so crotchety.

The man she'd hoped to find was there, in the back corner, exactly where she'd seen him during their last exchange. She dropped into an empty chair at the table occupied by James Lazarus, proprietor of the bar and the RCMP's one-time key to breaking open a deeply rooted smuggling ring in the area. Jimmy and his two companions stared at her.

"Mr. Lazarus."

Dark eyes narrowed, flickered in surprise, then lit with a lazy smile. "Well, well, well. If it isn't little Kate Dexter. I almost didn't recognize you with all your clothes on."

A heavy, possessive hand settled on Kate's good shoulder. She ignored it. Jimmy did not. His gaze lifted, turned speculative, returned to her.

"So. Come back to work for me, have you?" he asked, reaching for the coffee cup in front of him.

Kate snorted. "You know I have the utmost respect for you and your establishment, Jimmy, but no. Not in a million years."

"Too bad. You were a damned fine waitress. One of my best." The bar owner took a sip, then set the cup back in its saucer. He grinned at her, his leer as practiced as it was obvious. "Looks like you'd still earn yourself some decent tips."

Jonas's grip on Kate's shoulder tightened. She winced and pried his fingers loose.

"Relax," she said. "Mr. Lazarus is just trying to get a rise out of me."

Jimmy chuckled. "Not you. Him. Looks like I'm succeeding, too." He smoothed the fringe on the front of his black, western-style shirt. Kate couldn't see the rest of him, but she knew his pants would match the shirt, and that the cowboy boots on the feet tucked under the table would be of the finest leather money could buy. James Lazarus's establishment made him a lot of money, mostly because—thanks to Kate—it was still up and running.

"So, Katie my sweet, to what do I owe the honor? I doubt you've come just to introduce your boyfriend to me."

"He's not my boyfriend, he's—" Kate stopped and shot a look at the other table occupants, both young and male, both too interested in her words by far. She recognized neither. "Do you mind if we speak alone?"

Jimmy regarded her for a moment, then tipped his head sideways. Without question, both young men rose and headed toward the stage.

"My nephews," Jimmy said, shaking his head, "but you're right not to trust them. I don't, either. Not as far as I can throw them."

"Trouble?" Kate asked.

"Arrogance. Think they know better than their old uncle. I'm trying to keep them honest, but it's an ongoing battle." Jimmy took another swig of coffee. "Enough about me. What do you need?"

Kate grimaced. "I look that desperate, do I?"

"No. But he does." Jimmy jerked his chin in Jonas's direction, then kicked a chair toward him. Kate noted she'd been right about the boots. "Sit," Jimmy told Jonas. "If you keep looking at the door like that, people are going to think you're running from something."

Jonas went even more rigid than he'd been, and Kate brushed her fingers against the back of his hand. Their gazes locked, mistrust shadowing his. Then, his lips drawing tight, he positioned the chair between Jimmy and Kate. He sat.

"That's better," Jimmy said. He divided his attention between Kate and his coffee. "So. What is it you need?"

"Transportation across the river. Tonight, if possible."

Jimmy nearly choked. Black eyes bored into hers. "Excuse me? You're not serious."

"Deadly so. We can pay, but not much."

Jimmy banged the cup into its saucer. His gaze darted around the bar. "What the hell is this?" he demanded. "Another operation? You know I don't make runs. I didn't three years ago, and I don't now, and if anyone's said otherwise, they're a goddamn liar."

"This isn't about you, Jimmy. It's about me. Us. We're in trouble."

The man whose life she'd turned upside down with her undercover presence in his bar three years before regarded her suspiciously. "Do you really think I'm that naive? You're a—" he broke off, glanced around, and lowered his voice to a hiss. "You're a cop, damn it, and cops don't come to one-time informants for help."

"They do when they have no other options."

He stared at her, then he shook his head. "No. No way. I'm not falling for—"

"Jimmy." Kate reached out to lay a hand on his forearm, the cotton of his sleeve smooth beneath her fingertips. "You owe me."

Lazarus's mouth pulled tight. After a long moment, he lifted his free hand to beckon over a waitress, and they all waited while she poured fresh coffee for him. When she'd retreated, he stirred two packets of sugar into the cup before he scowled at Kate again.

"I want your word this isn't a setup."

"You have it."

Another silence. A sigh. "I may know someone, but it will cost you. A grand each. Up front."

Kate shook her head. "I don't have that much. Three

hundred for both of us. And we need a car on the other side."

Jimmy snorted. Kate waited. She sensed Jonas's eyes on her, but she kept her attention on Lazarus. On willing the bar owner to come through for her. For them. Jimmy's gaze flicked between them.

"He owes me a favor, so I can get him to agree to five hundred for both," he said at last. "But the car will cost you extra."

She hesitated. Heaven knew how long this little adventure of theirs was going to last. Dave had said there was a thousand available in his account. If they blew through five hundred of that just to cross the river, it wouldn't leave much to see them through. And even more for a vehicle?

"Agreed," Jonas intervened. Kate turned to him, startled, and he said, "We'll be good once we get to...where we're going."

Of course. The emergency stash he'd mentioned. All good undercover operatives had one, just in case things went south on the job and they needed a fast out. She nodded and turned back to Jimmy.

"It has to be tonight," she said.

Hard eyes stared at her. "I have your word. No bullshit."

"No bullshit."

Lazarus stood up. With deliberate care, he straightened his shirtfront and adjusted his belt buckle, a large silver rectangle with an eagle stamped on it. Then he caught the waitress's attention, pointed to the coffee cup on the table, and held up two fingers. The scantily clad girl nodded and headed for the bar counter. Jimmy looked down at Kate.

"I'll make the call," he said. "Coffee's on the house."

TWENTY-EIGHT

Jonas shouldered through the heavy wooden door, holding it open barely long enough for Kate to emerge onto the sidewalk beside him. He drew a deep lungful of chill autumn air. It did nothing to cool the temper that had been simmering since they'd sat down at that table with Lazarus. The door swung shut behind them, muffling the thud of the music.

He glowered at his partner, who studied the traffic, her features calm but watchful, seemingly unaffected by the surroundings they'd just left. No matter how long he worked undercover, places like that always managed to make him feel like he needed a shower...or fumigation...or both.

Surroundings Kate had once worked in, where men had come on to her. Made lewd suggestions to her. Slid their hands over her.

He knew it shouldn't bother him, but it did. It bothered him a lot. He shoved his hands into his jeans pockets.

Kate glanced his way. "Everything okay?"

"Peachy," he muttered.

She regarded him narrowly, then shrugged and went back to watching the traffic. "I did some calculations, by the way. By the time we pay Jimmy's friend, we'll have a grand total of thirteen dollars and sixty-seven cents left in Dave's account. We'd better hope that car has a full tank of gas. And that your stash is where you left it in Jersey."

"Jennings said there was more in the savings account. Take that. I'm good for it," he replied, his tone curt to the point of rudeness.

Kate pressed her lips together, and for a second he thought she might call him on his foul mood. He almost wished she would. A good argument might distract him from the "me Tarzan" urges that made him want to march back inside and take on Lazarus and every other male in the place.

But Kate said nothing. Stuffing her fingertips into the pockets of her jeans, she started walking back toward the alley where they'd left the SUV. Irritated all over again, Jonas fell into step beside her.

"I'd forgotten how loud that place is," she remarked, sticking a finger into her ear and wiggling it. "Can you believe I lasted six months there? It's a wonder I had any hearing left by the time I was done."

"I can't believe you worked there, period," Jonas retorted. "Please tell me you broke the fingers of anyone touching you the way that jackass in there was doing."

She dimpled a grin up at him. "And put my tips at risk?"

"It's not funny," he snapped, his hands bunching into fists in his pockets.

Kate stopped walking. She crossed her arms. "Right," she said, her good humor dissolving. "You've been like a bear with a sore ass ever since breakfast, Burke. Just what the hell is your problem?"

Jonas looked down at her. For the first time ever, he noticed a smattering of tiny freckles across the bridge of her nose. He swallowed hard and grated out the truth. "You. You're my problem."

Then, because she might read too much into the words—and because they had somehow robbed him of air and he could think of no other way to rescue himself —he added in a snarl, "You working there. Dealing with those perverts. Being touched like that. What the hell did . you think you were doing, Kate?"

She scowled at him. "My *job*." Her enunciation was precise. "Damn it, Jonas, yesterday you looked down your nose at me because you thought I was a desk jockey. Now you're ticked off because I got my hands dirty—"

"It's not your *hands* I'm concerned about!"

"Well, the rest of me is none of your business either!"

The fact that she was right made him even angrier. The fact that at this moment he desperately wanted her to *be* his business made him downright furious.

Heat crept up from under his collar into his cheeks. His fists curled tighter. He didn't want this. Hated that she could do this to him, tie his insides into knots like this. Hated himself even more for the part that wanted to give in to the possibilities...the promises he'd seen in her eyes and felt in the brush of her skin against his.

The part of him that made him reach for her not because he cared, but to prove he didn't.

The startled query in her eyes as he hauled her roughly against his chest might have made him recon- sider if she hadn't lost her balance and fallen against him. But the wonderfully soft, feminine fullness pressed against him, coupled with the feel of her hands clutching at his shoulders and the scent rising from her, cost him the last vestiges of control.

He kissed her.

For an instant—a brief, world-spinning, reality-altering instant—she responded. Her mouth opened to his rough invasion, her tongue tangled with his, her body melted into him, and Jonas tasted both heaven and hell in the same heartbeat. Heaven because he held Kate in his arms; hell because that's where he'd be when she was gone.

But he barely had time to register the quasi-poetic thought before Earth and reality were simultaneously and unceremoniously restored with a bone-jarring thud. From an ignominious position flat on his back on the sidewalk, Jonas blinked up at the sky.

"Dude," drawled a teenage boy with a snicker as he shuffled past, hitching up his drooping jeans.

Kate was nowhere to be seen.

Jonas's brain kicked back into gear. She'd dumped him. Dumped him on his ass and left him here, and he'd been so consumed by dizzying, never-before-reached heights that he hadn't seen it coming.

He should have, however, because he'd sure as hell deserved it.

How dare he?

Kate ground her teeth together as she stomped along the sidewalk, swiping at the tears blurring her vision. One spilled over, tracking down her cheek, and she sniffled inelegantly. Fury churned with betrayal in her breast, becoming into a quagmire of emotions she didn't know how to even begin sifting through.

Damn him to hell and back...*how dare he*? She'd had her share of kisses over the years, but never one that compared to what had just happened. Never one that carried such anger behind it.

Or such longing.

She thrust aside the secondary thought. Whatever it might have morphed into, whatever it might have stirred in Jonas—

Or in you, the little voice added. She snarled at it in her head and brushed away another tear. It didn't matter what it might have become, only that it had been delivered with such fury. Such—

Possessiveness? her voice inquired, and something in the pit of her stomach gave a traitorous flutter. Her breath snagged in a throat that had tightened painfully. Damn. Damn Jonas for kissing her like that, and damn her body for responding, and damn, damn, *damn*.

Taking a deep breath, Kate paused in the doorway of a building to get her bearings. Nothing looked familiar. She closed her eyes. Great. Now, on top of everything else, she'd managed to get herself lost? She took another steadying breath. *Easy does it, Kate. This is Cornwall. It's not big enough to get lost in, remember?*

Besides, she was nowhere near ready to return to Jonas just yet. A walk would do her good. Steeling herself, she stepped back onto the sidewalk, aiming her steps toward the river and the path that ran for miles alongside it. She wondered whether Jonas would be looking for her, or whether he would return to the SUV to wait. Then she wondered whether he and the SUV would even be there when she did return.

She scrubbed the last of the tears from her face, telling herself she didn't care. Knowing she lied.

Damn him. Just...

Damn.

Jonas melted into the shadows, his back hugging the grimy brick wall at the rear of the vacant store where

Kate had parked Jennings's SUV. He stood rigid, not daring to breathe. Had the two cops seen him? Seconds ticked by. The low murmur of voices reached him, but he couldn't make out any of the words. No footsteps approached.

He edged forward and risked a peek around the foul-smelling Dumpster that separated him from the vehicle —and from the police car parked beside it. Cardboard boxes lay strewn across the ground, the remnants of his and Kate's failed attempt to hide their vehicle for a few precious hours.

One of the cops stood beside the four-by-four, shining a flashlight into the interior. The other sat in the cruiser, talking on the radio. The light from the cruiser's interior dome showed no one in the back seat. They didn't have Kate. Yet.

Jonas leaned against the wall again. So if they didn't have Kate, where the hell was she? She'd been gone for hours. He'd been sure she'd head straight here—he'd picked himself up and dusted off his butt within a few seconds, then set out after her, but she'd been nowhere to be found. He grimaced. Nowhere that she *wanted* to be found, he corrected.

The sound of soft, careful footsteps reached him, not from the direction of the cops in the alley, but from the street behind him. One of their colleagues?

He drew back to listen, waiting. The stealthy steps drew closer, then paused. Jonas braced himself. Ran through his options if it was another cop. None of them were good. Bloody hell, where was K—

A head poked around the brick, and the light from a street lamp glinted off blond curls. Swiftly, reflexively, Jonas reached out and snagged Kate, pulling her against him. His other hand covered her mouth, muffling her squeak.

"It's me," he whispered as her heat wafted up to surround him. Kate stiffened, then nodded. He took his hand away and she stepped back, taking her warmth with her. *I'm sorry,* he wanted to add. *So very, very sorry.* But too many words increased their risk of discovery, and apologies would have to wait.

Silently, hoping she could see him in the shadows, he pointed toward the SUV, then held up two fingers. Kate's form nodded. She jerked her head toward the street, and the two of them picked their way back out to the pavement.

They walked quickly but in silence, sticking to the side streets where there were fewer cars. Fewer lights. More time for Jonas to absorb Kate's presence beside him and try to shunt aside his relief at her return. Shit, but things were spinning out of control fast. He cleared his throat. *Save the panic for later, Burke. First things first.*

"They'll be combing the town for us now they've found the vehicle," he said. "They'll go to Lazarus's bar."

"Jimmy's cool," Kate replied. "He owes me."

"So you keep saying. It must be quite a debt."

"I was put into place in his bar because he'd been implicated in a smuggling ring. The investigation proved he wasn't involved, and he got to keep his place."

"*The* investigation, or *your* investigation?"

Kate shrugged one shoulder as they passed beneath a corner street lamp. "I asked the right questions of the right people. That was my job."

Jonas suspected it had been more than that, but he didn't argue. "Even if he stays quiet about us, someone else at the bar will talk."

"Probably."

And their ride across the river wasn't scheduled for another two hours. The cops could talk to a lot of people in that time. Jonas followed Kate's turn onto another side street, matching his stride to hers.

"This is going to be one hell of a long night," he said.

She gave a soft snort. "Oh, yeah."

More walking. Then it was her turn to break the silence.

"They'll tow the SUV," she said, her voice quiet. Subdued. "And we still need to get to the rendezvous point for our ride. I'm thinking we find a bank machine, then see if we can get a taxi driver who's willing to keep his mouth shut. Does that work for you?"

"Absent any other options, it works fine. But first..." Jonas reached out and caught hold of her hand, pulling her to a stop and curling his fingers through hers. "First, I owe you an apology, Kate. And then—" He looked down at her. "Then I think we need to talk."

TWENTY-NINE

K ate stepped out of the phone booth, careful not to brush against Jonas, who was leaning against the booth's corner. He straightened up and quirked a brow at her.

"Well? Is he still speaking to you?" he asked.

"Dave? Yeah, we're speaking."

"And do you still have a job?"

Kate lifted a shoulder in a shrug she hoped looked more careless than it felt, but it took all she had to inject a light note into her voice. There wasn't a whole lot in this situation that was even remotely light anymore, least of all that talk with Jonas hanging over her head. Her gaze slid away from the electric blue eyes studying her so intently.

"To quote my partner, 'My father-in-law is an assistant commissioner, not the bloody Wizard of Oz!'"

Jonas didn't laugh. She hadn't expected him to. Restlessly, she scanned the deserted street, watching for the cab she'd called after ending her conversation with Dave. She flinched at the memory of the anger in her partner's voice when she told him their plans for getting across the river. The worry. If she went through with this—

No. Not if. When.

When she went through with this, she'd be burning

every bridge she'd built in her entire career, and no one—not Dave, not his father-in-law, not anyone—would be able to undo the damage.

Jonas cleared his throat.

Kate closed her eyes. Right. The Talk. She did a brief assessment of her remaining internal fortitude, confirmed what she'd suspected about not having any left to deal with this, and held up a hand to forestall Jonas's words. "Can we not?" she asked. "You've apologized. I've accepted. It's done."

"Kate—"

"Jonas," she cut him off. "You've made your position clear. You're not looking for a relationship. I get it. So let's just get across the river, find the evidence you need to take down Lewis and Ramirez, and then we can be done, all right? And speaking of getting across the river..."

She lifted her chin toward a set of approaching head-lights, and Jonas turned to look.

"Saved by the taxi," she told him, her cheerfulness buoyed by sheer relief. Jonas didn't respond.

At one-twenty a.m., the taxi pulled away from the end of a rough dirt road nearly obscured by the night and a tangle of bushes that stirred in the breeze. If it hadn't been the end of October with most of the leaves gone already, Kate doubted they would have seen the opening at all. As it was, the taxi driver had refused to take them any further, leaving her and Jonas with a tight window of twenty minutes to hike the final kilometer.

The red glow of the taxi's taillights disappeared down the paved road toward town, and the dark closed in on them like a tight fist. Kate shot a look at the sky. There was a full moon up there somewhere, but the cloud cover blocked it. It smelled like rain was coming, too. She shivered, wishing she'd thought to buy a jacket of some kind. And a flashlight.

"Cold?" Jonas asked.

"I forgot about it being cooler away from town," she replied, "but I'll be fine. We should get moving."

She peered into the dark to locate him, but it was no use. While she could hear him breathing, he was nothing more than the sensation of a shadow among shadows. Then his hand brushed her arm, making her jump, and his fingers twined with hers in a strong, reassuring grip. The rich timber of his voice came from a point somewhere above and to the right of her head in the night's blackness.

"This way."

Kate felt oddly disembodied as she followed Jonas along the narrow road that was little more than a well-used path. In a dark so deep she couldn't see her own hand if she held it up before her, Jonas's grip seemed the only link with reality, the only thing that bound her to an earth she knew was there, but couldn't perceive. Well, that and the branches slapping at her face. And the sharp, twiggy fingers tearing at her hair. She was pretty sure she was leaving half her curls behind, dangling blond clumps that marked their path to the river.

Another branch snapped back from Jonas to smack her cheek and she swallowed a squeak of pain.

"You okay?" Jonas asked. "That one got away on me."

Eyes watering, Kate nodded. Then she remembered he couldn't see her in the dark. "I'm fine," she said. "But we should pick up the pace. Lazarus said they wouldn't wait for us."

Jonas didn't reply, and for a moment, Kate thought he hadn't heard. Then, with an unidentifiable noise deep in his throat, he let go of her hand and slid his arm around her waist, snugging her in against his hard, muscular length. Everything in Kate softened, and only sheer force of will kept her from melting against him.

"We'll move faster like this," he muttered. Using his body as part bulldozer and part battering ram, he forged ahead, dragging Kate with him, branches snapping beneath his onslaught. But while she stumbled along the rutted, overgrown road, Jonas's steps were unerring.

The man had the night vision of a cat.

Fitting, given that he also had the lean, lithe muscles of a panther. She knew that for a fact, because said muscles were molded to her side right now. Or she was molded to them. Or—

Kate sucked in a quick breath. Jonas's warm, faintly musky male scent filled her nostrils. She stumbled again and would have fallen, but his arm tightened around her, holding her upright. Heat scorched her cheeks.

Just how far was it to that damned river, anyway?

The clouds parted to reveal the moon as she paused to disentangle her mess of curls from yet another grasping branch. Through the trees, she glimpsed the white glow reflected on water. The St. Lawrence River. Finally. And somewhere in the distance, fifteen minutes away by boat, the U.S. shore and the land transportation Jimmy Lazarus had promised them..

"We're here," she said unnecessarily.

Jonas joined her efforts to extricate herself from the tree's persistent clutches. The moonlight cast his face into a complexity of planes and shadows as it hovered above hers, and Kate's breath snagged in her throat. Traveling with this man under dark's cover this way was beginning to take its toll on her libido.

Although, if she was honest, she didn't fare much

better in broadest daylight when he stood this close to her. She held back a sigh. Maybe he was right to worry about what would happen when they parted ways after this. Maybe she should start worrying, too.

She felt her hair come free and stepped away from him.

"We're here," Jonas agreed, his voice grim, "but where the hell is Lazarus's friend?"

Kate glanced around. Maybe they had the wrong place? No, she was certain they'd got their directions right. Even the taxi driver had seemed to know exactly where he was going on the drive out. An indication of the number of passengers ferried across here?

Hell, she certainly hoped not.

She filed away the idea for future reference—assuming she lived and remained in her job—and focused again on the immediate. No, they had the right place. There was the dock Jimmy had told them about, solid and well maintained, jutting twenty feet out into the water.

And empty of any kind of a boat.

Clouds scudded across the moon again, cutting off their only source of light. Kate's heart sank.

"Still think Lazarus is cool?" Bitter frustration tinged Jonas's hard voice.

Kate didn't know what to think.

"One of us had better retain some faith in humanity, don't you think?" she countered, her calm voice belying her crossed fingers.

"Blind faith is for idiots, Kate. All it will get you is hurt."

Kate paused. As far as veiled warnings went, that one was a doozy. It hung in the air between them while she debated her response. She decided she couldn't ignore it.

"Maybe," she replied. "But the way I see it, faith figures right up there with caring, trust, love. The things that make life worth living."

Jonas didn't pretend not to understand. "You know nothing about my life," he bit out. "You haven't lived it."

"You're right. I haven't. But I don't see you living it, either, Jonas. You've given up, plain and simple. All you do now is survive."

There was a short, tense pause before he replied.

"Survival doesn't hurt as much."

"Doesn't it?" she asked, and then she tilted her head. From out on the water came the low, steady thrum of an outboard motor, its pulse slowing as it neared the shore. Jonas had heard it, too.

"Seems you were right," he said. "This time."

Kate opened her mouth to reply, then snapped it shut as another sound reached her ears. A vehicle engine. No, two—maybe three. The crash of brush being mowed aside. And in the distance, the wail of a police-boat siren.

"Jonas...?"

"I heard." Jonas's hand clamped around her arm like a steel band. "*Run.*"

THIRTY

K ate's feet hit the wooden dock a step behind Jonas's. Over her shoulder, she saw headlights slanting through the trees, bobbing and weaving as the approaching vehicles navigated the almost nonexistent road. Two vehicles. One with a flashing blue and red bar atop it.

"Cops," she gasped at Jonas.

"I saw." He skidded to a halt at the end of the dock. Kate teetered beside him, searching the dark waters beyond for the boat they'd heard. The distant siren of the police craft wailed closer.

A lantern came on, moving gently with the waves fifty feet off shore. Behind Kate and Jonas, car doors slammed, and powerful flashlights beamed into the night, moving their way. Shouts reached them. Jonas's fingers tightened on Kate's arm.

"Christ!" he muttered. "Get the damned boat over here!"

The flashlights were just down the shore now, closing fast. The outboard motor thrummed to life again, but the boat didn't move.

"Can you swim?" Jonas demanded.

Kate hesitated. Her shoulder already throbbed from Jonas's many attempts to keep her upright on their hike here. Would it hold up to the St. Lawrence's current? She reached behind her to tuck the nine millimeter more snugly into her waistband.

"Let's go," she said.

The water closed around her with an icy force that knocked every atom of air from her lungs. Her fingers and toes burned with cold by the time she broke the surface, gasping for air. Frigid didn't even begin to describe the St. Lawrence in late autumn. She blinked the river water from her eyes and scanned the dark, finding the yellow lantern light again. It had moved further away from shore.

Shit.

Jonas surfaced beside her. "You okay?"

She forced a reply through jaws locked against the cold.

"My jeans weigh a thousand pounds, but I'm fine."

"Come on, then."

Matching his powerful strokes to hers, he paced her as they swam toward the bobbing light. As long as she focused on his rhythm, she was able to ignore the ache in her shoulder and the drag of water-logged runners and half-ton jeans. But the insidious, mind-numbing cold was another story altogether, and the current as strong as she'd feared. It took an eternity to reach the boat.

At last Kate's fingers brushed against fiberglass, and with a last, monumental effort, she lifted herself out of the water high enough to grab hold of the boat's side. The lantern doused, plunging them into dark. Then, from shore, a flashlight captured her in its brilliant beam. She held up a hand against its glare, her heart skipping a beat. They were freaking sitting ducks out here.

Hot on the heels of the thought, a shot cracked out over the water. Its sharp report reverberated through the still, liquid darkness. Beside Kate, Jonas spat out a curse and heaved himself aboard. The boat bucked in response, and Kate almost lost her grip. Almost slid under. Almost missed the glint of moonlight on steel.

But it was there. A dull, cold gleam in the hands of one of the men Lazarus had sent. A rifle. Kate lunged upward, catching hold of the gun barrel and dragging it down so it pointed into the water.

"No guns!" she croaked. "Those are cops out there!"

The dark eyes of a stranger looked down at her in the moonlight—flat, expressionless. Their owner shrugged. "They shot first."

He tried to lift the rifle, but Kate clung to it stubbornly.

"No guns," she repeated. "Just get us the hell out of here."

The man stared back at her. From the corner of her eye she saw Jonas seated on the floor of the boat, another man at his back—with, she had no doubt, another gun. The blood in her veins chilled. So did her lower body as it continued to dangle in the frigid water. She debated the wisdom of reaching for her own weapon, but didn't dare let go of either the boat or the rifle in her frozen grip. Hell, she didn't dare so much as blink.

Of all the tenuous positions she'd been in during her years on the force, this one rated right up there as the most bizarre. Cops on the shore ready to arrest her, her wanted-for-murder partner held at gunpoint, and herself half-in and half-out of an icy river, clinging to the side of a boat. A boat that, in all likelihood, belonged to someone she'd devoted her career to taking down. Kate's grip on the rifle shook as she fought off fatigue and a hysterical giggle-snort.

Now would be a hell of a time to discover that Jonas's theories on humanity might have merit after all.

The man holding the rifle relaxed his grip and the rifle barrel dipped, dunking her under the water again. "I'll give you this, lady," he said as she came up gasping. "You've got balls."

He grasped her under her near-ruined shoulder, hauled her into the boat, and dumped her beside Jonas.

"Let's go," he ordered. The powerful outboard roared to life as someone opened it full throttle, and the boat leapt forward.

Violent shivers wracked Kate's frame. Hard fingers closed over her wrist and pulled, and then equally hard arms wrapped her close against a torso almost as chilled as her own. Jonas.

"You, Kate Dexter, take more goddamned chances than anyone I've ever met," he muttered in her ear. He rubbed his hands over her arms, but the friction did little to warm her. The weapon she'd tucked into her waist-band dug into her spine.

She ignored the discomfort. There were more impor-tant things at hand, such as the fifteen minutes it would take them to go around St. Regis Island and across the river with a police boat still coming for them. Not to mention the news she had to share with Jonas. She pushed away from his hold.

"Wasn't a cop who fired," she mumbled through numb lips and teeth chattering with cold. "Not OPP. Wouldn't shoot at a boat headed for Mohawk territory. Not unprovoked. Too political."

But whoever it had been was sure as hell traveling in the company of cops, which left little doubt as to their identity. She pulled her arms inside her soaked sweat-shirt and wrapped them around herself, looking over her shoulder at a silent Jonas. Moonlight slanted across the hard planes of his face.

"We'll have to move fast when we dock," he said at last, staring out over the water at the shore they'd left. "They'll already be on their way."

Kate thought it more likely the head of the local OPP detachment was currently reading Lewis and Ramirez the riot act for that ill-advised shot, but it was easier just to nod agreement. That way, she could focus on keeping her teeth from slamming together. The boat bounced over a wave, and she fell sideways against Jonas's hard, lean length. His arms came around her again, and she settled into them without objection, a dim part of her exhausted brain wishing she had enough feeling left in her body to enjoy the proximity—or at least feel his warmth.

The police boat screamed into view down the river, its lights flashing in the dark.

Outrunning the police boat turned out to be easier than Jonas thought it would be—maybe because their transportation providers had practice at it? For whatever reason, twenty minutes later, he and Kate stood in the woods on the opposite shore, staring at the vehicle Jimmy Lazarus had provided for them. Jonas slanted a look at Kate, finding his own incredulity mirrored in her expressive features—along with sheer horror.

"You're kidding me," she said at last, lifting her gaze to Lazarus himself, who sat on the hood of the orange and yellow, flame-painted Mustang. "This was the best you could get us?"

Lazarus shrugged in the glare of headlights from a pickup idling nearby. "You didn't give me much notice."

"Freaking hell," Kate muttered.

Jonas rubbed the back of his neck. "Look at it this way," he said dourly. "No one will be expecting us to drive something like this."

"Probably because I wouldn't be caught dead driving something like this," she retorted. She returned her attention to Lazarus. "Are you sure it's not hot?"

"She's clean," Lazarus assured her, patting the bright hood. "And registered and insured. You have my word."

Jonas looked down as she expelled a breath on an unintelligible mutter. "Why, Kate Dexter, are you beginning to lose faith in your fellow man?" he murmured.

She fished a soggy wad of bills from her jeans pocket, ignoring him, and tossed the money to Lazarus.

"You'll have to trust that it's all there until it dries out enough to count it," she said. "But you have my word."

Lazarus turned the wad of bills over in his hand, staring down at the ground. Then he threw a set of car keys to Jonas. "You'd better get your lady out of those wet clothes and warm her up," he advised. "Agent Burke."

Jonas went ramrod stiff, his gaze seeking out Lazarus's friends in the shadow by the pickup truck. None of them showed the slightest sign of surprise. They'd all known. But if so, why had they helped out? Why not dump both him and Kate into the river?

"You knew?" Kate asked.

"A couple of his friends came looking for you guys in the bar about two hours after the OPP did. Gave me the impression you wouldn't be missed if there was an accident of some kind, if you get my drift."

Jonas got his drift, all right.

"The locals must have steered them toward the pickup point," Lazarus continued. "It's no great secret in these parts."

"So when the OPP talked to you, you didn't—?" Kate's voice trailed off.

"Nah." Jimmy tossed the money up and down a couple of times, then launched it at Jonas, who caught it out of sheer reflex. "Like you said, Katie. I owed you. And now we're even."

He slid off the Mustang's hood, and his booted feet hit the ground with a muffled thud. "There's a phone number in the driver's visor," he said. "Call it when you're done and let me know where to pick up the car. Registration and insurance are in the glove box."

Without waiting for a response, he and his friends climbed into the waiting pickup truck. A second later, they rumbled down the road. Jonas stared after them in silence for a long minute before he became aware of Kate's convulsive shivering and remembered his own chill.

"Come on," he said, twining his fingers with hers. "Lazarus is right. We need to get you warmed up."

She let him lead her to the car and help her in, even letting him do up her seatbelt. Jonas's jaw tightened as he took in her pinched face in the glow from the dashboard lights. She'd been soaked and half frozen for the better part of an hour. They'd be lucky if she didn't catch pneumonia. He slammed her door shut, headed around to the driver's side, and slid in beside her.

The car sprang forward with a powerful, throaty grumble under his foot, fishtailing and spitting up gravel in its wake. Flashy or not, this baby might come in handy yet. Something Jimmy Lazarus had perhaps foreseen? He glanced sideways at Kate.

"Your friends are making me rethink my trust philosophy, you know," he remarked.

"I wouldn't be too quick with a change of heart, if I

were you." Kate stared out the side window. Her reflection's gaze met his surprise, and she lifted one shoulder in a shrug that seemed oddly defeated. Vulnerable. "Jimmy might have been right about the locals knowing where to find us, but that doesn't explain how they knew when we'd be there."

The cold of Jonas's skin seeped into his gut. Shit. She was right. If Lazarus had told the truth about not informing on them—and after that little display back there, he found it hard to believe the man had lied—then there was only one other who'd known the time of their rendezvous with the boat and wouldn't avoid talking to a cop.

Dave Jennings.

THIRTY-ONE

I t turned out that the one thing their "rental" car didn't have was a working heater. Kate's shivers became uncontrollable shaking as they drove through the woods to the highway, tremors so intense that every muscle in her body screamed in agony. Jonas cursed and turned off the cold air blowing through the vents.

"We'll stop at a motel in Malone," he said. "It's about forty minutes from here. Are you okay for that long?"

Kate forced her rigid neck into a small nod, then she settled against the car door to watch the trees slide past. She wasn't okay. Far from it, in fact, but even if she could have unlocked her cold-spasmed jaw enough to tell Jonas so, there was no point. They had no dry clothes for her to change into, no blankets to wrap her in, and nowhere they could turn for help. She would just have to tough it out until Malone.

Surely she'd survive that long.

Even if she could no longer feel her extremities at all.

Damn.

Closing her eyes, she distracted herself with thoughts of the hot shower she'd take. She could almost feel the heat of the water sliding over her. Motels had an unlimited supply of hot water, right? She could stand under the shower for as long as she wanted. Or maybe she could take a bath instead. A long, leisurely soak in water as hot as she could stand. Water so hot it almost burned, turning her skin pink, its heat seeping into her bones...

Bliss.

How long had Jonas said it would take to get there? She frowned. She couldn't remember. Couldn't remember how long ago he'd said it, either. She thought about asking, but she was warmer now—markedly so—and she couldn't seem to rouse herself enough for conversation.

Her frown deepened. Wait. Confusion. Apathy. Those were signs of something. Damned if she could remember what, however. Or why it mattered. Especially when all she wanted to do was sleep. With a sigh, she succumbed to the cottony softness waiting for her brain.

A hand shook her shoulder gently. Then not so gently. Then with annoying forcefulness. A voice called her name, too loud, too close.

"Kate! Damn it, wake up."

She surfaced into reluctant consciousness. "What?"

"Look at me, Kate," the voice demanded. A hand brushed back the hair from her forehead. She batted away the touch.

"Go 'way," she muttered.

"Open your eyes," the voice persisted. "Tell me how you feel."

"Tired."

"I know that. Can you be a bit more specific? Where are we? And what day is it?"

Jonas. It was Jonas talking. And not very nicely. Tears started to Kate's eyes. She blinked them back and sniffled. "Don't yell at me. I'm tired. And how the hell do I know where we are? You're the one who was driving!"

Jonas nodded. "Good. You're not completely out of it.

Let's get you into bed and go from there. Sit tight while I get us a room, all right?"

He'd exited the car before her fuzzy brain kicked into gear enough to comprehend his last words. What room? And *"Let's get you into bed"*? As in one bed? Together? Why—

Wait. Hypothermia. That's what she was supposed to worry about. But she was warm now. Hot, even. Or was that one of the signs? Hell. She couldn't remember. Was that what Jonas meant? Her brain mulled over the problem for a few seconds, but it was no use. She really was too tired to care. Not about the bad guys, not about her career lying in ruins, and sadly, not even the idea of Jonas and bed in the same sentence...

As she slid back under the mantle of sleep, one final thought surfaced. *What a waste.*

Jonas slumped into the chair he'd placed beside the window overlooking the front of the motel, his attention divided between the parking lot entrance and Kate. Not that he had to worry about her any more. She slept peacefully now, her breathing deep and even, her body warm to the touch.

A far cry from this morning, when he'd held her curled against him in the double bed, her skin as cold as that of a corpse, her chill seeping into him until it became his own. For a while he had despaired of ever warming her—and cursed himself for his lack of vigilance.

He'd been cold too, damned cold, coming out of the river and staying in those wet clothes until they'd reached the motel. It hadn't occurred to him that Kate would fare so much worse, that the eighty or so pounds of disparity in their body weights could mean the difference between life and near death.

And she'd come very near death. Too near.

Jonas suppressed a shudder. He'd never been so relieved in all his life as when her skin had finally warmed to normal, an achievement that had taken almost eight hours. Eight hours of imprinting Kate on his own body. Every curve, every line, every hollow, every softness...

Indelibly.

He blew out a breath. He had to stop doing this to himself. At best, he'd go nuts if he kept thinking about her this way, and at worst, he'd get them both killed if he kept thinking with his anatomy rather than his brain.

A car pulled up on the darkening street outside, and Jonas wrenched his attention back to the present, his entire being on high alert. The car waited, then pulled away from the curb again in a wide arc, making a U-turn in a break in the traffic. It disappeared down the street. Another false alarm. The third in the last hour. He was getting jumpier by the minute. And no wonder, with all the time he'd had to go over their predicament.

As soon as Kate's body temperature had returned to normal, he'd left the bed and taken up this post, from which he could monitor both her and the street outside. That had been at noon. Roughly—he glanced at the digital clock beside the bed—seven hours ago.

Plenty of time for thinking about Kate's little bombshell.

Because ever since she'd linked her partner to a possible set-up, the details and possibilities had been bouncing around his brain until he felt like a pinball machine dangerously close to tilt. But nowhere near an answer.

No matter how he looked at it, he couldn't find a solid link to Dave Jennings. Ramirez and Lewis had shown up at Kate's apartment long before Jennings had known of Jonas's existence in her life. And if Jennings was involved, he'd had plenty of opportunity to either nail Jonas himself at the club in Ottawa, or tip someone off when they'd left the city. He sure as hell wouldn't have turned over his vehicle, bank account, and weapon to someone he wanted dead—nor would he have warned Kate to get off the bridge.

Jonas sighed. On the other hand, as Kate said, the only way Ramirez and Lewis could have known their exact rendezvous time at the river was through her call to her partner. So if Jennings hadn't passed it on to them himself, there remained only one other conclusion—and it wasn't much prettier than the first.

Someone had tapped Jennings's phone.

Staring out the window, Jonas rubbed a hand along his jaw. To get a phone tap in Canada, an ATF agent would need to have a Canadian contact. Another cop—or cops. Most likely someone in the RCMP. But who? And how had Ramirez and Lewis convinced them? Had they needed to convince them, or were they somehow involved? Wearily, his mind skittered sideways at the last thought. He didn't have enough intact synapses to sort through that theory. Not right now. Not on his own. He glanced over at the lump of covers on the bed.

Wake up, Kate.

The irony of wanting to discuss a situation with a partner didn't escape him.

He rubbed a hand over his face again, this time grimacing at the prickle of three days' growth along his jaw. The rub became a scratch. This was why he didn't grow a beard. The itch was enough to drive him insane.

Still, if he could hang tough past the discomfort stage, he might have a disguise of sorts. Add a pair of sunglasses and a baseball cap...

On the other side of the room, the shadowy pile of blankets on the bed stirred and moaned. A pale, slender arm appeared from under the covers, trying to push them away.

She was awake.

Casting a last glance over the parking lot and street outside, Jonas climbed to his feet and stretched. Dusk was descending, and streetlights had begun to blink on, casting pools of light onto the handful of cars that passed beneath them. No one turned into the motel lot. He turned toward the bed and Kate. God, he was stiff. Neither his leg nor his side had taken well to their night-time swim, and sitting all day hadn't helped. He didn't imagine Kate's shoulder had fared much better.

The two of them made a fine pair.

He reached the bedside table and switched on the lamp. Dazed cat's eyes blinked up at him from a face almost as white as the pillow on which Kate lay. The shadows cast by her lashes emphasized the bluish circles under her eyes, and blonde curls stuck out every which way in the most bizarre hairstyle Jonas had ever seen. She looked lost, fragile, and utterly beautiful.

Ignoring the shock of desire that kicked him square in the solar plexus, he hid behind a half-smile. "Morning, stranger."

The golden eyes blinked, then moved past him to sweep over the room.

"It's dark."

"It's just after seven p.m. You've been pretty out of it."

Kate was silent for a moment. Then a peculiar look crossed her pale features. "I have no clothes on."

"You don't know the half of it," he muttered. "But at least you didn't need a sponge bath."

Well, that certainly put some color back into her cheeks.

Taking pity on her, he moved back to the window, his eyes scanning the street and lot quickly. Still nothing, but for how long? He swung back to Kate.

"How are you feeling?"

"Like I swam the St. Lawrence at the end of October." She pulled a face. "But I'll live. We should get going."

"Do you feel up to traveling?"

Her mouth twisted, and she sighed. "Do I have a choice?"

She wrapped the sheet around herself and struggled to sit up. Jonas gathered up her clothes from where he'd hung them over various furnishings to dry them out. He carried them to the bed. His heart contracted in his chest.

Even after her marathon sleep, she still looked tired. He had no business taking her on the road yet. She belonged right here, right in that bed, for at least another day. His gaze trailed over the haphazard curls, touched on eyes still hazy with sleep, and fell to devastatingly bare shoulders gleaming in the lamplight. Heat slammed into him, low and heavy, startling him into a cough.

On the other hand, maybe getting back on the road was best.

For both of them.

"I'll wait outside," he said, averting his eyes. "Let me know when you're ready."

THIRTY-TWO

Kate popped the last French fry into her mouth, then scrounged in the paper bag for a napkin. Sitting back again with a sigh of contentment, she caught Jonas's amused, sidelong look in the headlights of a passing vehicle.

"What?"

"I think that's the most I've seen you eat since I met you."

Was it any wonder? The way her stomach tied itself in intricate little knots in his presence was enough to put any girl off her food. It was also one of those things she was probably wiser not to mention.

"I told you I was hungry," she said instead. It had also been easier to concentrate on her food than to try to hold a conversation with the man she'd just slept naked with, conscious or otherwise. Jonas may have only been following standard protocol for the treatment of hypothermia, but she still doubted she'd ever fully recover from the idea.

A half-full French fry bag appeared under her nose.

"Would you like the rest of mine?"

Kate hesitated. She would, actually. But it seemed rude to take his dinner away from him. She shook her head, but the rumble of her stomach belied her refusal.

Jonas deposited the bag in her lap and returned his hand to the steering wheel. "I insist."

She took a fry. "Thank you."

"How are you feeling now?"

A reference to how she'd almost passed out at his feet when she'd first stood up from the bed.

"Better for food."

"Good enough to discuss how Ramirez and Lewis keep finding us so quickly?"

The half-chewed fry in Kate's mouth turned to sawdust, and she had to force herself to swallow it. As inevitable as the discussion might be, she would have liked to postpone it just a little longer. There was a camaraderie to riding through the dark and sharing French fries with Jonas that she was loath to give up. A companionableness she wanted to cling to.

Especially in the face of what was to come.

She shot a glance at the man beside her. The dashboard lights illuminated the hard set of his jaw. She looked away. Regrettably, Jonas took her silence for agreement.

"I don't think it's just my bureau in on this, Kate."

Betrayal churned in her gut. Tightened her voice. "Nothing new about that idea. I'm the one who connected Dave to them in the first place, remember?"

She still couldn't believe her longtime friend and partner could have—

A hand settled over her own as it clenched the napkin.

"It's not Jennings. At least, not directly."

She frowned. "I don't get it."

"I think they may have tapped his phone, but I don't think he knows anything about it."

Cold trickled through her veins. "You think someone else in the RCMP is involved?"

"When I was checking those files in Jersey, I did a bit of snooping around some of our other offices, too. New York City, Detroit, Chicago. There's a high rate of bad deals in this part of the country."

Which happened to be rather near her own part of the neighboring country.

"Just what kind of bad deals are we talking about?" she asked. "Dealers getting off? Agents taking bribes?"

Silence. A darkened gas station slipped past on the passenger side, closed for the night. The empty stretch of secondary highway unwound before them. Jonas cleared his throat.

"The kind of bad deals where arms go missing and dealers end up dead," he said. "I think agents are dealing arms, Kate. And cops, too."

With a trembling hand, Kate moved the bag of fries off her lap onto the console. Her stomach rolled around the hamburger and fries she'd fed it as denial reared in her. Agents dealing arms? Conspiring with cops on her own side of the border? Her own colleagues? *Impossible,* she wanted to say. *No way in hell.*

But she didn't believe that, did she?

"How many?" she asked instead. "How big is this thing?"

"I don't know. A lot. The way things have stayed buried this long...the way they're tracking us..." Jonas slammed the heel of one hand against the steering wheel, and the car swerved across the middle line. He made a visible effort at self-control, and the vehicle straightened out again. "I don't know how big, Kate. I don't know anything anymore."

"If you're right," she said, "We can't do this alone."

Jonas pulled onto the shoulder of the road and turned to face her, his eyes hidden in the shadows. "You're right," he said. "We can't. Not as cops, anyway."

Her jaw dropped. "Excuse me?"

"This changes things, Kate. It's not just Ramirez and Lewis gunning for me—for us—anymore, and the closer we get to Jersey, the worse it'll get."

"What are you suggesting?"

Jonas shook his head. "It doesn't matter, because you're not going to be a part of it." He reached across the car, sweeping his hand feather-light across her cheek. His voice dropped to a rumble. "This is my battle, Kate Dexter. And it's time you bowed out so that I can fight it my way."

"Your way how?" Kate made herself ignore the ache that stirred in her breast at his touch.

His reply was evasive. "I didn't make the rules," he said. "They did."

She batted away the distraction of his hand. "Exactly what is that supposed to mean? What are you planning to do?"

In the glow from the dashboard, his jaw flexed. "Whatever I have to do to get my life back."

His intent slammed into her gut like a fist.

He wouldn't. He couldn't.

"No," she said, and his shadowed gaze flicked back to her. She shook her head in emphasis. "No way, Burke. You're a cop, and I am damned if I'm going to sit back and watch you trash what's left of your life. I'm sorry you stumbled into a hornet's nest, I'm sorry you got shot, and I'm sorry you don't think you can trust anyone. But that does *not* give you carte blanche to lower yourself to the level of the likes of Ramirez and Lewis and whoever else is involved in this—this"—she waved a hand

—"whatever this mess is. And it doesn't give you the right to take the easy way out."

"The *easy* way?" Jonas gave a bark of laughter that held no amusement. "You really don't get it, do you? I stopped being a cop when they left me for dead, and *you* stopped being one when you didn't call the OPP after you picked me up off that road. You're aiding and abetting a suspected felon, Kate. That makes you an accomplice, not a cop. Going after them on their terms isn't the *easy* way out, it's the *only* way."

"Bull. I might not be a cop for a living anymore, but it's still *who* I am. Just like it's who you are." Kate folded her arms and jutted out her chin. "I'm not leaving, Jonas. We find another way. Together."

Heavy silence followed her words, and then Jonas wrenched open his door and hurled himself from the car. In the glow of the headlights, he paced the shoulder of the road, the internal war he waged evident in every rigid line of his body. Kate watched him for a few minutes, then she switched off the ignition, leaving the headlights on, and slid from the car. Jonas rounded on her as she joined him at the front of the vehicle.

"None of this was my idea, damn it," he snarled. "They've taken away my entire life, Kate. All of it, along with all my options. What am I supposed to do, sit back and let them? Not fight back? Is that what you want?"

He towered over her, his face cast in fierce, shadowy angles. Kate shrugged.

"I want you to do what you think is right," she said. "It's that simple."

It was like watching a balloon deflate. First Jonas's jaw unlocked, then his fingers uncurled, then his shoulders sagged. He opened his mouth, closed it, turned away, swiveled back.

"That phrase," he said, in the most reasonable tone Kate thought she'd ever heard from him, "has got to be the biggest killjoy there is in the English language."

She blinked at the transformation he seemed to have undergone. "Um...I'm sorry?"

"No, you're not."

"No," she agreed. "I'm not."

Not if what she'd said had made him rational again. *If.*

Shoving his hands into his pockets, Jonas regarded her narrowly. "Mike would have liked you," he said, making it sound like a pronouncement.

"Mike?"

"The Chicago cop I told you about. The one responsible for my career path. Do you know how sick I got of hearing those words from him?" He grimaced. "*'Do what you think is right.'*"

"Does that mean...?"

"It means I won't go taking pot shots at my enemies," he replied. "*Yet.* But you'd better have an alternative, because I'm fresh out of ideas at this point."

Kate levered herself onto the hood of the hot rod, the metal warm from the motor's heat. She rested her feet on the bumper. Then she hesitated.

Jonas watched her for a moment. Then he sighed. "You do have an alternative."

Kate nodded.

"And I'm not going to like it."

She shook her head.

Jonas rested hands on hips and tipped his head back to stare up at the sky. "Out with it."

"We call the FBI."

Jonas snorted. "Are you kidding? We walk into an office with those warrants out on us, and they'll arrest us first and ask questions later. Only we won't likely get a later. Unless..." He lowered his head to look at her. "You know someone there, don't you?"

Define know, she wanted to say, thinking of her former fiancé.

"Yes," she actually said. "I do."

THIRTY-THREE

Jonas hovered in the doorway of the restaurant, every muscle tensed for flight. Kate was putting way too much trust in this former relationship of hers, in his opinion, and he fully expected a dozen armed undercover cops to be waiting for them. He scanned the interior, looking for the telltale signs of interest: a covert glance, an exchange of looks, a barely there nod.

He saw nothing but people eating their lunches.

His tension remained.

Kate touched his arm and nodded toward a table along the far wall. A solitary, dark-suited man sat watching them, a salad before him, a water glass to his right, his hands out of sight beneath the table. So. That was him. The man who had once shared Kate's bed. The knot in Jonas's gut wound tighter.

"You're sure we can trust him?" he asked, trying to dislodge the image of Kate in the other man's arms. "You dumped the guy. What if he's ticked with you? He could be setting us up."

Kate snorted. "Trust me, Grant Douglas is not the kind of man to carry a grudge that far. Even if he was ticked with me—which he's not—he wouldn't fly up from New York just to get back at me. It would be far more *sensible* to have the local cops do the honors."

Jonas slanted a sideways glance at her. She hadn't offered much of an explanation about her former engagement to FBI Agent Grant Douglas, but the dry emphasis in that last sentence spoke volumes. It also helped ease the knot a tiny bit as Jonas followed her across the restaurant.

The man stood as they reached the table. He was shorter than Jonas but powerfully built, and he held himself in a way that spoke to his own tension. His gaze slid past Kate to settle on Jonas, turning hostile.

"Grant." Kate reached up to kiss the man's cheek, and his arms went around her in return, holding her close for a long moment. The gesture of familiarity twisted through Jonas with all the subtlety of a prison-made shank. He exhaled a slow breath, his gaze locked with the other man's.

Kate stepped back. "Thank you for coming," she said quietly. She looked over her shoulder, her expression inviting Jonas into the conversation. "This is—"

"He knows who I am," Jonas said.

Douglas shrugged. "I knew before I left the office. You two are pretty unpopular with law enforcement agencies in these parts."

"Have you told anyone?" Kate asked.

"No." Grant Douglas looked down at her. "Not yet. You have ten minutes to tell me why I shouldn't."

"Then we should get started." Kate pulled out the two chairs opposite her ex-fiancé, settled into one, and shot a pointed look at Jonas.

He hesitated. Douglas remained standing. Kate cleared her throat. Jonas tightened his lips and dropped onto the chair—but only its edge. Across the table, Douglas sat, pushed away the uneaten salad, straightened his tie, and rested his elbows on the table. Then, as Kate took a breath to begin, he held up a hand.

"First things first," he said. "Are you sleeping with him?"

Jonas was half out of his seat, hands curled into fists, before Kate's hand stopped him. He shook her off and leaned across the table, his face inches from the other man's, fury leaping through his veins.

"What the hell does that have to do with anything?" he snarled. He felt the eyes of other patrons on him, sensed the unease, but didn't care. He knew his reaction was extreme. He didn't care about that, either.

Nor was he about to analyze why.

Douglas looked past him at Kate. "Well?" he asked. "Are you?"

Jonas straightened, drawing back a fist, anticipating the pleasure he would derive from wiping that supercilious expression from—

Again Kate's hand stopped him, her fingers digging into his rigid forearm. He couldn't shake her off this time.

"No," she said. "We're not sleeping together, and no, my judgment isn't compromised."

Jonas's breath left him in a hiss.

Oh.

The response put Douglas's question in a whole other light. Of course he needed that reassurance; Jonas would want the same if the tables were turned. Any decent cop would.

But it didn't mean he liked the FBI agent any better.

Fingers uncurling, he subsided into his seat again. Kate's hand moved from his arm to his thigh, pressing lightly, then remaining in place. As the gesture of comfort and encouragement he suspected she intended it to be, it failed miserably. But it certainly succeeded in distracting him.

Grant Douglas studied him as if he knew exactly where his former fiancée's hand sat—and what it did to the man it sat on.

"I'm listening," he said.

With all his being, Jonas wished he could stand up and walk out. He didn't want to be beholden to this man. Didn't want anything to do with him, apart from the lingering urge to deck him just on principle.

But Kate—Kate, who had come so far and given up so much, Kate who trusted him but also trusted Douglas—Kate needed them to work together if she was going to survive this. And so Jonas swallowed his anger, along with what he would have liked to say, and in a low voice, began laying out the facts as he knew them, the theories as he supposed them, and the conclusions he'd had no choice but to reach.

Douglas stared at the tabletop for long, silent seconds when Jonas was done, toying with the butter knife beside his wilting salad. Beneath the table, Kate's fingers remained on Jonas's thigh. They tightened as Douglas shook his head.

"It's not enough," he said.

Jonas was unsurprised by the words, but Kate almost came up out of her chair in objection.

"What? But the tap on Dave's phone line, and the—"

"I can't do anything on the Canadian side, Kate. You know that," Douglas interrupted. "And as big as the rest of it—what your...friend is telling me—is, I can't open an investigation into another agency based on hearsay from a fugitive. Hell, he's a rogue agent. Most people would say he's just trying to put the blame elsewhere."

"It's not just his word, Grant. It's mine, too."

"And what exactly do *you* know? You have no more evidence than Burke does—a lot less, in fact," Douglas pointed out, speaking as if Jonas wasn't sitting right there with them. "He's fed you everything you know. I can't go to my director and ask for people based on that."

"Can't or won't?" she asked, weariness edging her voice. Making it catch. "Damn it, Grant—"

"He's right," Jonas cut her off, his words made abrupt by Kate's defeat and his own disillusionment. They should have known better. *He* should have known better. "It was a long shot at best. We don't have—"

"Hold on." Douglas held up a hand, and for the first time since they'd sat down, his gaze encompassed both of them. "I'm not saying I won't do anything at all; I'm just saying I can't do anything official. I'll make some inquiries—discreet ones," he assured Kate when she opened her mouth to object, "and see what I can dig up. If I find anything, however remote, I'll take it to my director. You have my word."

Kate did a slow slump in the chair next to Jonas. Her gaze sought his. He read the question in it, saw the half-hearted reassurance. He considered pulling her aside so they could discuss her former fiancé's offer—then he sighed. They didn't need to discuss anything. He knew what she was thinking, just as she knew what he thought.

It was like they were partners, or something.

He sat back in his chair and looped an arm across the back of hers. "Go for it," he said.

She turned back to Douglas. "All right. But only because we don't have a lot of choice right now."

Douglas nodded satisfaction and took a notebook from his inside breast pocket. "Right. Burke, can you think of anyone I can start with? Someone in your bureau who owes you a favor, maybe?"

Honeyman, Jonas thought. But he shook his head. "No. No way. If I send you directly to anyone, I may as well be painting a target on their back. First, you find a way to make this official and guarantee their safety, and then we'll talk."

Grant Douglas regarded him in silence for a long moment, then looked to Kate. "What's your cell phone number?"

"I don't have one. It was in the vehicle they impounded in Cornwall."

"The vehicle they—then how did you—no, never mind." Douglas waved a hand to ward off a reply. "I'm better off not knowing." He replaced the notebook in his pocket, then stood, pulled a twenty dollar bill from a clip, and dropped the money on the table. "Give me twenty-four hours, then call me. We'll decide where to go from there."

"And what exactly do you suggest we do for those twenty-four hours?" Kate asked.

Bitter disappointment laced her voice, echoing Jonas's own. Despite his misgivings going into this meeting, he'd allowed a tiny part of him to share Kate's optimism. He'd *wanted* to share it, damn it, because they'd needed this. Because without it...without it, they would lose. It was that simple. That definitive.

"Lie low," Douglas replied to Kate's question. "Find somewhere to stay out of sight."

Kate exchanged a sardonic look with Jonas. When Douglas raised an eyebrow, she explained, "We don't exactly have a great track record at that."

Once again, Douglas's gaze traveled back and forth between them. Then, with a sigh, he took pen and notebook from his pocket for a second time. He stooped, scribbled some notes, then tore the paper from its binding and slid it across the table to Kate.

"Directions to a friend's fishing cabin," he said, straightening. "It's about halfway between here and Jersey. No one uses it at this time of year. There's a key on the window frame to the left of the door. Top right corner. You'll be safe there."

Kate stood as Douglas tucked pen and notebook back into his pocket. She stepped away from the table and reached up to hug her ex a second time. "Thank you."

Douglas returned the embrace, then pulled back. "Twenty-four hours," he repeated. "And Katie...be careful."

Jonas doubted the real meaning of his words was lost on any of them.

THIRTY-FOUR

J onas lifted a log from the woodpile beside the shed at the side of the cabin and balanced it on top of the load in his other arm. With luck, that would be enough to keep the fireplace—their only source of heat—going until morning. He certainly hoped so, because the October air held a distinct chill here in the Adirondacks. He'd be willing to bet on frost overnight.

He looked over his shoulder at the cabin. A light glowed from the kitchen through the dark, as warm and inviting as the company of the woman it silhouetted. Kate, doing dishes, waiting for him to return. Kate, who had him feeling tighter than an over-wound clock spring on the verge of tearing apart its housing. Bloody hell.

Jonas shifted his hold on the load of wood and turned his collar up against the cold.. At first, he'd quite liked Douglas's suggestion they stay here, for a couple of reasons: First, there was safety in the cabin's isolation; and second, the peace of a lakeside cabin offered an undeniable reprieve from the insanity into which he and Kate had been thrust.

The idea had seemed perfect—until they'd pulled up in front of the solid, squat log cabin, Kate had switched off the rumbling engine, and solitude had settled around them—quiet, absolute, and knife sharp with the tension that had been building between them.

Far from finding themselves rested or relaxed, he and Kate had circled each other all afternoon with exaggerated care, barely spoken during dinner, and pushed the food around on their plates until by mutual, unspoken consent, they'd given up any pretense of eating. He, acutely aware of every move she made, every look she gave him through lowered lashes. She—hell, he didn't know what she was thinking, and he didn't dare speculate. Not when his thoughts alone had him waffling out here in the cold, yearning to return to the cabin and dreading it, all in the same mangled breath.

He shifted his weight to the other foot, exhaled in a fog, and started toward the cabin. Desire intensified with each step, licking through his belly, adding its traitorous whisper to the sound of the wind rustling the trees. Would it really be so bad? They were both adults, after all. Experienced, with their eyes wide open. Surely they were capable of handling a brief relationship before they went their separate ways...

Except that wasn't how it would go. Not if he was honest. Kate wasn't the brief relationship kind—and worse, he didn't want her to be. If he got involved with her on any level, he'd want more. He'd want it all— forever. And he, of all people, knew there was no such thing. Not where he was concerned.

He tipped back his head to stare at the night sky. Billions of pinpricks of light dotted the dark like specks of dust scattered across velvet. He breathed in. Breathed out. Centered himself. Then he climbed the stairs and crossed the porch.

No. He had no intention of opening himself up to

another lesson in the kind of pain that went along with the death of a dream. And that was what someone like Kate ultimately amounted to: a dream. Balancing his load in one arm, he twisted the door handle and pushed into the cabin's darkened living room. He just needed to hold out for a few more days. He'd get his evidence, he and Kate would part ways, and he could go back to his life. Maybe look up someone for a little companionship of the distracting kind—maybe Valerie, if she wasn't married yet. It had been a couple of years since they'd dated, but—

Jonas stopped dead in his tracks as Kate half-turned from the fireplace she'd been tending. She'd changed from jeans and sweatshirt into a nightgown she'd found somewhere. Voluminous folds of fabric stretched from multiple ruffles under her chin all the way down to her toes. It should have looked ridiculous. Should have, but didn't.

Instead, backlit by the firelight, the garment had become a magical, translucent creation, draped over and simultaneously highlighting every line, every contour. The curve of her breast, the gentle swell of her hip, the long, slender legs. Jonas damned near dropped the armload of wood. Then he clung to it as he might a shield between him and certain doom.

Damnation.

Fireplace poker gripped in one hand, Kate looked over her shoulder. "I thought you'd gotten lost."

A throat that had gone dust-dry refused to let him respond. Kate straightened up, replacing the poker in its stand.

"Jonas? What's wrong? Is someone out there? Did you see—" She started toward him, but stopped when he held up his free hand.

"We need to talk," he said. Using his foot, he shoved the door shut behind him and stalked across the room. He dumped the wood into the box sitting by the fireplace, then toured the living room, turning on every lamp he could find.

"Again?" she asked warily. "What about this time?"

"You. Me." He stopped moving and faced her, fireplace between them and the room as bright as day. The nightgown had turned opaque again. Thank God. He raised his gaze to Kate's. "Us," he said.

It was funny how a single word could tip a person's entire existence on its head and knock the air from their lungs. Kate went still, trying to process that one word. To decipher it.

To breathe.

"Jonas, I—"

"No. Let me talk." Jonas turned away to lean both hands against the brick of the fireplace.

Us. The word hung in the air between them.

Kate felt for the couch near her and sat down, staring at his back. *What ifs* whispered through her mind. What if she stood and joined him by the fire? What if she ran her hands over fabric drawn tight across muscular shoulders? Tugged it from the waistband of his jeans, slipped her hands beneath it and around his waist, and then slid them up to caress the deep, powerful chest?

What if she stopped worrying about emotional involvement, threw caution to the wind, and just—

"It would be all too easy to fall in love with you, Kate Dexter," Jonas said. "But I can't let that happen."

Kate blinked at his back. He couldn't have said what she thought she'd just heard...could he?

"I don't trust myself to give you the kind of love you deserve," Jonas continued, still not looking at her. "I don't think I'm capable of it. Hell, I'm not capable of *trust*, period."

Her heart twisted. "Jonas..."

"No, Kate. I'm not looking for pity or sympathy. I'm just stating facts. My life is what it is. I've come to terms with that. I also refuse to inflict it on anyone else."

At last he looked her way, his jaw set like hardened concrete and his gaze determined. "I *could* fall in love with you," he said, "but I won't. Because if we become involved, I guarantee it's only a matter of time before I hurt you, and I won't be responsible for that. I can't be."

Kate didn't respond for long, silent seconds. She stared down at the rolled arm of the couch, tracing the faded tapestry pattern with one fingertip. She'd known for a while that she was already in too deep where this man was concerned, and Jonas's words at breakfast had confirmed he wasn't entirely immune to her, either. But this latest admission really took the proverbial cake. He didn't trust himself to fall in love with her? She didn't know whether to admire him for his honesty or sock him one for being so incredibly obtuse.

Or maybe she could just throw herself at him and see how long his ideals lasted. She wiped slick palms against the cotton of the nightgown.

"In other words, all you can offer me is pure, unadulterated sex?" she asked.

Jonas's eyes widened. He coughed, spluttered, made a visible effort to recover. "That wasn't quite what I meant," he said, "and you know—"

"What if I say yes?" she interrupted.

A host of conflicting emotions played across Jonas's face. White-hot need warred with decency. Desire wrestled with a lifetime of distrust. Yearning struggled against resignation. Kate twisted her hands into folds of fabric.

"What if I don't need all the rest?" she pressed, ignoring the little voice screaming *"Liar!"* in her head. "What if I'm okay with just this, what we have just now?"

Blue eyes glittered at her, and corded tendons stood out along the side of Jonas's neck. Kate waited. Willed him to—

He turned his back on her. "We'll go into town and call your ex after lunch tomorrow," he said. "You should sleep in if you can. You need it."

She gaped at the back of his head. Was he seriously not going to—? She closed her eyes and gathered her scattered thoughts. Maybe he hadn't understood. Maybe she hadn't been direct enough. She cleared her throat.

Jonas cut her off before she could speak. "Go to bed, Kate. Please."

For a long moment, she didn't move, and the room itself seemed to hold its breath. Her gaze traveled the taut length of the man across from her. The rigidity of his shoulders, the way his hands were clenched into fists at his sides, the shudder of a long inhale. She knew it wouldn't take much to crumble his resistance: a touch, a whisper, a reassurance, a plea.

Her entire body thrummed at the thought of breaking down that final barrier between them after their days of dancing around one another. The imagined feel of Jonas's hands sliding over her body. The ecstasy she knew he would wring from her, and she from him...

But there her thoughts paused and her heart skipped a beat. Then it skipped another. Because just as she knew Jonas would give in to her, she also knew— without a trace of doubt—that he would hate her for it afterward. And that she would hate herself for doing that to him.

With a whisper of fabric and a last, lingering look at the maddening, complicated man who claimed not that he didn't love her, but that he didn't *want* to love her, Kate rose and left the room.

THIRTY-FIVE

K ate surged awake to a hand across her mouth. Within the space of a single heartbeat, she shoved free, scrambled out of bed, and danced out of reach, filling her lungs to bellow a warning to Jonas. Her shout died in her chest as a whisper came from the darkness.

"Kate, it's me!"

She froze, bedside lamp poised over her head to throw at the vague shadow among shadows. "Jonas?"

The adrenaline faded from her system, leaving confusion in its wake. Why was Jonas in her room? Had he changed his mind? Was he here to—

"Keep your voice down," he whispered. "We have company out on the road. They just got here. If we move fast, we'll have enough time to get out the back door to the lake."

Company?

She lowered the table lamp to her side. "How did they find us here?"

"Only one person knows we're here, so how the hell do you think? Come on."

He thought Grant—? Kate blinked at the idea. Grant might be as dull as dishwater and totally lacking in imagination, but he was loyal to a fault. How else could he have continued their friendship even after she'd called off their engagement? She shook her head in the dark. No, he would never have informed on them. Not without talking to her.

"Kate!" Jonas urged.

Argument would have to wait. She tossed the lamp onto the bed. "I need my clothes."

"Just wear the nightgown. I have your shoes for you."

"I'm not wearing anything at the moment." She shivered in the cool night air.

There was a tiny silence, followed by a muffled curse.

"Where?" Jonas asked curtly.

"Bureau by the door. Jeans and sweatshirt." No time for life's little niceties such as the underwear she'd dropped onto the floor. Her clothes hit her bare chest and she clutched at them.

"Be quick," Jonas said.

She didn't need to be told twice. She scrambled into the clothes and then felt her way across the room to shadow-Jonas and took her running shoes from him. She tied them swiftly and straightened. "Ready."

A warm hand closed unerringly around hers. She pulled away. "Wait—my gun."

"I have it."

The hand closed over hers again, and she followed Jonas through the dark cabin, relying on him to steer her through doorways and around furniture until they stood at the patio door overlooking the deck and lake beyond. Jonas paused.

"Hear anything?" he murmured.

Kate shook her head, her hair catching on his stubbled chin.

"Good. Me either." He slid the glass panel open slowly. Kate cringed at the metal-on-metal squeak, releasing it in a gust when there was enough room for them to slip through. Jonas went first, holding her back with one hand while he listened again to the silence. Then he tugged her after him and steered her in a path around the deck's perimeter.

"Shit," he muttered. "The whole deck is out over the lake. We're going to have to get wet again. You up for another swim?"

Kate could think of a lot of things she'd rather do after her dip in the St. Lawrence, but she didn't see many alternatives. She nodded, trusting him and his superpowered night vision to see her. Together, they slipped over the rail and lowered themselves into the lake. As dark as the night itself, the water closed around Kate's waist, then crawled up to cover her shoulders. Sheer, bone-numbing cold sucked the air from her lungs.

Jonas touched her arm. "All good?"

She nodded and struck out after him. Following the shoreline, they stuck to the deepest shadows where the ripples of their passing were less likely to be noticed. Lake-bottom slime oozed over the tops of her runners and crept between her toes like clammy, vile worms. Kate suppressed a shudder. Too late now, but it would have been so much better to carry their shoes rather than wear them.

Jonas's shadow glided through the water a few feet in front of her, leading her away from the cabin. When they had gone a hundred yards or so, he veered back in to the shore, where the trees hung low over the water. With the help of the branches there, they pulled themselves up and out onto land. Jonas's cold fingers closed over hers again.

"You okay?"

Kate gritted her teeth to keep them from chattering and nodded again. They forged ahead, picking their way through the underbrush, and every snap of a twig or rustle of leaves underfoot made Kate's heart miss another beat. Time stood still yet again—but for all the wrong reasons.

Then, suddenly, gravel crunched underfoot and no more branches slapped at them. The road. And if her bearings were at all correct, Jonas was headed back toward the cabin. She tugged him to a stop.

"We're going the wrong way!"

"We need the vehicle," Jonas replied. "It's our only way out of here."

She hesitated, then gave a nod of capitulation and fell into step behind him again. He was right. Even if they weren't soaked to the bone, they'd never be able to walk out of here. Not unless they wanted nature to finish the job Lewis and Ramirez had started.

The next time Jonas stopped, she nearly ran into him. He held up a warning hand and she looked past him to see the shadowy shapes of four cars parked along the road ahead—theirs plus three more. Only one of them had a light bar sitting atop it; the others were nondescript sedans. The kind driven by suits. Lewis and Ramirez? Kate's blood ran a little colder, and a knot settled in her chest. Could she have been wrong about Grant after all?

Later, Kate. Deal with it later.

Side by side, she and Jonas waited at the edge of the woods, but nothing moved around any of the vehicles or on the path leading down to the cottage. Nothing moved anywhere. Jonas pressed something into her hand, and her fingers closed around the handle of a jackknife.

"I'll get the radios, you get the tires," he murmured. "Leave us one of the sedans to get away in. Work fast."

Kate did. Within a few minutes, she had slashed three

tires on the state police car, three on one of the sedans, and three more on the gaudy hot rod. She joined Jonas beside the second sedan as the moon slipped out from behind the clouds. Damn. Moonlight was the last thing they needed.

"Done?" he asked, already on his way around the vehicle to the driver's side.

"Thoroughly," she replied. With one hand on the open passenger door, she lifted a foot into the car—and then froze at the unmistakable, distinctive sound of a shotgun shell being chambered. A powerful flashlight came on, capturing Jonas in its beam.

"That's far enough, folks," a terse male voice said. "Move away from the car, ma'am, and put your hands up where I can see them. You, too, Agent Burke."

Kate didn't move. She couldn't. She was too stunned. Too shocked. Too devastated. In the flashlight's harsh glare, Jonas raised his hands and locked them behind his head, resignation etched into his face. Her own hands curled into fists. Exhaustion curled through her. Cold, clammy, wet denim clung to her legs. Her sodden sweatshirt weighed her down. And she still had mud in her shoes. Her lips pressed tight.

They'd been so close to escape, to safety, and now this?

No. No way. She was damned if things would end like this.

Gravel crunched as the armed man behind her moved closer.

"I said move away from the vehicle!" he snapped.

Not bloody likely. Her gaze darted to the side mirror on the open car door, flicked away from the brilliance of the flashlight beam reflected there, rose to meet Jonas's. *Move,* she silently urged. He gave a tiny, barely perceptible nod and began edging to his left, away from the vehicle and toward the trees.

"That's far enough," the voice said. "Now down on the ground."

Jonas took another step. And another. More gravel shifted behind Kate, signaling rapid steps. She stopped breathing.

"Do it!" the voice barked at Jonas—closer now. Close enough?

Her gaze fastened on the mirror again. The glare of the flashlight had become a mere glow. She turned her head a fraction to the right, just until she could see the silhouette of a shotgun in her peripheral vision, held by a man who stood no more than a few feet away.

Close enough.

She whirled, her right arm coming up under the shotgun barrel and forcing it up. The gun fired into the air, the sound of its blast ricocheting through the forest night. Shit. There was no way the others in the cabin wouldn't hear that. But even as the thought registered, Kate's left hand slipped around the back of the man's neck, and her knee buried itself in his gut. The man doubled over with a grunt, and the gun flew from his hands, skidding down the road.

His hat—a state trooper's Stetson—tumbled onto Kate's feet. She stared at it in shock, panicking licking through her veins like wildfire. Double shit. She'd just assaulted a fellow police officer. Shouts erupted from the direction of the cabin.

"Damn it, Kate, get out of the way!"

Jonas's voice. Kate twisted to look over her shoulder and saw him coming at her—at the state trooper—her gun in hand. For a fraction of an instant, shock held her immobile. He wouldn't—he couldn't—

Common sense kicked in, along with a fresh rush of adrenaline, and she jumped out of Jonas's path. The gun in his hand came down, connecting with the back of the cop's skull with a muffled *thunk!* Enough to put him out cold and ensure he had a nasty headache when he woke up. Not enough to kill him.

She couldn't believe the possibility had entered her head, however briefly. The cold condemnation in the eyes now turned on her assured her it had. And that Jonas knew it.

Instinctively, impulsively, she stretched out her hand to him. "Jonas—"

He pulled his arm away. The shouts in the woods grew nearer.

"We need to go." Jonas shoved the gun at her, and she accepted it automatically, her brain still trying to recover from the chaos of the past few moments. From the unforgivable leap it had made. Jonas rounded the vehicle and slid behind the steering wheel. He pulled down the sun visor, and a key dropped into his lap. The small part of Kate's brain that still functioned thanked the sloppy, overconfident cop who'd left it there.

The engine turned over. Caught. Headlights illuminated the road and the canopy of trees above.

"Kate!"

Kate cast a last glance at the flashlights bobbing along the path from the cabin and got into the car. She slammed the door shut as Jonas jammed his foot down on the accelerator and the car surged forward in a spray of gravel. In the side mirror, the flashlights broke free of the woods. Two pops sounded. The mirror exploded.

"Get down!" Jonas's hand snaked around Kate's neck, forcing her head down. She didn't need to be told twice.

Wrapping arms around knees, she tried to stay in her

seat as the car slewed first left, then right. More pops followed, growing fainter. A sharp turn pressed her rib cage against the door handle, and then the vehicle straightened out. She ventured a peek at Jonas from between straggly strands of wet hair.

"Are we clear?" she asked. In the glow of the dashboard lights, she saw him check the rearview mirror.

"For now."

She straightened in her seat and fumbled for her seatbelt with fingers numb from cold. A metal-on-metal clunk made her pause. Freaking hell. She was still holding the gun Jonas had given her, her fingers clamped around it so hard that—now that she'd noticed—she could feel the bite of the grip against her palm. A bubble of laughter rose in her chest, and she clamped her teeth together to keep it from erupting. She and Jonas may have laughed together once over a narrow escape, but there would be no repeat of shared relief. Not after—

A navy trench coat dropped into her lap.

"Change into that." Jonas stared stonily ahead. "I'm not up to another bout of hypothermia."

"I'm okay."

"Just do it, Kate."

She flinched from his flat tone. "Jonas, about what happened back there—"

"Forget it."

"No. It wasn't what you think. It was—"

"Save it, Kate." His mouth took on a bitter twist in the pale green glow from the dashboard lights. He didn't look at her. "It doesn't matter anyway."

She scowled at him. "It does matter. At least to me. Yes, the thought crossed my mind—for about a hundredth of a second. I was in the middle of assaulting another cop, for God's sake. I wasn't exactly at my most logical!"

His lips pressed tighter. "I told you, it doesn't matt—"

White-hot anger flared in Kate. "Screw you, Burke," she snarled. She slammed the gun onto the console between them, heedless of safety precautions, and started peeling off her wet sweatshirt. She was naked beneath, but she didn't care about that, either.

"You don't want to be a reasonable human being?" she continued, her voice muffled by the soggy fabric as it caught around her ears. "*Fine*. Go ahead and believe what you want. You will anyway, because heaven forbid you run out of reasons to keep me at arm's length, which is what this is really about."

She gave the sweatshirt a final, vicious tug, and it slipped off with a suddenness that made her hand smack his shoulder. The car swerved on the gravel road. Shivering at the chill against her wet skin, she tossed the balled-up shirt into the back seat. She'd hit the proverbial nail on the head with her words—she had no doubt about it. She also had no earthly idea what to do about the realization, and she was too goddamned exhausted to even care anymore.

Tomorrow she'd care again, but not tonight.

Tonight, Jonas Burke could go pound sand.

"*I'm not capable of trust,*" the memory of Jonas's voice reminded her as she picked up the trench coat that had slid to the floorboards.

"No shit, Sherlock," she muttered under her breath. If Jonas heard, he didn't let on, and Kate unsnapped her jeans, lifted her hips from the seat, and commenced the near-impossible task of separating wet denim from skin.

THIRTY-SIX

Damn it to hell and back. Jonas's jaw ached from being clenched, but he couldn't relax it. Not with Kate wiggling in the seat next to him like that. Every time she lifted her hips up to coax the wet jeans down a little further, the trench coat she'd put on fell wide open. So far he'd managed to refrain from outright gawking, but he could still see the pale glow of her skin from the corner of his eye.

Soft, supple skin, chilled now, but oh so receptive to being warmed. He knew that from experience. An experience his traitorous mind was determined to relive despite his best efforts.

Kate, naked against him. Kate, taking her warmth from him. Kate, relaxing into—

Hell. There he went again.

Kate lifted off the seat and inched her jeans down another notch. Jonas gripped the steering wheel until his fingers protested. He didn't want to be so aware of her. *Shouldn't* be, given how she'd looked at him back there, when she thought he'd been going to shoot that state trooper. She'd all but branded him a murderer—

"Screw you, Burke!" The memory of her voice intruded. *"Heaven forbid you run out of reasons to keep me at arm's length..."*

Jonas scowled at the road unfurling in the headlights before them, self-righteousness hot in his chest. And what if she was right? It wasn't as if he didn't have good reason to want to protect himself. How many times in his life had he let his guard down, only to have things go wrong like this? As far back as he could remember, when something had gone missing or been damaged in one of his foster homes, or when there had been an altercation at school, he'd been the first one they turned to for answers. The accusing eyes, the pointing fingers...the lack of trust had followed him right up to and through his career to where he was now, running from his own colleagues.

No, he had every reason to protect himself. Even from Kate.

In the seat next to him, the woman in question successfully peeled off the troublesome jeans and tossed them into the back seat—leaving her naked as the day she was born under the trench coat.

Jonas's mouth went dry. Who was he kidding? He needed to protect himself *especially* from Kate.

Damnation.

Kate jolted awake as the car slid to a halt, its passenger tires scraping along the curb. She sat up, surreptitiously wiping the corner of her mouth as she took in the flow of traffic around them—cars on one side, pedestrians on the other—and buildings piled up everywhere. It was a far cry from the woods they'd still been driving through when she'd drifted off. She blinked the last of the sleep from her eyes and looked over at Jonas.

"Where are we?" she asked.

"Newark."

She raised an eyebrow at the terse response. So. Their surroundings might have changed, but someone's mood hadn't followed suit. She tried again, motioning at the sign on the building beside them—an Italian restaurant. "Isn't it a little early for lunch?"

"I have to see a man about a key." Jonas opened his car door. "Stay here. I'll be back in a minute."

Without so much as a glance in her direction, he rounded the vehicle, crossed the sidewalk, and banged on the restaurant's glass door with the flat of his hand. The door opened a second later, and he disappeared inside. Kate stared after him, then sighed and leaned her head against the seat. She closed her eyes.

They hadn't spoken again after their heated exchange last night. Jonas had driven in tight-lipped, rock-jawed silence, and she'd stared out the window until—much to her relief—sleep had claimed her. She wished she could have continued.

The driver's door opened again, making her jump and open her eyes. Jonas slid in beside her and reached for the ignition. Kate sighed. She cleared her throat. Jonas hesitated, and a muscle flexed in front of his ear. He looked at her.

"Good morning, Jonas," she said.

He stared at her. She stared back. Think what he might, they were still partners in this, which meant they had to at least be speaking to one another. Jonas looked away, then back again. He exhaled a long, slow breath.

"Good morning, Kate," he replied wearily.

A pang of guilt shafted through Kate. The man hadn't had a decent sleep in days, and they were both running for their very lives—was it any wonder they'd reached a breaking point of sorts? She rested an elbow on the car door and cradled her forehead in her hand.

"We can't work like this," she said. "Last night—"

"Last night doesn't matter," he interrupted. "I know you didn't mean anything by it, and you were right. I was looking for reasons to—for—" His gaze moved to the windshield. "I was looking for reasons. I didn't mean what I said. Not then. But I did mean what I said earlier. I won't get involved with you, Kate. I can't."

Well. That certainly made working together easier.

Kate joined him in staring out at the street. "I know."

I just don't agree, a little voice whispered in the back of her mind.

She coughed, and Jonas sighed. "Kate—"

"I need food," she announced, because she didn't want to hear anything more—not from him, and not from her inner voice. "I'm starving."

Jonas looked as if he might pursue the conversation, but then he shrugged. His gaze dropped to the trench coat she wore. A spark of amusement glinted. "Clothes first, I think. And the bank before that, because we're officially broke at the moment."

"You have no ATM card," Kate reminded him as he switched on the engine. "Or am I about to add bank heist to my list of transgressions?"

"I keep a safety deposit box for emergencies."

"The key you picked up at the restaurant?" Of course. She should have realized.

Jonas nodded as he pulled out into the flow of traffic. "There's enough in there for us to lie low for a few days and figure out what comes next."

An hour later, infinitely more comfortable in leggings and an oversized cotton sweater, Kate slid the remains of an all-day-breakfast platter away from her. Then she drained the last dregs of coffee from the mug and leaned back in her seat with a blissful sigh. Jonas's mouth curved upward.

"You look happier."

"You have no idea."

"Actually, I suspect I do." He bit off a piece of toast piled high with scrambled eggs, chewed, and swallowed.

"Actually, no, you don't." Kate gave a delicious wriggle in her seat and wrapped her arms around the warm sweater enveloping her.

"Dry clothes feel good, do they?" He picked up his cup.

"*Clothes* feel good," she responded. "Never underestimate the comfort level of underwear."

Jonas almost choked on his coffee.

"Sorry," she said.

"No, you're not."

She grinned. "No, I'm not. Did you see that sales clerk's face when I told her I wanted to wear the underwear out, too? How much do you want to bet she's already told the story to everyone she knows?"

"And probably put it on Facebook," he agreed. He balled up the napkin and dropped it on his finished plate. "Along with her theory of how you came to be in that predicament—and quite possibly a store video."

Amusement dropped away. Hell. She hadn't thought of that. Had she looked up at the store camera at all? Given a clear shot of her face? If the woman's post somehow went viral, it could be seen by anyone. Uneasily, she looked around the diner. Welcome to the Internet age, where privacy was just a suggestion...and a weak one at that.

"We should go," she said. "We need to keep moving."

"We need a plan first." Jonas set his empty coffee cup on the plate and folded his arms along the edge of the table. He leaned forward and dropped his voice. "We're not going to be able to disappear for very long, Kate. Even without a store video, Lewis and Ramirez will have figured out I was trying to get back here. They'll be closing the net as we speak."

Kate nodded, then she jutted her chin toward the envelope sitting near his elbow—the one he'd picked up at the bank before they'd gone shopping for her new clothes. "I suppose it's wishful thinking to imagine you have enough in that envelope of yours to get us out of the country."

"Not for both of us, no. Even if I did, you have no passport."

She raised an eyebrow. "And you do?"

"Jonathan Blake."

Her other eyebrow followed the first. "Fake ID? That's not part of a standard stash. You've been worried about things for a while."

"I told you I have trust issues."

Kate suspected the comment was only half in jest. "So. About that plan."

"First, we need to find a new car."

"Find?" If she'd had a third eyebrow, she would have raised that one, too.

A smile threatened at the corner of Jonas's mouth. "You prefer borrow?"

"I prefer not to think of committing yet another felony crime," she retorted.

He chuckled. "You can relax. I plan on renting this time. And after that, I think we should—"

"Wait," she interrupted. "It's my turn. You came up with the first step in the plan; I should get the second."

Jonas's eyes narrowed. "Why do I get the feeling I'm not going to like this?"

"We need to call Grant."

Jonas nearly choked. "You've *got* to be kidding!"

"I'm serious. It's been twenty-four hours. He'll have a decision—"

"For Christ's sake, Kate, the man ratted us out!"

"No." Kate tensed for battle. "I know Grant. He wouldn't do that. Even if he decided to move against you, he would have given me a heads-up beforehand."

"So you could separate yourself from me?"

"He wouldn't have put me in jeopardy," she allowed. "So no, he didn't tell them where to find us. We need to call him, Jonas."

Jonas stared down at the tabletop for a long, silent moment. Then he sighed, lifting his gaze to hers, his shoulders sagging. "You're not going to let this go, are you?"

Kate shook her head. "I trust him. And you need to trust me."

"Fine. But I need to talk to someone first." He held up a hand against her objection. "It's a compromise, Kate. And you need to trust *me* on this. Honeyman is—was my handler. He'll have access to files. Things we need."

"And *he* can be trusted?"

Jonas's mouth became a tight line. "I sure as hell hope so," he said.

THIRTY-SEVEN

K ate stepped past Jonas into the short-term rental unit they'd acquired. One week, the agreement said. An agreement Jonas had paid for in cash and signed with the name Jonathan Blake. The clerk had accepted the money without batting an eyelash, making Kate wonder what kind of clientele frequented the place. But she hadn't asked. She'd just accepted the duplicate key he'd handed across the counter, nodded understanding about the renovation work being done between seven a.m. and six p.m. daily, and then followed Jonas to the stairs.

Now, three flights up and standing inside the door, she surveyed their temporary home. A tiny kitchenette to the right opened onto a tinier cubby that housed a bistro-style table and two chairs; a couch, chair, and ancient television passed for a living room; and three closed doors led, presumably, to a bathroom and the two bedrooms Jonas had asked for. All the comforts of home.

Becoming aware she blocked Jonas's own entry, Kate moved into the living room and dropped her load of bags on the sofa. While not enough to take them out of the country, Jonas's stash was substantial, and after breakfast, he'd insisted on buying more clothing for both of them. They didn't know how much longer this situation was going to last, he pointed out, and he for one had no intention of living in the same set of clothes for days on end. Kate had settled for extra undergarments and a lightweight, charcoal gray sweat suit along with a sports bra. When she was ever going to exercise again, she didn't know, but the clothes were comfortable and inconspicuous.

She dropped onto the sofa beside the bags as Jonas flipped the security bolt into place on the door. Letting her head fall back against the cushions, she closed her eyes, allowing exhaustion to gain the upper hand. Damn, but she was tired. And edgy. So edgy. Hovering somewhere between hyper-vigilant and downright paranoid, if she had to take a guess.

A cupboard door slammed a few feet away, and Kate's eyes shot open. She stared across the room at the broad-shouldered man surveying the meager management-supplied cupboard contents in the tiny kitchenette. From where she sat, she saw salt, pepper, instant coffee, and what looked like powdered creamer. They'd have to do something about groceries, she supposed, but not now. Not until they'd both gotten some much-needed sleep, because yeah...paranoid. She uncurled fingers from the gun at the small of her back where her hand had gone when Jonas opened the cupboard.

Definitely paranoid.

She levered herself up from the couch, and Jonas looked over his shoulder.

"I'm going to lie down for a while," she told him. "You should, too."

"I'm—"

"Jonas."

He stopped.

"You've had even less sleep than I have," she said

wearily. "And this may be the only chance we have. I'll get groceries when I get up—enough for dinner, at least—and then we'll talk about when you want to see Honeyman."

"I don't want you going out by yourself. Wake me."

"There's a convenience store across the street. I think I can manage."

"Kate—"

She turned at the bedroom door, arms crossed. Jonas pressed his lips together and shook his head.

"Never mind. Sleep well."

Sure.

Later that afternoon, Kate divided her attention between the apartment building across the street and the man in the driver's seat beside her, who also watched the building. She and Jonas had been sitting in silence for twenty minutes—longer, if she counted the ten-minute drive to get to Rick Honeyman's home. She studied the brooding man behind the wheel. Jonas had picked up a disposable razor in their travels, and after their nap, he'd shaved off several days' worth of growth, exposing the stubborn jaw line and the tiny muscle that flickered in front of his ear when he was tense. And she'd never seen him tenser than he was right now. She cleared her throat.

Jonas flicked her a sidelong look, then turned his gaze back to the building. "What?"

"You're procrastinating."

He scowled. "I'm making sure—"

"There's no one watching the building, Jonas. One of us would have picked them out by now if there was."

The muscle in his jaw flickered.

Kate sighed. "Are you sure seeing him is the wisest thing to do if you don't trust him?"

"I never said I didn't trust him."

"No, you said you don't trust anyone."

"Honeyman was my handler for more than two years, Kate. I think I would have picked up on it if he was screwing me over." He turned to look at her. "The only reason I'm being cautious is that I don't want to put anyone else in Lewis and Ramirez's sights."

"If we call Grant—"

"No. Not until I talk to Honeyman." He reached across her to the glove compartment and took out the pistol—a Glock—that he'd retrieved from the safety deposit box along with his emergency stash. He tucked it into the waistband of his jeans, then pulled his shirt out to cover it. Then he reached for the door handle.

"Fifteen minutes," Kate said, "and I come looking for you. Apartment seven-oh-two."

"Thirty minutes," Jonas countered, one foot out the door and on the street. "Honeyman—"

"Twenty," she interrupted. "Final offer."

She pulled out her own weapon, removed the clip, checked it, and snapped it back into place. Then, unflinchingly, she met Jonas's gaze. "Someone helped Lewis and Ramirez set you up, Jonas. A handler is in the perfect position to be that someone."

As soon as the words left her mouth, Kate gave an inward groan. Great. Now she was starting to sound as paranoid as he usually did. She steeled herself and repeated, "Twenty minutes."

Jonas's gaze slid away to the building across the street. His lips tightened. "Fine," he said.

And then he was gone.

* * *

Uneven, heavy footsteps sounded on the other side of the door marked with the number 702, their approach interspersed with the lighter thud of a cane—Rick Honeyman's trademark tread since the car accident more than a year ago.

Jonas took his hand from the butt of the pistol tucked into his waistband, and rolled his shoulder muscles to loosen them. It was no use. He was perpetually tensed for fight-or-flight these days, unless he was near Kate. Then he was tense for a whole other set of reasons. He shook off the thought as the door opened and Honeyman's familiar frame filled the opening.

A burly man who looked like he'd be more at home in a boxing ring than in the suit he wore, Honeyman would have had Jonas outgunned six ways to Sunday if it wasn't for his shattered leg. Except Jonas's own healing wounds rather leveled the playing field right now, so he eyed his handler with caution, hoping Honeyman would be willing to hear him out and not attempt an arrest.

"Jonas." Pale gray eyes surveyed him with an odd lack of surprise. "I wondered when you'd turn up."

Honeyman opened the door wider, then turned and limped into the belly of the apartment, leaning on his cane, leaving Jonas to follow. Jonas frowned, hesitating. Honeyman would know about the warrant for him, of course, but he'd expected Jonas to come to him? Why?

He glanced at his watch. Fifteen minutes left before Kate came after him. Bloody hell, he should have held out for the half hour. He stepped across the threshold and closed the door. Hand back on the pistol's grip, he followed Honeyman down the hallway to the kitchen. His handler opened the fridge door and took out a can of beer. He held it aloft in Jonas's direction. Jonas shook his head.

Honeyman shoved the fridge door shut with his elbow and popped the tab on the can. His gaze remained on Jonas. "So when did you figure it out?" He raised the can to his lips and took a swig.

Figure what out? But even as the question arose in his mind, Jonas felt himself slipping into undercover-cop mode. He'd played along for more information so many times in his career, it had become automatic. He shrugged and leaned a shoulder against the doorframe.

"It wasn't difficult," he said, his voice betraying none of the churn going on in his brain. "Just a matter of putting two and two together."

"I suppose." Honeyman looked thoughtful, then nodded. "I knew it wouldn't last forever. Something that big never does. Too many players, too many loose ends." The ghost of a smile crossed his face. "But I have to say, it was good while it lasted."

He took another slug of beer. Unease began a slow, sickening swirl in Jonas's gut. The way Honeyman talked made it sound like—no. No, he couldn't have been that wrong. About Lewis and Ramirez, yes. He'd never worked that closely with them. But his handler?

"If it makes any difference," Honeyman continued, "it wasn't my idea to kill you. I tried to tell them you were too stubborn to die out there."

Full comprehension slammed into Jonas like a sucker punch. He *had* been that wrong. And Kate had been right. He dived across the kitchen, shoving his handler up against the counter, one hand at Honeyman's throat, the other holding a pistol to his head. The cane clattered to the floor. Beer sloshed across Jonas's shirtfront.

"You damn son of a bitch!" he snarled. "You were in on it? You set me up?"

Gray eyes stared into his, showing surprise at last.

"Shit," breathed Honeyman. "You don't know a thing, do you?"

Jonas pressed the gun muzzle harder against his handler's temple. "Not yet, you prick," he said. "But you're going to tell me. You're going to tell me everything."

THIRTY-EIGHT

Despite her warning to him, Kate gave Jonas significantly more than the twenty minutes she'd promised, figuring he would need it, secure in knowing no one else had entered the building. At the forty-five-minute mark, however, she could wait no more. Leaving the car locked behind her, she dodged through the traffic to the other side of the street and the apartment building into which Jonas had disappeared. The elevator took forever to arrive, and even longer to ascend to the seventh floor, during which time her imagination decided it needed to conjure possible reasons Jonas hadn't come out yet.

None of the scenarios were good.

When the doors finally opened, she stepped into the corridor and came up short against a broad chest. Before she could do more than register Jonas's identity, rough hands clamped onto her shoulders and set her aside, and without either speaking or looking at her, Jonas stepped into the elevator she'd vacated.

Kate blinked as he jabbed at one of the buttons. Then she recovered her balance and stepped back through the door he held aside for her. The elevator lurched into motion.

Kate studied her companion as they descended, but Jonas gave no sign that he noticed. She cleared her throat.

"I take it things didn't go well," she said quietly.

"Drop it, Kate."

"Jonas—"

"I said *drop it*." Blue eyes flicked over her like a whiplash, their color deepened to the slate blue of the ocean on the brink of an ugly storm.

Kate sucked in a quick breath. So. She'd been right about his handler. Damn. Above the doors, the number four lit up, then three, then two. She braced herself and reached a hand out to him. "I can't drop it. You know that. We're partners, Jonas, and partners—"

"*Partners*," he snapped, shaking her off, "are like everyone else in the world. They can't wait to screw you over as soon as it suits them."

The elevator bumped to a stop, and he shouldered his way between the doors before they'd opened half way. Hesitating, Kate watched him stalk across the lobby and out the front doors. She glanced at the control panel. If she went to Honeyman's door, would he let her in? It wasn't likely. And even if he did, it was less likely that he would tell her much.

The elevator doors began closing. With a sigh, she slipped between them and followed in Jonas's tracks. By the time she emerged onto the sidewalk, he was already at the car. The driver's door stood open, but he hadn't gotten in, instead standing with hands braced against the roof, shoulders slumped, head bowed. Kate's heart twisted inside her, and her footsteps halted. Gnawing on her bottom lip, she stared at the broad back turned to her, ignoring the pedestrian traffic that parted to flow around her.

Damn, damn, damn. For every one step forward she

managed with Jonas, the universe seemed determined to send him back four. There was no way he'd agree to calling Grant now. Not when life had proved his trust wrong yet again.

A woman pushed by onto the stairs Kate blocked. Kate murmured an apology and stepped aside, but the woman was already halfway up, tossing long red hair over one shoulder. She didn't so much as look back, let alone respond. Kate sighed.

Welcome to the big city.

She waited for a good minute for a break in traffic long enough to make a run for the other side of the street, but Jonas still stood by the car with head bowed when she arrived. She regarded him across the roof. As if he felt her eyes on him, he lifted his head and met her gaze.

"I'm sorry," he said.

You are? Kate blinked at him. His mouth took on a wry twist.

"That bad at apologizing, am I?" he asked.

She shrugged. "You're getting better at it," she replied. "With practice."

He snorted. "Funny."

She studied him. The fury was gone, taking most of the intensity with it, but the betrayal remained, underlined by an air of defeat she hadn't seen before. She didn't like it.

"Are you going to tell me what happened?" she asked.

Jonas's hands curled into fists on the vehicle roof. His expression turned stony again. "Exactly what you said would happen. It turns out Honeyman was in on the whole thing from the start. Although killing me wasn't his idea, apparently."

Kate flinched from the words. Jonas tightened his lips

in a grimace she thought he intended as a smile, but she couldn't be sure.

"You were right about Douglas, too, by the way," he said. "He didn't roll on us about the cabin. That state trooper we took out spotted us when we stopped for groceries and decided we looked suspicious. He called in our descriptions, and the rest is history."

Kate waved off the explanation. It didn't matter. What mattered was—

Jonas slammed a fist onto the rental car's roof. "Two years," his voice was raw. "Two years I worked with him, Kate, and I never suspected a thing. Can you believe it? How goddamned stupid *am* I?"

"I'm sorry," she said inanely. Inadequately.

His fist came down a second time, and she glanced around them, afraid they might be drawing attention. No one so much as looked in their direction.

"He made sure I was in on every one of the deals they put together," he said. "Know why? So if something went wrong, they'd have someone to pin it on. Hell, they had this thing set up so sweetly, it's not even funny. Three years they've had it going. One before I came on the scene, and two with me earmarked as their patsy." He shook his head, a hint of disbelief shadowing his expression. "And I never suspected a thing. God, was I gullible!"

"You're going to blame yourself for this, too?" The words slipped out before she could censor them, and Jonas's head jerked as if she'd slapped him. He glared at her.

"What the hell is that supposed to mean?"

"You were deliberately duped, Jonas. Honeyman and the others worked very hard to make sure you didn't suspect anything. How can that be your fault?"

"And—?" he prompted, his voice as dangerous as it was soft.

"And what?"

"And what did you mean, *'blame yourself for this, too?'*"

Kate looked away. Normally, she was such a reasonable person. She thought before she spoke, she was wise enough to keep certain ideas to herself—

"*Well?*"

She flinched. Lifted her chin. Met his gaze squarely. Like it or not, Jonas needed to hear a few truths in life. And if no one else was going to tell him, then she would.

But not without a frisson of trepidation.

"I meant that you can't keep taking the blame for everything that's gone wrong in your life," she murmured. "Whether you like it or not, you can't control the actions of everyone else in the world."

"I never thought I could," he replied.

"Didn't you? Think about it for a minute. *You* haven't done anything wrong here, so why are you coming down so hard on yourself? Rick Honeyman and his buddies are the bad guys, not you." Kate hesitated. Every line of Jonas's body shouted a warning at her to back off. The rigid set of his shoulders, the jawline that had turned to granite, the way he stared past her. But she couldn't stop. She had to finish. She had to try.

"You were never the bad guy," she continued. "Not when your father ended up in prison, not when your mother left, not when you were bounced around from one home to another, and not when you couldn't keep your sister with you. Things happen, Jonas. Life happens. You can't always control it."

His head snapped around at that and he glared at her. "Who are you to stand there and judge me? You have no idea—"

"That's your best defense, isn't it?" Kate interrupted, her own temper flaring. "No one knows what you've been through, so no one can understand. It makes a hell of an excuse for alienating yourself from everyone, doesn't it?"

"I think you've said enough."

"I haven't said nearly enough," she corrected. She leaned her elbows on the car roof and threaded fingers through her hair in frustration. "Damn it, Jonas, how long can you live like this?"

"As long as I bloody well want to!" he shouted. "It's my life, Kate. Butt out!"

Silence, thick and heavy, followed his outburst. Kate felt the eyes of the curious on her back as they passed by. Stared into the eyes that reflected a lifetime of defense. Finally understood the man behind them...and knew his truth.

Jonas Burke was not about to change. Not now. Not ever.

And not for her.

A tiny hope she hadn't wanted to acknowledge died a quiet death in her breast. Whatever it would take to make this man want to live, and not just survive, it wasn't something she could give him. She pushed upright from the vehicle and looked down at the sidewalk, gaze unseeing, mind unfocused.

"I think I'll find my own way back," she said.

Jonas didn't argue.

THIRTY-NINE

Two hours after leaving Jonas at Honeyman's apartment, Kate closed the hotel door behind her, then tiptoed past the long form stretched out on the couch. One of Jonas's forearms covered his eyes, the other rested across his chest. She couldn't tell if he was asleep or not. She tried to tell herself she didn't care. Knew she lied.

His voice stopped her at her bedroom door. "Kate."

She leaned her forehead against the doorframe, her eyes closed, listening to the shifting of his body as he sat up.

"We should talk."

She laughed at that, not even trying to hide the bitter amusement in the sound. "No. No, Jonas, I don't think we should talk anymore, because every time we talk, you get angry, and I get in deeper, and now I'm done. Let's just do this thing and get it over with so I can go home. Please."

Silence.

"I meant about Honeyman," he said at last. "And Douglas."

Kate squeezed her eyes tighter. Freaking hell. She stayed where she was, praying for divine intervention of some sort. Any sort. But when no lightning bolt struck and the floor stubbornly refused to open up and swallow her, she pried her fingers from the doorframe and turned. Jonas had sat up on the couch, elbows supported on his thighs, hands clasped between his knees.

Summoning every ounce of willpower she possessed, she walked over to drop her jacket onto the back of a kitchen chair. "I'm listening."

"Honeyman will help. He'll talk to Douglas and tell him everything in exchange for a deal. And he'll get us evidence. All the files and paperwork we need. He's going to the office tonight."

"And you trust him? After what he's done?"

"Do I have a choice?" Bitterness warred with defeat in his voice, in the weary gaze, and in the slump of his shoulders. "Without him, we—*I*—have nothing."

Kate gripped the chair back to hold herself in place. To keep from going to him and wrapping him in her arms and—

She looked away from him to the phone on the counter that divided the kitchenette from the living room. "I'll call Grant."

Her ex-fiancé answered on the first ring. "Douglas."

"Grant, it's Kate—"

"Where the hell are you?" Grant's voice roared across the line. "Why didn't you call me when we agreed? And where the *fuck* is Burke?"

Shock robbed her of a response. In all the years she'd known Grant Douglas, she'd never once heard him raise his voice—not even when she'd broken off their engagement. In fact, she hadn't thought him capable—

"Goddamn it, Kate, answer me!" Grant bellowed, making her jump.

"I'm in Newark," she said. "Jonas is with me. We had to leave the cabin when—"

"Never mind that. Has he been with you all day?"

"Who, Jonas? Yes, of course."

"You're sure."

Belatedly, Kate's instincts jolted to life. "What's going on, Grant?"

She turned as Jonas stood up from the couch, shaking her head and shrugging.

"Just answer the question," Grant ordered. "Has Burke been with you all day? Yes or no."

There was nothing friendly about his tone. Nothing even remotely familiar. A chill slithered down Kate's spine, but she didn't hesitate.

"Yes," she said, because she was damned if she'd throw Jonas under whatever bus Grant Douglas was driving. Not before she knew what was going on. Across the room, Jonas's eyes narrowed. She turned away.

"He didn't go to see anyone?" Grant pressed.

"We went to see his handler. That's why I was calling you. Rick Honeyman—"

"Rick Honeyman is dead."

It took a moment for Grant's words to sink in. Then Kate's knees sagged, and she felt behind her for one of the chairs at the bistro-style table. "What?"

"He was shot this afternoon in his apartment—about two hours ago. The police received an anonymous tip, with Burke's description given."

"Oh, my God." Kate tried to think, but her brain had turned to sludge. "Oh, my God," she repeated softly.

"Kate, were you with Burke when he went to see Honeyman?"

"Yes—no—sort of." She bit her lip. As much as she wanted—no, needed—to protect Jonas, she knew that lying to Grant would only make things worse. "I waited in the car."

"So he went in alone. *Damn* it!"

Kate swallowed. "Rick was going to get us files," she whispered. "Papers. Everything we needed to prove—"

"Is that what Burke told you?"

"It's what I *know.* And you do, too. You've met him, Grant. You know he didn't kill Honeyman." She felt Jonas's gaze on her, but she couldn't bring herself to meet it. Couldn't face the fresh defeat there.

"I don't know what I know, Kate," her ex said heavily. "I've been digging into every corner I can think of, and I can't find anything."

"Nothing at all?"

"Not enough to open an investigation—not on the timeline Burke has."

Strong fingers closed over the hand holding the receiver, and Kate looked up in surprise as Jonas tugged the instrument from her grasp. Her gaze searched his face, but she found none of the defeat she'd anticipated. Only a cold, hard determination as he put his hand over the mouthpiece.

"Do you trust him?" he asked.

She nodded.

Jonas's lips pulled tight. "Right. Then let's get this over with." He put the receiver to his ear. "Douglas, it's Burke. I know how to end this."

Long after Jonas had given Grant Douglas the hotel address and hung up the phone, he stood with his hand on the receiver, staring at the chipped counter-top. Part of him wished he could recall the words he'd just spoken. Most of him just didn't want to face the questions he knew Kate would have. At last, he turned.

Kate sat at the table, tracing a circle with one fingertip on the wooden surface. She didn't look up.

"Kate—"

"So that's it?" she interrupted. "You paint a target on your back and put yourself out there as bait? That's your plan?"

He folded his arms and leaned back against the counter. "We've run out of options. With Honeyman gone—"

"How do you know he didn't already tell them he gave you nothing?" She looked up, amber eyes flashing fire. "What reason will they have to believe you have anything on them? And why in hell would they believe you've suddenly decided to change sides?" She stood abruptly, and the chair crashed to the floor as she threw her arms wide. "How can you think—for so much as a second—that this will work?"

"Because I have no other choice. *We* have no other choice. We can't live the rest of our lives hiding from Lewis and Ramirez."

"We can't, or I can't?"

His jaw hardened. "Like it or not, I'm the one who got you into this. And like it or not, I'm getting you out of it."

"Even if it means getting yourself killed?"

The ache in her voice reached out to wrap itself around his gut, and for a moment, he couldn't draw breath enough to respond—and then he couldn't find the words. While he had every intention of walking away from this alive, they both knew there were no guarantees, and he couldn't promise otherwise. He watched Kate cross the short distance separating them. Braced for her touch as she reached a hand toward his knotted forearm.

"Don't do this," she said quietly. "Please, Jonas. We'll find another way. Together."

Together. He let himself absorb the word, staring at the creamy, slender fingers against his skin. Felt the stir of possibility in his belly, his chest. Knew from the quick intake of Kate's breath that she felt it, too. His heart rate kicked up, and he raised his gaze to hers. In ageless, tacit invitation, her eyes softened and her lips parted. Ever so slightly. Oh, so temptingly.

Jonas closed his eyes. For a moment, he remembered the silk of her skin against his when he'd warmed her frozen body. The taste of her lips when he'd kissed her in Cornwall. Her words at the cabin: *"What if I say yes?"*

For a moment, he considered what it might be like—what it *could* be like. Here, now, with no barriers and nothing to stop them.

For a moment, *together* seemed possible.

And then reality returned.

Who the hell was he trying to kid? Even if he survived this fool's errand he'd set himself up for, he wouldn't be doing Kate any favors by giving in to her fantasy. Not when he still had every intention of going his own separate way. And damn it, he *would* go his separate way, because no matter how much it hurt to do so, it would still be infinitely better than watching Kate slowly destroyed as he dragged her down with him.

"I have work to do," he said, pulling away from her hand. Away from her. Amber eyes blinked at him, then narrowed. Kate crossed her own arms.

"That's it?" she asked, frustration giving her voice an edge. "We can't just keep dancing around one another like this, Jonas. How much longer do you think we can ignore this—this *thing* between us?"

"As long as we have to. I've told you before, Kate, you don't want to get involved with me."

"And I've told you, I can make my own decisions about who I get involved with."

Raking both hands through his hair, Jonas paced the room, putting a safer distance—and a sofa—between them. "Be realistic. Even if I—" He broke off, inwardly cursing his lack of tact as a shadow crossed her expression. He sighed and tried again. "Best case scenario, anything that happened between us would be over in a matter of days. Do you really think you could live with that?"

"Why?" she demanded. "Why would it have to be over? You said it would be easy to fall in love with me. Would it be so awful if you did?"

Eyes closed, Jonas rested one hand on his hip and pinched the bridge of his nose with the other. He thought back over a lifetime of failures. Failure to keep his family together, failure to stay connected to his sister, failure to live up to the expectations of everyone around him, failure to see he'd become the target of his own colleagues. The people he'd trusted.

Would it be so awful to fall in love with Kate?

It would be the worst, because he couldn't live with the thought of failing her, too.

The sound of footsteps broke into his thoughts and, once again, he steeled himself. But there was no need, because no touch followed. Not this time.

This time, there was only the soft closing of a door.

"I still say it's a bad idea." Kate paced the length of the apartment's living space with short, angry strides. "There has to be another way."

"We've gone over it a hundred times, Kate." Jonas scrubbed a hand over his face and sighed. "There *is* no other way."

"Do feel free to jump in with suggestions if you have them, however," Grant Douglas added, a note of impatience edging his voice.

Kate glowered at him. They'd been at this for three hours, going over every detail, everything that could possibly go wrong—but she was damned if she'd make it easy for Jonas to get himself killed. Or for Grant to help him.

"You can't seriously mean to let him do this," she said. Foreboding tangled with a growing helplessness in her belly. She crossed her arms over it and scowled at her ex. "It's not like you to take chances like this. When the hell did you become such a goddamned maverick?"

Grant's lips tightened. "I'm not a maverick. I just think Jonas is right. This is the fastest way to—"

"It's the only way," Jonas interrupted. He rose from the table and intercepted her agitated pacing, his grip firm on her shoulders. Kate's knees wobbled at his touch, and it took all she had not to lean in against him. To hold him. Tightly, so she never had to let him go. But he wouldn't let her. He'd made that crystal clear.

"You're not thinking objectively, Kate," Jonas said, his brilliant blue gaze steady. Focused. Calm. Missing the point altogether.

She crossed her arms in sheer self-preservation.

"Step back for a minute and be a cop again," he continued. "If this thing is as big as we think it is, we have no other choice. People are going to start burying evidence—if they haven't already—and the longer I'm in the wind, the more chance they have to do so. We don't just need to move fast, we need to move *now*. Before they realize we've brought in the FBI."

Kate blinked back sudden hot tears, swallowing against the hard lump in her throat. For an instant she almost hated the quiet strength of the man before her —did hate the wordless compassion he extended. She didn't want to step back and be a cop, didn't want to be objective. Not when the thought of what he was about to do filled her with a fear unlike any she'd ever known. Not when she was about to lose the man she—

She lifted her chin. "Then let me go with you," she said.

"No."

She knew argument would get her nowhere. Knew with absolute certainty he wouldn't change his mind. She hated him for that, too.

Over Jonas's shoulder, she saw Grant still sitting at the table, studying the cellular phone in front of him as if it held the utmost fascination for him, and looking like he'd rather be just about anywhere else in the world. He wouldn't try to change Jonas's mind, either. Defeat settled over her like a suffocating blanket. She turned her face away.

Jonas's grip on her shoulders hardened for a second, and then he released her. "I'm ready," he told Grant.

In silence, Grant held out the cell phone to him—a burner he'd brought along so Lewis wouldn't be able to trace it back to anyone. Jonas punched in a number, put the phone to his ear, waited.

Then, "Lewis," he said. "It's Burke."

Kate walked to the window and stared down at the stream of glaring headlights and flickering taillights below the apartment hotel, mentally tuning out the conversation on the other side of the room. She didn't need to hear it, knew already what Jonas would tell the man on the other end of the phone line.

Rick Honeyman had given him information, he would say to Lewis. Files. Papers. Hard evidence. He wanted to deal, he'd tell him. The evidence for a cut of the profits—enough to let him disappear. For good.

He'd give the address of an abandoned building chosen by Grant's team for its ease of surveillance. He'd give a time, too—ten tomorrow morning—and go in alone, wired, trying to get someone to say something they could use. Trying to get someone to confess, or at least give them enough to open an investigation, obtain a search warrant, start the long process of nailing Lewis's and Ramirez's asses to the wall.

Trying not to get killed first.

Kate drew a quick, reflexive breath against the pain that lanced through her. No. He'd be fine. He had to be fine, because the alternative was unthinkable—especially knowing she couldn't be there to prevent it.

"Kate?" Grant's voice and cleared throat brought her back to the present. She turned and found him at the door, trench coat on, briefcase in hand. Jonas no longer held the cell phone to his ear. The plan was set. The damage was done.

"I'm going," Grant said. "Do you want me to pick you up on our way to the stakeout in the morning?"

The FBI team would be at the location three hours before the meet, setting up their stakeout. Waiting for Lewis and Ramirez and the others. Waiting for Jonas to—

Kate pressed her lips together and nodded.

"I'll be here at six-thirty," Grant told her. "Try to get some sleep, okay?" He turned to Jonas. "You, too. I'll bring someone with me in the morning to get you up and running with the tech we'll need you to wear."

The door closed behind him. Silence descended on the room, deafening in its totality. Jonas looked across at her, the physical distance between them made a thousand times greater by his remote expression. An ache settled into her heart, deep, hollow, awful. She had no idea how to breach the gulf, and Jonas had no intention of doing so.

"I'm going to bed," she said. She passed him on her way to her room, near enough to feel his warmth brush against her skin. Hoping, wanting, needing him to reach out a hand to stop her.

He didn't.

Jonas propelled his torso off the floor on his third set of push-ups. A thin sheen of sweat bathed his body, sensitizing his skin to the whisper of air moving past as he descended again, pushed up again. He set his jaw against the quiver of fatigue in his arms and across his chest, against the nagging tugs of pain that still plagued him, against the reason he was doing calisthenics at three in the morning in the first place.

He'd been tossing and turning since midnight, unable to settle into a sleep that didn't center around dreams of car chases and cabins and filmy white nightgowns. Dreams of rising from his bed and going to the room next to him. Going to Kate...just once.

Awake wasn't any better. Lying in a tangle of covers, staring at the ceiling, listening for signs of her presence on the other side of the wall. Distraction had seemed the only answer, and so for twenty minutes he'd punished his body with the most intense exercise he could dream up in the cramped living space of the hotel apartment. And still he wondered...

Abandoning the push-ups, he levered himself into a sitting position and rested his arms across bent knees in the dark. This was useless. He could run a marathon right now and it wouldn't do a damn bit of good. He stared at the closed bedroom door only a few feet away. Of all the roads Lewis and Ramirez could have dumped him on, why did it have to be the one Kate Dexter was traveling that night? Things could have gone so differently if someone else had found him...been so much less complicated.

Right, because anyone else would have taken the same chance on your sorry ass that she has, a snarky voice said in his head. *Picked you up, believed your story, not turned you in, given up half her life for—*

A soft scrape sounded against the door to the hallway. Jonas stopped breathing. He waited. It came again, accompanied this time by a muttered exclamation and a metallic jingle. The blood in his veins ran cold. Someone was trying to get in.

He pushed himself up from the floor. He thought of

his gun, still in the nightstand drawer by his bed, then glanced at Kate's closed door. No, warning her came first.

But even as he took a step toward her bedroom, the apartment door edged open, and he changed direction, swiftly crossing the room to flatten himself against the wall behind the door. A shadow stepped into the apartment. Jonas waited until it cleared the doorway, then threw himself forward, slamming it into the wall.

The intruder grunted under the impact, then recovered and looped a leg behind his, dropping him to the floor. His grip tight on a zippered sweatshirt front, Jonas pulled the figure down with him. The carpet had barely brushed his back before he gave a mighty heave and rolled over, pinning the other person beneath him. With his left hand, he slammed both the intruder's hands against the floor, then he leaned his right forearm across the vulnerable throat, applying enough pressure to leave no illusions about his superior power. Or his ability to cause great damage.

"Now," he snapped, glaring down at the hoodie-sheltered face, "suppose you tell me who you are and what the hell you're doing here."

The shadow sucked in a quick, ragged breath. "Jonas?"

Jonas stiffened, and in the span of a heartbeat, he became aware of the distinctly feminine curves of the body between his thighs. The gentle rise of the chest beneath his. The softness of the belly pressing against his—

"Kate?" he croaked.

FORTY-ONE

The pressure of Jonas's forearm lifted from Kate's throat, and she heard him fumble for something on the wall beside them. The overhead light came on, and she blinked in the glare. She would have held up a hand against it, but he still held both of hers pinned to the floor over her head. With his free hand, Jonas pushed the apartment door closed.

"Damn it to hell, Kate, I could have hurt you!" he growled. "What in God's name were you doing?"

"I couldn't sleep. I went for a run."

"You *what*? At three in the bloody morning in a strange city? Are you out of your mind? What if I'd been someone else?" His grip tightened on her. "Anything could have happened to you out there."

"I know how to look after myself," she reminded him. "And I was careful."

He didn't look impressed.

Kate sighed and tugged at her hands. "Do you mind?"

His gaze moved to the hold he still had on her. He let go, but he didn't move away. She eased her arms down and rubbed at her shoulder.

Jonas frowned. "Did I hurt you?"

She shook her head. "Not really. It just doesn't like being in one position for too long."

"Show me."

The request was as unexpected as it was abrupt, and Kate stopped massaging her shoulder to stare up at the tiny muscle flickering in front of Jonas's ear. Then she tugged aside the hoodie and the strap of her sports bra to expose the shiny, puckered remains of the bullet hole just above the midpoint of her collarbone. Jonas stared at it in silence. His gaze returned to hers, a question in the shadowed blue depths. Kate cleared her throat.

"It was a freak thing," she said. "There was a gap at the neck of my vest. It entered there. A one-in-a-million shot."

"Hollow point?"

She gave a terse nod of her head. "When it fragmented, it took out something called the coracoid process, part of the shoulder blade that helps stabilize everything. They pieced it back together as best they could, but..." She trailed off, still coming to terms with knowing it would never be the same.

"It missed the artery?"

"Nicked it." Kate held back a shudder at the memory of bright red arterial blood spurting from her body when they removed her vest. So much blood.

"You're lucky to be alive." Jonas's voice was gruff.

"So are you," she pointed out.

His mouth twisted. "Touché."

Conversation fell away, and quiet settled between them, its seconds marked by the soft tick of the wall clock. *Tick. Tick. Tick. Tick.* Ten seconds. Twenty. Thirty.

The silence morphed into a beast stalking its prey. Stalking them.

And still Jonas remained. A half-naked Jonas, his chest sprinkled with crisp, curling hairs, skin gleaming beneath the harsh light above them. Kate blinked.

Breathing failed. How in heaven's name had she not noticed the semi-nakedness before?

In the space of a single heartbeat, awareness flared in her belly and spread to her every nerve ending. Suddenly, acutely, she felt every inch of the hard, muscled strength of his legs pressing against her sides. Saw the lean fingers resting on his thighs, tantalizingly near her ribcage, her breasts. Felt the unmistakable swell of his—

Oh, dear lord. Her eyes snapped shut. *Move*, her mind urged him. *Stay*, her body whispered. She tried to swallow, but her tongue had glued itself to the roof of her mouth. Above her, Jonas exhaled on a long shudder. His legs tensed as if readying to rise, and she braced herself for his retreat from her yet again.

But this time, he didn't. This time, he remained. This time, gently, magically, his fingers brushed her collarbone, traced it, rested on the puckered scar. She opened her eyes and stared upward, into the brilliant blue of his.

"Kate," he began.

She placed her fingers over his lips, stilling his words. She shook her head. "Don't," she said.

Another long, deep shudder rippled through his frame.

Kate raised her other hand to his shoulder. She traced her fingertips over his collarbone, slid them over the swell of muscle, skimmed them across the scattering of rough hair. She hesitated as his jaw contracted, then boldly let her touch drift lower. Her fingers grazed the denim edge of his jeans, slid beneath the stiff material.

Jonas's stomach muscles contracted, and he inhaled sharply, covering her hand with his own, catching it tight. "There are so many reasons we shouldn't," he muttered.

And so many more they should—but Kate kept the thought to herself. "I know," she said.

"Do you?" His expression was both bleak and filled with yearning at the same time. "I don't want to hurt you, Kate."

"Then don't."

Surprise flashed through his eyes. Resignation followed it. He tightened his jaw and nodded. "You're right," he said. He braced a hand against the floor on either side of her, preparing to push himself up. Away.

Kate curved her hands over his shoulders and pulled herself up to meet him. "That's not what I meant," she whispered. Then, before she could think better of it, she kissed him.

Jonas went rigid beneath her touch. His mouth tightened against hers, and for a moment she thought she had failed. Thought that he would pull away after all, that she would be denied even this one moment with him. In desperation, she softened her mouth, opened it ever so slightly, and slid the tip of her tongue against his bottom lip.

He pulled back, conflict clouding the brilliance of his eyes. "Damn it, Kate, you're not playing fair."

"There's no such thing as fair," she retorted. "Not anymore, and certainly not tonight. You don't want this to go anywhere? Fine. But you owe me, Jonas Burke, and I'm collecting. Now."

The war in Jonas's gaze continued for a few seconds more, and then, just as Kate was wondering what more she could possibly do to convince him, it gave way to a smolder that darkened his eyes to the color of sapphires. Strong hands cupped her face, and he leaned forward, bearing her to the floor with unmistakable intent.

"Have it your way, Kate Dexter," he growled. "But be forewarned that I believe in paying my debts in full."

She had no time for more than a quick, surprised inhale before his mouth claimed hers and his tongue slid between her lips to tangle with her own. A groan broke from her as his hands spanned her ribcage, thumbs sliding over her breasts through the fabric of her hoodie and the sports bra beneath.

Too much fabric.

As if in agreement, Jonas undid the hoodie's zipper and pushed the garment from her shoulders. Strong fingers slid under her bra, fought for a second against its snug fit, then shoved it impatiently up and out of the way. Then his mouth left hers, traveling down, trailing over her throat, lifting to bypass the bra, closing with mind-spinning accuracy over first one rigid peak, then the other.

Kate wanted to object, to tell him to slow down, but need arched her back, driving her against him. His hands roved her body, stroking and teasing, evoking sensations one after another, so fast she couldn't catch her breath between them. Couldn't keep up with her own body. She buried her face against the thick muscles of his neck, tasting the salt of his skin. Her fingers found the snap of his jeans. The hardness of his body beneath the zipper.

The already taut muscles of Jonas's stomach went rigid, and his fingers closed over hers, stilling her efforts.

"Not yet," he murmured, his voice hoarse with restraint and his breath hot against her cheek. "I'm too close to the edge. You deserve more—"

Kate stopped his words with her lips.

"To hell with that," she murmured against his mouth. "I'm already over the edge—and I'm not going alone."

She tugged free of his hold and found the jeans snap

again. This time, Jonas didn't try to stop her. He lifted to give her access, and she slid his zipper down, the metallic rasp loud in the silence that had fallen between them. She wrapped her fingers around him, reveling in his thick heaviness. The throb of his heat. His breathing turned ragged.

He rolled to the side, and anticipation curled through Kate as he peeled off his jeans, tossed them aside, and turned his efforts to her own clothing. Hoodie and sports bra followed in the wake of the jeans. His fingers slipped beneath the elastic waistband of her sweatpants. They stilled.

"Bloody hell," he muttered against her shoulder.

Kate thought she might scream. "What?" she asked, fighting to keep the frustration from her voice—and from adding *now* to the question.

"Protection," he said. "I don't have—"

"Hoodie pocket," she interrupted. Jonas pulled back to stare at her. Heat scorched her cheeks, and she waited for his comment. Waited for the questions. Wondered how she would phrase her intent to seduce him tonight, because she'd known it would be her one and only chance to be with him.

Even if he survived tomorrow.

But Jonas said nothing. Instead, with a speed that would have left her breathless if his touch hadn't already done so, he tugged the sweatpants from her ankles, reached for the hoodie, sheathed himself, and enveloped her in his arms.

And then he was bearing her back onto the carpet, and his body was covering hers, and his mouth and hands were everywhere at once, touching, teasing, stroking, trailing liquid fire in their wake. Kate tried to reciprocate, but blind need stripped her of any capacity to do more than rise to meet him. To take him into her. To clutch frantically at his shoulders as she tried to draw him ever deeper.

They moved as one. Her body became molten, merging with his as he abandoned any attempt at control. Heat swept through her, carrying her to dizzying, spiraling heights, until the entire world fell away into nothing but her and Jonas and all the exquisite sensations flowing between them, over them, around them. From far away she heard Jonas's hoarse voice, but words meant nothing now. She teetered for an instant on a precipice, somewhere between reality and eternity.

Then Jonas's voice came again, clear this time, calling out her name, and she toppled, free-falling through a kaleidoscope of timeless, whirling colors, her own cry mingling distantly with his.

FORTY-TWO

J onas set the mug of coffee on the nightstand beside Kate. Her eyes opened and she stared first at it, then at him. He pushed away the memory of how the amber gaze had clouded with desire the night before. Passion. Need.

He cleared his throat. "Douglas and the others will be here in half an hour," he said. "I thought I should wake you."

Kate's eyebrows twitched together. "Good morning to you, too."

Jonas shoved his hands into the pockets of his jeans. He looked away from the tousled hair and intriguingly bared shoulders. His lips pressed together.

After a long moment, Kate said quietly, "I see. So last night—"

"Last night should never have happened," he said. "I shouldn't have let it."

Not the first, desperate coupling on the living room floor, and sure as hell not the slow exploration and discovery that had followed here in his own bed.

He turned to leave. "I'm sorry," he added gruffly.

Kate's voice stopped him at the door. "You're kidding me, right?"

His hand rested on the knob, every muscle in his

body screaming at him to go back to her. To take her in his arms again and—

"Last time I checked, what we did last night required two parties," she said. "I'm pretty sure I was a willing partner, so I don't see where you get to claim full responsibility."

The sheets rustled, and he wondered if she'd sat up. If she held the covers against her, or—

Feet thudded to the floor behind him, and the air left his lungs. She'd been naked under those sheets. If he turned around...

His fingers tightened around the doorknob.

"Damn it, Jonas." Frustration laced Kate's tone. "I wasn't expecting an undying declaration of love from you this morning. I get that last night doesn't change anything. I didn't expect it to. But I'm damned if I'll let you regret it."

He closed his eyes. She hadn't thought it would change things? That was just bloody ironic, because it sure as hell had. Long after Kate had fallen into a deep, sated sleep, he'd stayed awake, watching her in the semi-darkness of the streetlamp-lit room. Imagining her in ten years, thirty years. Imagining the house, the kids, the dog, the camping trips. Thinking that maybe, just maybe, his life had finally turned around. But he'd been wrong.

The cold light of dawn had brought an even colder realization with it. A realization that, in every single one of his visions, one thing had been consistently missing. Him. No matter how hard he'd tried, he hadn't been able put himself into any of the pictures he painted of Kate's future. Because no matter how much he wanted it, he didn't belong.

Not with the kids, not with the dog, not with Kate. Just as he hadn't belonged in any of those homes when he was growing up, or, ultimately, with his sister. He was meant to be alone, and people were better off without him. Time, circumstances, fate—call it what he liked—had proved that to him again and again.

"You're right," he said now, without turning. Without looking at her. "It doesn't change anything."

He opened the door, stepped out, and closed it again behind him. Then, with grim determination underlined by desperation, he headed for the phone on the kitchen counter. Nothing had changed, and nothing *would* change, because he wouldn't let it. Kate might think she was willing to take a chance on him, but he knew better than to let her.

And he'd do whatever it took to hold onto his determination.

Before he could think better of the idea, he punched in a number on the phone's keypad and then leaned a shoulder against the wall as he listened to the ring at the other end of the line.

In the wake of Jonas's departure, Kate tugged a rumpled sheet from the bed and wrapped it around herself. She dreaded the trek to her own room, but with her clothes still scattered across the floor by the front door, she had little choice. Not that she needed to worry about Jonas's reaction to her unclothed state, after that little exchange.

Freaking hell. Had there ever been a more stubborn man? She compressed her lips, holding the sheet in place with one hand as she reached for the knob with the other. She pulled open the door. What the hell did you do with a man who admitted he *could* fall in love with you and yet refused to do so? And who went out of his way to—

"Valerie? It's Jonas Burke."

Valerie? Kate stopped in her tracks as the man with his back to her gave a low, rumbling chuckle. A sound of intimacy he'd never shared with Kate.

"Yeah, I know. It's been a while," he said.

He pitched his voice low...to keep from being heard in another room? Kate put out a hand and curled fingers around the painted wood of the doorframe. She should go back into the bedroom and wait. Or say something. Do something to let him know she was here. Listening.

But she did none of those things, because she couldn't. Couldn't move, couldn't breathe, couldn't speak.

"I've been away a lot," Jonas continued. "Business stuff. Anyway, I was hoping you were still unattached, and maybe free this weekend?"

A date. He was making a date. Pain lanced through Kate, so sharp it sucked the remaining air from her lungs. Her grip on the doorframe tightened, and she held herself upright through sheer force of will.

"Dinner? Show? You name it," Jonas continued. He straightened up from the wall he'd been leaning against. "That's great. I'll pick you up on Saturday night at seven."

Kate watched him turn toward her as if she viewed a slow-motion sequence—or an unavoidable car wreck she couldn't stop. His gaze met hers. Widened. Turned hard. A handful of seconds ticked by.

Then he said to the phone, "Val, I have to go. I'll see you Saturday. Yeah, you have a good rest of the week, too." He replaced the receiver in its cradle and cleared his throat. He looked away from her.

"I didn't mean for you to hear that," he said.

She almost laughed at that. Might have done, if there hadn't been so much pain in the way. She lifted her chin.

"Yes, you did," she said. "You wanted me to hear it. It

was your way of proving that last night changed nothing." She knew the truth of her words even as they left her lips, even as the brilliant blue gaze flashed back to hers, guilt and denial visible in equal measure in its depths.

"That's not—" Jonas began, but a knock at the door interrupted him. Neither of them moved to answer it. Jonas raked both his hands through his hair. "Kate—"

Another knock, louder this time. Jonas muttered something under his breath and stalked across the room. He threw open the door, then turned his back on Grant Douglas and the suit standing beside him without so much as a *hello*.

"Damn it, Kate," he began again, quiet desperation in his voice.

She waited, but he didn't continue, and after a moment, her gaze slid past him to their expected guests and settled on Grant Douglas's tie clip. "I'm running late," she said. "Sorry."

Her ex-fiancé cleared his throat. "Bad timing?"

"Yes!" Jonas snapped. He shoved his hands into his jeans pockets and scowled. "No. Hell, I don't know. Ask Kate."

Grant's eyes took in the jumbled pile of clothing discarded on the floor. He raised an eyebrow.

"Coffee?" Kate asked. "I think there's some left."

Grant stared at her, then shook his head. "We should get in and set up. Agent Kelvin can set up the tech on his own."

Kate nodded. She looked at Jonas on the other side of the tiny living room that might as well have been an ocean, it seemed so vast. He stared back at her, tension weaving itself into the fine creases about his mouth, and myriad emotions warring in his eyes.

Kate recognized his hurt even through her own pain. She just couldn't deal with it. Not right now. Not while her own agony was so fresh, and not while they both needed to focus on the job at hand. Especially Jonas.

"You're sure you want to go in alone?" she asked.

He stared at her. "You'd still go in with me? After—"

Her heart twisted at how very screwed up this man's thinking had to be for him to doubt it even for an instant. She pushed away the knowledge.

"I came along to watch your back," she said. "I could do a better job if I could actually *see* your back."

Measured silence. Then Jonas shook his head. "No. This way's best."

She nodded acceptance of his decision, her voice failing her as all the foreboding she'd been holding at bay threatened to swamp her. If something went wrong, if he didn't make it back—

She turned and went into her own room to get dressed. When she rejoined the others, Grant Douglas and the technician were studying a suitcase of equipment they'd opened on the kitchen table, and Jonas was pacing the living room floor. The clothing scattered across the floor had been scooped up and deposited in a pile on the couch.

Grant looked up at her reappearance. "I'll be with you in a second," he said. "Why don't you call the elevator for us? That thing is as slow as molasses in January."

Kate hesitated, not wanting to miss anything but knowing she had nothing of value to add. She slid her arms into the hoodie she'd retrieved from the clothing pile. Whether she heard everything now or not wouldn't matter. After all she and Jonas had been through, her part was done. Jonas was on his own. By choice. As he'd always wanted to be.

She zipped up the hoodie, then hesitated. Jonas had stopped pacing, but he stood with the room between them again. She wrestled with all the things she wanted to say but knew he didn't want to hear, settling in the end for a simple, "Be careful."

Then, without waiting for his reply, she left their suite. Jonas caught hold of her arm halfway down the hall to the elevator.

"Kate, wait."

She stared at the faded paisley-patterned carpet.

"I don't want us to end like this," he said, his voice tight. "Not after all you've done for me. If I don't—"

"Don't," she croaked. "Don't you dare say it, Burke. Hell, don't you even *think* it. You're going to walk out of there when this is done, do you understand? Under your own steam and in one piece."

She tugged away before he could argue, turned, and continued toward the elevator. Jonas followed.

"Damn it, Kate, this is exactly what I didn't want," he muttered. "I tried to warn you—"

Down the hall, the apartment door opened. Grant stepped into the corridor and began striding toward them. Kate punched the elevator call button.

"You did warn me," she agreed. "And I meant what I said. My problem, not yours."

Grant joined them at the elevator as the doors slid open. He flicked a glance over Jonas, then turned to Kate. "All good?"

Kate swallowed a laugh she suspected would have bordered on the hysterical. "All good," she replied.

She followed him into the elevator and turned to face Jonas as the doors began to rumble closed again. Then, as if of its own volition, her hand shot out. The door bumped into it, resisted for a moment, then reversed.

Kate stepped back into the corridor beside a rigid, unmoving Jonas.

"You know what's so sad about all of this?" she asked softly.

The muscle in front of Jonas's ear flickered.

"It isn't just my heart breaking here," she said. "It's yours, too. And I don't how to help either of us."

Standing on tiptoe, she reached up to press a kiss to his cheek, then rested her forehead against the powerful chest one last time, absorbing his warmth, feeling the strong beat of his heart against her skin. Finally, throat aching with unshed tears, she stepped back into the elevator.

"Be safe, Jonas," she said. "Please."

FORTY-THREE

I t was the longest two hours of Kate's life.

While Grant had allowed her to be at the FBI's surveillance post, she had no official capacity there, and thus, no role to play. She could do nothing but watch the team set up their equipment in the office they'd taken over for the day, drink way more coffee than was probably wise, and watch her ex-fiancé with new respect.

The meticulous attention to detail that had once driven her to distraction was evident in spades here, but with Jonas's life hanging in the balance, she had a whole new appreciation for it. Operating on an unbelievably tight timeline, Grant had still managed to secure the perfect vantage point: an office on the fourteenth floor of a building behind the abandoned warehouse where the meet would take place. High enough to offer an unobstructed view of the entire alley between the buildings and reduce the risk of being spotted from below; low enough to give them a clear sightline through the warehouse's main floor windows.

According to the sign stenciled on the office's door, an accountant normally occupied the premises, but he was absent for the day, no doubt enjoying his unexpected time off at government expense. Though he'd enjoy it somewhat less if he saw what that same government had done to his workspace, Kate suspected.

Shelves and filing cabinets had been shifted aside to give access to the windows overlooking the alley, and the desk had been summarily cleared of everything on it, papers and equipment alike dumped into a large cardboard box. Sophisticated listening equipment sat there instead—their sole link to Jonas when he arrived.

Kate glanced at her watch. Ten minutes. She stared down at the littered passage below. Dumpsters lined the edges on both sides, some overflowing with cardboard boxes and other debris. Dried stalks of plants poked through the broken pavement. Sheets of newspaper drifted randomly, blown by the wind that funneled between the buildings.

A radio handset hissed and crackled to life.

"Base, this is Unit One. We have a blue sedan entering the alley. Three occupants, one female."

The agent manning the equipment picked up the handset and acknowledged, "Ten-four, One."

Grant joined Kate at the window.

"You okay?" he asked.

She nodded. As okay as a stomach tied in knots and a cold sweat would allow, she supposed. She loosened her white-knuckled grip on the window ledge.

Fourteen floors below, the sedan came into view from the west and stopped at the warehouse's back door. Kate took the binoculars Grant offered. She focused on the emerging occupants. One man had his back to her, but she recognized the driver and female passenger from the gym at her apartment.

It seemed a lifetime ago, now.

"It's them," she said. She handed the binoculars back to Grant, fighting the tremble in her hand. "It's Lewis and

Ramirez. Jonas identified them to me in Ottawa. I couldn't see the other man."

Grant nodded confirmation to the other team members over his shoulder. Tension in the room ratcheted up several notches. Kate threaded shaking fingers through her hair.

"This is insane," she muttered. "They've already tried to kill him once. How do we know he's not walking into an ambush?"

"We don't."

Grant's admission buried itself in her gut like a fist, and she sucked for air, every fiber of her being demanding that she stop Jonas from—

"But we do know Burke," Grant's quiet voice continued. "And if everything I've heard about him is true, he can handle this."

No, she wanted to deny.

"He's good at what he does, Kate. You know he is. He wouldn't have survived as long as he has undercover if he wasn't."

Kate closed her eyes. *That's not the point.*

Grant's hands settled on her shoulders and squeezed gently. "Let him do his job," he said. "And you do your job. Here. With us. He needs to know you still have his back."

Kate drew a deep breath. Through sheer, dogged force of will, she steadied the internal vibration that had plagued her since their arrival. Then she nodded. Grant was right. She needed to do what she could to make sure Jonas came through this alive. She needed to have his back, because he had her heart.

She took the binoculars from Grant again and turned back to the window.

* * *

Jonas paused at the battered metal door and scanned the alley. In a world of dull brick and duller pavement, the blue sedan parked outside the warehouse meeting place was the only splash of color. A chill prickled down his spine and raised the hair on his arms. The last time he'd tangled with Lewis and Ramirez had been a day just like this one. Bleak, cold, gray.

His gaze traveled over the sedan again. He also seemed to remember an intimate acquaintance with the trunk of a car just like that one, right after he'd been shot. He shook off the sense of *déjà vu*. This time was different, he reminded himself. This time, others knew about Lewis and Ramirez, knew he was here, watched over him.

He risked a quick glance up at the building on the other side of the alley and the rows of windows that stared down on him. This time, others had his back—*Kate* had his back—and he knew what he was dealing with.

This time, there would be no surprises.

He gripped the doorknob, cold against his palm, and turned it. Then he pulled open the door and stepped into the warehouse.

"Carmen. Lewis." Jonas's measured tones filtered through the equipment on the desk, rich and vibrant, filling the office. Kate turned to stare at the receiver that had become the center of her entire universe. Grant went to stand beside the desk.

"Burke." A male voice spoke. "You're a brave man, coming out into the open like this with so many people looking for you."

"So why not be a hero and take me in?"

Kate pictured the belligerent expression that would have accompanied Jonas's words, and her skin tightened.

The man snorted. "I think we can do without the games."

"I was hoping so."

"Why don't you start by telling us what you want?" a woman's voice suggested. Carmen Ramirez.

"Three million," Jonas replied. "Cash. If I'm going to live with the accusations, I should be able to enjoy the spoils, don't you think?"

There was a moment's silence.

"And in return?" asked a new male voice.

"Sorry, I don't think we've met?"

"You don't need my name."

"Then you don't need what I have."

Footsteps.

"Hold on, Burke," said Lewis. "This is Hal Peters."

"Never heard of him. Is he Bureau?"

"Canadian."

Kate sucked in a sharp breath, the name and nationality coming together in her mind with explosive force. Corporal Henry Peters, RCMP Customs and Excise, going by the nickname Hal. He'd been a part of the investigation into Jimmy Lazarus—and the reason the investigation would have failed to turn up the real suspects if Kate hadn't been there to contradict him. At the time, she'd put his errors down to sloppy work, but now...now it made more sense. And she wasn't in the least surprised to learn he was their Canadian connection.

She grabbed a pad of paper and pen from the box of desk contents, jotted down a note, and passed it to Grant. He glanced at it, then at her. A single nod conveyed understanding. They focused again on their eavesdropping.

"—and he gave me all the papers to back up what he told me," Jonas was saying. "Those are what you get in exchange."

"You really think we're that stupid?" Lewis laughed. "We checked the files, Burke. Honeyman never removed them from the office."

"Do you really think Rick was that stupid?" Jonas countered. "He told you not to go after me in the first place, and when you screwed up, it made him nervous. He copied everything as a backup and kept it at his apartment. With good reason, apparently."

Another silence, longer this time.

"You're bluffing," Lewis said at last.

"Maybe. Maybe not. You can part with some of your profits to find out, or you can kill me and wait to see if my partner takes the evidence to the feds—along with my signed statement as to what it all means. Your choice."

"Kate Dexter has the files?" Hal Peters gave a derisive chuckle. "Now I know you're lying. If she had anything, she'd have already turned it in. They don't come any more uptight than Dexter."

"Just like she turned me in?" Jonas asked. "Kate's blown any career she once had by helping me, Peters, and you know it. She needs the money to drop out and start fresh somewhere, just like I do."

The pause this time lasted so long that Kate began to think they'd lost their connection. The air knotted in her chest.

"If I'd never seen you in action, Burke, and if I didn't know what a damned good liar you are, I might believe you," Lewis said at last. "But our partners would be less than happy if we handed that much money over to you without proof of what we get in return."

Partners? Kate exchanged another look with a grim-faced Grant. It was their first evidence that others were involved. But how many? They needed more information. Jonas had to get names.

Lewis was speaking again. "I tell you what. Let's have your friend bring us a sample. She provides us with one file, and we'll talk business."

"You really think I'm stupid enough to put both of us in the same room with you?" Jonas gave a short bark of laughter. "Forget it. Kate stays out of this. You want a file, I'll get one for you. But *I* get it, not Kate." Footsteps sounded as he added, "You kiddies stick around. I'll be back in an hour."

"Hold up there a minute, Burke."

Lewis's voice had hardened, and Kate's heart dropped to her toes at the unmistakable sound of a gun leaving its leather holster. The footsteps stopped.

"I think we'll do this our way, if it's all the same to you," Lewis said. "You call Dexter. She brings the file here to all of us. You stay. Peters, why don't you take Agent Burke over to one of those chairs and see that he's comfortable while he makes his call?"

Heavier steps crossed concrete, and Kate suddenly remembered Hal Peters as a veritable mountain of a man. Much larger than Jonas. A brief scuffle sounded, and then—

"What the hell is that?" Peters's voice demanded. "Lewis, that belt buckle. Isn't that—?"

"Issue," Carmen Ramirez responded. "It's goddamned issue, Lewis. I *told* you we should've scanned him for tech. He's freaking wired!"

Other sounds poured through the radio connection. An angry bellow—Jonas's? More scuffling. The muffled crunch of a blow being struck. A thud. Labored breathing. And then—

"Get the damn thing off him, for chrisssake!" Lewis shouted. "Peters, check the—"

His words cut off abruptly, and the quiet static of radio silence took their place. Kate turned to Grant in disbelief, but he was already in full swing, barking out orders as he pointed at various agents.

"Tell them to block the alley!" he snapped at the first. "Both ends!" He pointed at another. "You—get me Jack Lewis's cell number. You three, clear everyone out of this side of the building. And for God's sake, someone get me the assistant director! Move, people, *move*."

Agents sprang into action, one pulling out a cell phone as she headed into the corridor on the heels of three others, one issuing terse instructions over the radio, another handing a cell phone to Grant. Two more headed for the windows with binoculars in hand.

Sound and movement roared together in a hideous blur around Kate. The floor bucked beneath her feet, threatening to pitch her to her knees. She remained upright through sheer force of will, moving out of the way, claiming a third window for her own, fighting down hysteria.

She remembered Jonas's face as she'd first seen it, blood spattered and pale beneath caked mud—but this time she saw it not through the eyes of the stranger she had been, but through those of the lover she had become. Her gut twisted. She struggled to draw air into lungs that had all but forgotten how to function.

God, please, no.

A shout went up from one of the other windows, and Kate leaned forward too fast, her forehead connecting sharply with the glass. She blinked away tears of pain as four people emerged from the warehouse below. Her gaze fastened on Jonas, one arm slung over Hal Peters's shoulders, feet bouncing as the larger man dragged him over the doorsill.

Unconscious.

Even as she registered the fact, the group stopped, and Lewis and Ramirez both gesticulated wildly. They pulled their weapons from their holsters and made a hasty retreat back into the building. The battered metal door slammed shut, cutting them off from the cops that had blocked the alley. Cutting her off from Jonas.

She jumped as a hand closed over her shoulder.

"We'll get him out, Kate," Grant said. "You have my word."

She wanted to believe him, but the cop in her had been in his shoes before and knew he could make no guarantees. She didn't reply.

Grant released her shoulder. "The assistant director is on his way down. I'll let you know when he gets here."

Kate turned back to the alley and the empty sedan sitting outside the warehouse door. She crossed her arms against the icy cold that had settled in the center of her soul. Thought about how Lewis and Ramirez had already tried to kill Jonas once and how they had nothing to lose by finishing the job now. They'd already be going to prison for so long at this point that his murder would make no difference to anyone except them.

And Jonas.

A knife blade slipped between her ribs.

And me.

"They won't let him out." She hated herself for being the one to speak the words—the truth—on everyone's minds. Movement and noise subsided behind them. She felt Grant's eyes on her. Braced for his denial, the empty assurances he would feel obliged to make.

He cleared his throat. "I'll let you know when Assistant Director Fraser arrives," he said again, and he moved away.

Kate rested her bruised forehead against the cool glass and stared at the warehouse door across the alley.

FORTY-FOUR

It took long, excruciating minutes for Jonas's awareness to come back online. Hal Peters had handcuffed him to the post in the center of the floor, but not until the man had buried his fist in the still-healing gut wound left by Lewis's bullet. Twice.

The first time had left Jonas unable to breathe. The second had left him unable to function—physically or mentally. Jonas risked a shallow inhale as the agony in his belly subsided. The pain stabilized into a deep, dull throb. Slowly, the haze between him and the rest of the world dissipated. He took another breath and then, chin resting on his chest, cracked open his eyes enough to take stock of the situation.

It wasn't encouraging.

Sheets of plywood, braced by scrap lumber, had been placed over the windows lining the alley wall, cutting the already murky daylight to almost nothing. Jonas made out the figures of Ramirez and Peters at gaps in the wood, their weapons drawn and their faces grim in the little light that penetrated. A dozen feet away, Lewis paced the concrete floor, cell phone pressed to his ear, his voice angry—and desperate.

Jonas's hands twitched in the metal cuffs. Desperate wasn't good. Desperate led to impulsive moves. Stupid decisions. Choices that got people killed. People like Jonas. He tuned into the one-sided conversation.

"I know how this works, Douglas," Lewis said. "And I'm telling you now, I'm not interested in negotiation."

A pause while Lewis listened to the voice at the other end of the line, and then, "No, I don't want to make a *deal*. I don't give a flying fuck about reduced sentences. I've seen what happens to cops who get sent up, remember? There's one deal on the table, and one deal only. We get a plane out of the country, you get Burke. Take it or leave it."

Another pause. Another snarl. "I said no. You have our terms. First sign of activity in that alley, I put a bullet in Burke's head. Don't call again until our plane is ready."

Lewis ended the call, and Jonas closed his eyes, pretending continued unconsciousness.

"You really think they'll go for it?" Peters asked. "Maybe we should—"

"No," Lewis cut him off. "We roll over on the others, we die. You know it, and I know it. Our only option is getting the hell out of the country."

Peters was silent for a second, then said, "Ramirez?"

"Jack's right. You don't give up names like Zabatoff and live to tell the tale."

Zabatoff? These idiots are in bed with one of Russia's most infamous arms dealers? The revelation was nearly Jonas's undoing, but he managed to remain still enough not to alert the others to his eavesdropping.

"You're a frickin' idiot if you think the feds will go along with this," Peters grumbled.

"I think we didn't give them a choice," Lewis said.

"And Burke? You'll really turn him over?"

"After the chase he's led us on?" Lewis snorted. "What do you think?"

Peters didn't answer. Jonas didn't need him to. In his mind's eye, he went over the warehouse setup again, examining the details he'd filed away as he'd entered, as he'd stood talking to Lewis. There weren't many. A cavernous space, empty but for piles of rubbish and the wood Peters and Ramirez had used to shore up the only windows. A solid concrete floor throughout. Metal roof. One pedestrian door at the front, through which he'd entered. A massive loading door at the rear, closed and padlocked.

What had seemed the ideal place for a meet was a virtual fortress when it came to a police assault. If Grant Douglas and the feds stormed the place—the likely scenario—he would almost certainly die along with the others. And even if they let Lewis think they'd caved to his demands in order to draw them out into the open, .there was no way Lewis would let him live.

Either way, Kate's last memory of him would be the aftermath of his phone call to Valerie. His denial of anything between them. Everything between them. His chest tightened, and he closed his eyes.

Oh, Kate.

"Constable Dexter?"

Kate wasn't sure what startled her more: the unexpected voice at her shoulder, or hearing her name and rank for the first time in what seemed an eon. She turned to face a short, thin, middle-aged man in a dark blue suit and charcoal overcoat. Blue eyes regarded her with calm professionalism.

"I'm Assistant Director Sean Fraser," he said.

Kate summoned a ghost of a smile and dutifully shook hands.

"Why don't you come and have a coffee?" A.D. Fraser suggested. "You've been through quite the ordeal."

Glancing out the window, Kate hesitated. She hadn't moved from her post in almost two hours because a part of her—the not altogether rational part—was convinced that if she did, Jonas would die in her absence.

A gentle hand cupped her elbow and urged her forward.

"It'll do you good," A.D. Fraser said, "and it's only on the other side of the room."

She eased cramped muscles into motion and allowed him to lead her to the far side of the office. A coffee station had been set up there, with percolator, foam cups, and a mixed heap of creamers and sugar packets. An open box of thickly frosted donuts sat to one side, but Kate's stomach churned at the sight of them, and she shook her head when offered one.

A.D. Fraser poured two coffees and led her to the quietest corner of the room, pulling two chairs over and waiting until she sat down before he did so himself.

"Constable Dexter—"

"Kate," she said.

Fraser started over. "Kate, you should know that I've been in touch with Assistant Commissioner Bennett."

Dave's father-in-law? Kate frowned. "Why?"

"Given the circumstances, we're setting up a joint investigation with the RCMP. The assistant commissioner says he can't guarantee you total amnesty, but he has named you to the task force as their primary investigator, retroactive to when you met Agent Burke. That should erase some of your...um..."

"Less horrendous escapades?" Kate supplied.

A faint smile tipped the corners of A.D. Fraser's mouth. "Something like that. Another of your colleagues is flying down with the memorandum of understanding. Constable Jennings, I think the A.C. said. He should be here within the hour."

"My partner." Great. If nothing else set her off, Dave Jennings's bear hug and bottomless sympathy were sure to do so. She began shoring up her defenses in anticipation of Dave's arrival. "I appreciate your help, sir—"

"Sean."

"—but what I really want to know is what's happening *here*."

"Not much so far. Special Agent Douglas is handling the negotiations."

"They want leniency in exchange for testimony?" she guessed.

"Not exactly."

Kate frowned. "Then what?"

"Total amnesty and a ticket out of the country in exchange for Agent Burke. No testimony."

Kate watched the other agents moving about the room. She sipped at the overly sweetened coffee. "If you let them leave with Jonas," she said finally, "they'll kill him and disappear, and whoever else is involved will get off scot-free."

Fraser nodded grim agreement. "And if we go in after them, they'll kill him, probably get killed themselves, and whoever else is involved will still go free."

Rock, meet hard place.

The cop in Kate already knew the answer to her next question, but she asked anyway, because the woman in her needed to hear it. Needed to know for sure.

"What are you going to do?"

The assistant director squared his shoulders, his expression going tight as if bracing for argument. "We've called in tactical," he said simply.

Kate set the cup down on the bookshelf beside him. "Thanks for the coffee," she said, and then she went back to her post at the window.

Within the hour promised by A.D. Fraser, a familiar voice spoke behind Kate. "You know, when I told you to be careful, this wasn't quite what I had in mind."

Dave. At last.

Bracing herself, she turned to greet her partner—and in an instant, all the mental preparation she thought she'd done for his appearance crumbled into relief, terror, and sheer hopelessness. Tears filled her eyes, and she gulped for air through a suddenly constricted throat. Without a word, Dave reached for her, and leather-clad arms wrapped her in the bear hug she'd both needed and dreaded ever since she'd learned he was flying down. A shudder wracked her frame. The arms tightened, and a chin rested on top of her head.

Kate stayed in the comforting embrace for long seconds, letting Dave's silent strength envelop her as she swallowed her tears and struggled to regain a semblance of control. She'd come too far with Jonas to dissolve into hysterics now. He needed her to be a cop, not some wilting flower. At last, she pushed back and offered Dave a crooked smile.

"Bet you weren't expecting that greeting," she said ruefully.

"Bet I was," Dave replied, his gray eyes warm with sympathy and concern. "How are you holding up, kiddo?"

"Good." She heard the wobble in her voice, cleared her throat, and repeated firmly, "Good. I'm good. Honest. And I hear you've been doing a magic act back home."

Dave grimaced. He snagged a chair and pulled it over to where they stood. Kate refused his wordless offer, and he straddled the chair himself, his arms slung over the back.

"Magic, hell," he retorted. "What I've pulled off is nothing short of a bloody miracle—including not getting my own ass fired."

Kate's eyes watered again. She swallowed. "Thank you."

He waved off her words. "That's what partners are for."

"So what exactly have they forgiven me for?" she asked. She didn't really care, but the conversation distracted her. Kept her mind off...other things. Her gaze slid toward the window and the still-closed warehouse door. To her relief, Dave played along.

"Let's see." He ticked her infractions off on his fingers, his brow creased with exaggerated concentration. "Aiding and abetting a suspected felon is gone; concealing is gone; and I think you're okay on illegal entry to the U.S., along with illegal possession of a firearm. They're still trying to iron out assaulting a peace officer and swiping his car, however." He grimaced. "Did I forget anything?"

"High-speed chase resulting in a wrecked PC."

"Ah. Yes. The police cruiser." Dave sighed. "Actually, that one may still land you in an Arctic posting. But you'll be in good company, because I'm pretty sure that's where they send constables who vault over the entire chain of command to cry on daddy-in-law's shoulder."

Remorse twisted through Kate's belly. "Hell, Dave—"

Again, he waved her off. "Don't worry about it. I happen to think dog sleds are a great way to get around." He glanced over his shoulder at Grant Douglas's approach, then stood to hold out his hand in greeting. "Douglas."

"Jennings," Grant responded absently, his attention already on Kate even as he shook hands with her partner. He looked nothing like his usual precise self, she noted. His suit jacket was long gone, he'd loosened his tie, and the top two buttons of his shirt were undone. And she could have sworn that was a smudge of chocolate frosting on the edge of his top lip.

"How are you holding up?" he asked.

"I'm okay. What's happening?"

"Tactical is on the way."

Kate narrowed her gaze. "They were on the way an hour ago."

"They got held up."

Dave put a hand on her arm before she could request clarification. "They're going in?" he asked her.

"We have to," Grant replied on her behalf. "His chances are zero if we let them take him out of there."

Dave frowned. "They don't seem much better if you go in."

"They're not," Kate said. She saw the questions forming in her partner's gaze, and she looked away before she lost it again. "What do you mean tactical got held up?" she asked Grant.

Grant hesitated, and his expression turned haggard. Unease uncoiled in Kate's chest.

"Grant?" she pressed. "What's going on?"

Her ex ran a hand over his close-cropped hair. "They were involved in an accident," he said, sighing. "The sniper was injured. We're flying someone in from Chicago."

She gaped at him. "That's two hours away! You must have someone closer—what about the local police?"

"Tied up with other incidents. Seems we picked a hell of a day for our little sting. They'll let us know if they come free. In the meantime, our guy is only an hour and forty minutes out."

"You have *got* to be freaking kidding me!" She stared at him for a second longer, then looked out the window. Almost two hours until the sniper arrived, another thirty minutes for briefing and set up, and—she glanced at the clock on the wall over the door—and it was already ten minutes to two now.

"It'll be after four by the time tactical is ready to go," she said. She shook her head. "That's too long. They'll know something is up."

"We have no alternative, Kate." Grant's voice was as gentle as it was weary. "I wish—"

She flapped a hand at him, cutting him off. "What about the rest of the team?" she asked. "Were they injured, too?"

"Three of them were. The other two are fine, but it's not enough to go in with. Especially not without a sniper to back them up."

"Damn it!" Kate whirled away and braced her hands on the windowsill, staring down into the alley. The beginning of an idea stirred. She shoved it away. It resurfaced stubbornly.

Impossible, she told it.

His best chance, it responded. *Maybe his only chance.*

Grant gave her shoulder a gentle squeeze. "I'll keep you posted," he said. "Hang in there."

"Wait," she said as he turned away. "I have an idea."

FORTY-FIVE

From the corner of her eye, Kate saw Grant turn back to her, but she kept her attention on the alley below, studying its every detail. Every nuance. The warehouse windows. The battered metal door. The blue sedan.

Angles.

Distances.

The scraps of paper dancing across the pavement.

"Kate?" Dave prompted.

"What if we draw them out instead of going in?" she murmured, her gaze darting to the unmarked SUVs blocking the alley entrance to the east. "If we convince them we're backing off, they might come out into the open. A sniper positioned here could take out the one holding Jonas and probably one other before they have time to react. That would give your team time to move in."

Grant shook his head when she glanced back at him. "I don't see how that changes anything. We still have to wait for our guy to—"

"I don't think she's talking about your guy," Dave interrupted, his gaze fixed on her.

Grant stared at him. Then at Kate. "You're not serious."

Her throat closed. *Was* she serious? Now that she'd

made the suggestion, a thousand voices screamed denial in her brain. She was nowhere near ready...her scores since the shooting had been mediocre at best given her prior skill level...she still had so far to go...what if she missed...what if she hit Jonas instead...

"She can do it, Douglas." Dave's calm voice penetrated the haze of panic. "You know she can."

But what if I can't?

The same question was etched across Grant's brow as he looked pointedly at her shoulder. "Can you?"

Kate sucked a deep breath into her lungs and forced her mind to still. She focused all her attention on the shoulder she'd barely given a thought to for the last few days. Carefully she rotated it forward and back, raised it, dropped it. Each of the movements met with remarkably little resistance and even less discomfort. Her mouth twisted. Talk about ironic. She'd come further since picking Jonas up off the road than she had after months of careful exercise, following the physiotherapist's every instruction. Who knew running for her life would turn out to be so beneficial?

She met Grant's gaze. "I think I can."

"You think." Grant folded his arms over his tie. "But you don't know. That seems an awfully big risk where Jonas's life is concerned, Kate."

Her heart gave an uncomfortable thud. "It is," she agreed, "but it's no bigger risk than your plan. I tested just shy of sharpshooter level two weeks ago. I know it's nowhere near my previous status, but I'm pretty sure I'm still the best shot here. And I *am* here."

Indecision flickered in Grant's expression, and then he gave a terse nod and unfolded his arms. "I'll talk to the assistant director," he said. "Wait here."

Grant's conversation with A.D. Fraser took forever.

The two men stood with their backs to Kate so that she could read neither their lips nor their expressions. Her only clues to the discussion came from the shake of Fraser's head, the shrug of Grant's shoulders.

She looked at the clock over the door. Five past two. She made an impatient noise under her breath. Dave's hand covered hers.

"Down, girl," he warned. "You're in their territory, remember?"

Kate shot him a dark look, but before she could respond, the two men on the other side of the room turned and made their way across to them. Her lungs gave up functioning.

A.D. Fraser came straight to the point. "Your shoulder. How bad was the injury?"

Kate saw no point in hedging. "The bullet shattered a bone and did extensive muscle damage. I'm expected to recover enough to return to active duty."

"But not as a sniper."

"No."

"I see." Mouth tight, Fraser looked past her, out the window. After an excruciating eternity, he met her gaze again. "And how is it today?" he asked. "Right now."

"Better than waiting for your Chicago guy."

"You're absolutely certain. No hesitation." Fraser raked a hand over his hair, the desire to believe her warring with indecision in his expression. "You have no jurisdiction here, Constable Dexter. If I put a rifle in your hands and you screw up..."

"I won't."

I can't.

Fraser held her gaze for another second before wheeling away and stalking back the way he'd come.

Kate blinked after him, then let her shoulders sag as she looked up at Grant.

"Is that a yes?" she asked.

"You'll have a weapon in twenty minutes," he said. "It's already on the way. I'll start trying to convince Lewis at we have a plane ready and we're pulling back."

The sniper's rifle rolled into the office at two twenty-three, on the lap of a man in a wheelchair who looked like he should still be on a gurney. His left arm was in a newly minted cast, and one eye and the side of his face were swollen and evolving from purple to black, even as another agent wheeled him into the room. Kate detached herself from the windowsill and met him halfway, beside the accountant's desk.

"You're the sniper," she said. "You didn't have to come."

"Brad Downing." The man in the wheelchair patted the rifle case with his good hand. "No one knows her like I do," he said, his words slurred a little, most likely from pain medication. "And I figured you'd need all the help you can get."

"The blind leading the halt?" Kate suggested wryly.

The uninjured side of Brad Downing's mouth tipped upward. "Something like that."

"May I?" She indicated the rifle case on his lap. He nodded, and she took it from him as he tried to lift it. She set it on the desk, flicked open the tabs, lifted the lid, and stared at the weapon inside. In a heartbeat, all the confidence she'd spent the last half hour shoring up in herself evaporated.

What in hell did she think she was playing at? Conditions here were nothing like the firing range. There were too many variables that she wasn't ready for: the wind, an unfamiliar weapon, the changing light as the clouds moved across the sky, the rain that had begun falling...

The fact that her target wasn't made of paper and neither was Jonas.

"Kate?" Dave's voice asked at her shoulder.

She tightened her hands into fists to hide their tremble. Swallowed. Looked over her shoulder at Agent Downing. "Tell me about it," she said.

As Downing talked her through the weapon's habits and idiosyncrasies, she began lifting the rifle parts from the case for assembly. Body, stock, dayscope...one by one, she fitted the pieces together and secured them in place, finishing as Downing lapsed into silence.

"Nothing else?" she asked, hefting the completed weapon in her arms. It nestled against her, both familiar and foreign, benign and deadly.

Downing shook his head. "Just...good luck."

Kate took a deep, steadying breath and, with Dave trailing her, returned to the window. She looked down at the alley. The wind had picked up, funneling through the narrow space in gusts, and the rain had settled into an unrelenting drizzle. She flexed aching fingers wrapped around the rifle's barrel.

One window over, two agents lifted a window clear of its frame. Behind her, Grant was on the phone with Lewis, telling him the police and FBI had withdrawn, convincing him that the coast was clear for them to leave.

The clock over the door ticked inexorably on.

Dave placed his hand over hers. "You're like ice."

"Right through to my core." She ran over the details Downing had given her, fitting them into what she observed. The rifle had a hairline tendency to pull to the left, he'd said. With the wind gusting in the same direction, she'd need to compensate for that, but not too much.

Dave's hand squeezed hers. "You can do this, Kate," he said.

Her gaze sought his. "What if I can't? What if—"

"Don't," Dave interrupted. "You can't afford to start second-guessing yourself, Kate. *Jonas* can't afford it."

Kate pressed her lips together and made her shoulders drop. Dave was right. If she wasn't a thousand percent sure when she took aim, she'd blow it for certain. Instead of almost for certain.

Freaking hell.

She closed her eyes. Nodded her understanding. Thrust away the cold, nerve-numbing dread.

"Constable Dexter? We're ready for you," said one of the agents at the next window.

Game on.

She positioned herself to one side of the opening where she had a clear view of the warehouse door below. She would've preferred to use a bipod on a solid surface, but it would have put her too much in the open, where she could be seen from below if one of the targets happened to look up. As it was, the windowless opening itself would be a dead giveaway if Lewis or one of the others studied things too closely.

She flexed icy fingers.

"You ready?" Grant asked, coming to join her and Dave.

She nodded.

"Good. We're all in position. Lewis is expecting us to provide safe transport to the airport. I'll have an SUV come in from the west. It will stop short of the sedan, but it can't be too far away or it will raise suspicions. That means Lewis and the others will be out in the open for a half dozen feet at most. You won't have much time."

Her gaze flicked over the scene below, calculating possible shots.

"I've got agents in the two doorways to the west of the warehouse," Grant continued. "And one to the east. Five in total."

She mapped out the locations in her head. "Got it."

"Lewis is waiting for our call."

Her stomach twisted violently, and she thanked her lucky stars that she'd turned down the earlier donut offers. She drew a deep breath. Held it. Exhaled again. Gave a single nod. "Let's do it."

As Grant turned away to set the wheels in motion, Dave took the rifle from her and handed her an elastic band. With fingers so steady they surprised her, she pulled her hair back into a ponytail and tucked away all the loose ends where they couldn't distract her. Someone handed her a radio headset, and she settled it into place, fitting the earpiece into her right ear and adjusting the microphone. Then she took back the rifle from Dave.

The cold metal warmed to her grip. Calm settled over her. Dave was right. She could do this. As long as she stayed focused. As long as she didn't think. She settled the rifle stock against her injured shoulder.

"We're on the move," Grant called out.

Kate's world narrowed to the warehouse door in her scope.

FORTY-SIX

R ain drummed against the warehouse's metal roof, the only sound in the tense silence that had fallen over the open space. Ramirez and Peters still held their positions at the boarded-up windows; Lewis still paced the floor, tapping his cell phone against his thigh. And Jonas, his ass cold and numb from sitting on the concrete, turned the entire mess over and over again in his head—reaching the same inescapable conclusion each goddamned time.

Kate was wrong. This whole situation *was* his fault. Not in the control-freak kind of way she'd accused him of, but in the inevitable kind of way that stemmed from his own behavior. His own stubborn independence. He'd been so busy guarding against betrayal that he'd failed to form connections—to anyone. He'd never waited for help, never worked *with* a partner. He'd been a man without friends. Untrusted and untrusting.

In short, he'd made himself the perfect patsy.

And if that was true...Jonas's breath caught in a painful lump beneath his ribs. If that was true, if he'd screwed up his past so thoroughly with his solitary existence, then maybe—just maybe—he ought to reconsider his future.

A future with Kate.

If he had one.

The sudden buzz of Lewis's cell phone underscored the last thought, bringing the imminent threat of his own mortality to hang over him as the other man answered the call.

Lewis listened for a moment, then snapped, "This better be for real, Douglas, or he's dead." Pocketing the phone, he turned to the others. "They're ready for us. An SUV, coming in from the west. One driver. Clear windows."

"I see it," said Hal Peters, peering between boards.

"Anything else moving out there?"

"Nothing since they pulled back," Ramirez answered. "We're in the clear."

"What about the windows across?"

"No movement."

"Right. Then it's time to move. I'll take Burke."

"I still think it's too easy," Peters growled. "They've had more than enough time to put a team together."

"A team would be coming in here to get us, not giving us a ride to the airport. We hold all the cards, Peters"—Lewis jerked his head in Jonas's direction—"and everyone knows it. So we can either hang around debating the issue until they *do* bring in a team, or we can move. I vote move."

Ramirez sighed and pushed back the hair from her face. "I agree. Sitting here is getting us nowhere except on each other's nerves."

"Two to one," Lewis said. "We move."

He crossed over to Jonas and crouched beside him, handcuff key in hand and pistol in the other. "One wrong move and I finish what I started, Burke. With pleasure."

Jonas nodded understanding. He had no idea what Kate and Grant Douglas had planned, but he knew damned well it didn't include driving Lewis *et al* to any airport—and he was damned if he would jeopardize that future he'd finally decided he wanted.

"You have my word," he said.

Lewis undid one cuff long enough to release him from the pole, then snapped it shut over his wrist again and roughly pulled him to his feet. "Let's go."

The warehouse door in Kate's scope opened, and every fiber of her being snapped to attention. Jonas emerged first, framed in the doorway for a split second before someone shoved him forward, into the alley. Kate's rifle scope followed, and for a moment, both time and her heart ground to a halt.

Jonas might have been standing right in front of her, he seemed so close. Close enough to see the shadow of stubble along his jawline, the thick fringe of dark lashes around his brilliant blue eyes, the tug of pain at the corner of his mouth, the livid purple bruise that highlighted one cheekbone.

"You have a green light, Kate," Grant's voice came through her earpiece, yanking her back to the task at hand. "I repeat, green light."

"Ten four," she acknowledged. This was it. Time to get Jonas the hell out of there and end this thing. She shifted her scope away from him, seeking her target. She found the pistol pressed to the base of his skull, the hand holding it, the brown sleeve that covered the arm attached to the hand...

And then, nothing. Jonas's superior height and breadth all but made the person behind him invisible. She had no shot.

"Shit!" She jerked back from the rifle scope. "No confidence, Grant. I repeat, no confidence! Get me another window. I can't even *see* the target from here!"

"No time, Kate," Grant said, his tone even. "The windows are all sealed in their frames. Even if we could get one out fast enough, they'd hear us."

Freaking hell. Kate dipped her head back down and swept the scope over the little group below. Carmen Ramirez and Hal Peters stood to each side of Jonas, their weapons drawn as they scanned the alley intently. That meant the brown sleeve belonged to Lewis—for all the good the knowledge did her.

"Just do your best," Grant's voice advised in her ear.

"There's no such thing as 'best'," Kate snapped. "I either make the shot or I don't, and right now there's no damned shot to make!"

Sweat trickled down her back, and her shoulder quivered with the strain of holding the rifle barrel aloft. She pushed away the ache forming along the edges of her consciousness. She pressed her lips together. Later, she could hurt. Right now, she had no time. Couldn't allow the distraction.

Tipping her head to one side, she peered past the scope at the bigger picture as Hal Peters walked around the front of the SUV to the passenger door. Time was running out. If she couldn't make the shot, Jonas would get in the vehicle with them, and they would drive away with him, and—

She suppressed a shudder. And she didn't need to think further than that, because it wasn't going to happen. Regardless of what Jonas did or didn't want for them, she wouldn't be another in a long line of people who had let him down.

Jonas stepped forward, and Kate returned to following his progress through the scope. The edge of the

SUV's black roof entered the bottom of her circle of vision. Jonas shifted to his right, and for a split-second, Lewis's full arm came into view. Kate caught her breath. The arm disappeared again behind Jonas. Despair slammed into her gut.

"Damn it!" she growled. "How much time do I have left?"

"Ramirez is in the car, rear seat, passenger side," Dave responded. His voice was controlled and even, but tight. "Her door is closed. Peters is standing by the front passenger door, not open yet."

"Come on, come *on*," she murmured, willing her target into view. Still nothing but that damned brown—

And then it was there. In view. A sliver of Lewis's face, just beside Jonas's head as he reached to open the SUV's back passenger door on the other side of the vehicle. Kate tightened her finger against the rifle's trigger, slowly, infinitesimally. But no more of Lewis appeared, and she eased off again. It wasn't enough.

"Kate?" Grant's voice in her earpiece, taut, questioning, prompting.

"Still no confidence. It's an unfamiliar weapon. I need a wider margin." Her voice was a bare thread of a whisper. She waited, willing herself to patience. She shut out the room behind, the world around, the turmoil within. Her focus became absolute. Unwavering. In the scope, Jonas's head lowered for his descent into the vehicle, and part of Lewis became visible—forehead, eyes, the bridge of his nose. It wasn't much, but it was enough.

She had a viable target.

Kate stilled the tremble in her shoulder.

She stopped breathing.

She squeezed the trigger.

* * *

Jonas felt the hairs on his head lift in the wake of the bullet a millisecond before the report of a rifle cracked through the alley and echoed between the buildings. Chaos followed on its heels. Shouts, another shot, the thunder of heavily booted feet.

His head snapped up long enough to register the presence of armed agents coming at them from seemingly everywhere, and then instinct kicked in. He dropped to the ground and rolled away from Lewis's body and the vehicle until the brick wall of the warehouse brought him up short. More shouts from many voices all muddled together, filling the narrow alleyway.

"Drop your weapon! *Now!*"

"On your knees!"

"Hands in the air—*in the air!*"

Jonas struggled to sit and wedged himself into a gap between the wall and a Dumpster. Only then, out of the immediate way of too many adrenaline-driven people waving guns, did he dare take stock of the situation.

The SUV blocked most of the activity from his view, but there was no mistaking the bright yellow *FBI* emblazoned across the chests and backs of the heavily armed and armored agents swarming the scene. No mistaking, either, the prone figure of Hal Peters, face down in a puddle with four of those agents pointing their weapons at him.

Or, a half-dozen feet away, the unmoving figure of Lewis on the pavement, a spreading pool of crimson beneath his head, a small hole punched neatly between his brows.

Jonas stared into the vacant, unseeing eyes of his former colleague. He waited for the expected sense of satisfaction to rise in him, but it didn't come. Nothing came. No anger. No relief. No anything, really, except a hollowness in the center of his chest where Kate's head had rested one last time that morning when she'd said goodbye at the elevator and told him to be safe.

Booted feet came between him and Lewis's corpse, and Jonas blinked as an FBI agent kicked the pistol away from Lewis's limp hand. The agent looked down at Jonas.

"Are you injured?" he asked.

Jonas hadn't thought to check, but there seemed to be no critical damage, and so he shook his head. "I'm fine."

"Good." The agent nodded. "Stay put. I'll send someone to get you in a minute."

Jonas watched him stride over to where Peters was being cuffed, and then he returned to staring at Lewis. So that was it, then. After all that had happened in the eternity since he'd been shot, it was over. Lewis was dead, the others were in custody, their operation would be blown wide open, and Jonas would have his life back. Except...

Except.

Except after spending these days with Kate—after having her be such an integral part of his every waking moment, his every thought—the life he'd had before her seemed beyond empty, felt like it had belonged to someone else. Someone he'd known a long time ago, but couldn't really remember anymore. He didn't think he wanted to remember. And he sure as hell didn't want to go back to being that person.

He scanned the blank windows in the building opposite, looking for her. She was up there somewhere, his beautiful, maddeningly stubborn Kate, who'd had his back throughout this whole ordeal, refused to let him shut her out, and shown him just what he'd been missing all these years.

But all the windows looked empty, and a chill that had nothing to do with rain or temperature shivered down his spine. She *was* up there, wasn't she? What if she'd—

A door banged open on the other side of the alley. He dropped his gaze to it as Grant Douglas emerged, followed by four more people Jonas didn't recognize, and then Dave Jennings.

Jonas blinked. Jennings? Where the hell had he come from?

The lanky RCMP officer sauntered across to him and, grinning from ear to ear, grasped him under one arm to haul him to his feet. Then, to Jonas's everlasting shock, Jennings pulled him into a hug and slapped him heartily on the back.

"Damn, but it's good to see you still breathing." Jennings set him away again but kept hold of his shoulders as he grinned some more. "You have no idea how close that was, my friend. No freaking idea."

Jonas's scalp tingled with the remembered passage of the bullet. "On the contrary," he said, "I think I do. We're sure that whoever took that shot meant to miss me, right?"

Jennings chuckled, turning him so that he could undo the cuffs. "Oh, I'm pretty sure she meant to miss, all right."

Rubbing at the marks on his wrists, Jonas turned back to him. "She?"

Jennings's grin grew, threatening to split his face in half. "I told you she was better than you thought. You *did* ask her about the shoulder, right?"

Jonas stared at him, trying to absorb words that made

no sense. Kate? He looked up at the windows of the building opposite. *Kate* had taken that shot? But how—

"Three years as a sniper with our emergency response team," Jennings answered as if Jonas had spoken aloud. "Until she took that bullet."

Jonas swallowed against a thickness in his throat. Kate had made it clear how she felt about him. To have made that shot, knowing the risk, knowing that if she missed...

He met the other man's calm gray gaze. Jennings's grin faded to a half smile, and he nodded.

"Hardest thing she's ever done," he agreed. "She could probably do with seeing you breathe in person. Thirteenth floor. Suite fourteen oh-six."

Jonas didn't need a second invitation.

FORTY-SEVEN

Jonas found the office halfway down the hall from the elevator. The door stood open, and the interior gave new meaning to the word chaos. Filing cabinets and bookcases had been shoved aside; radio equipment and an open rifle case littered the desktop. His gaze skimmed over it all and settled on the sole person in the room.

Kate.

She stood with a sniper's rifle in her hands, silhouetted against the gray daylight of the window out of which she gazed. Pausing in the doorway, he stared at her. At all of her: the woman, the cop, the partner. The full impact of the role she'd played in his rescue hit him square in the solar plexus. He owed her so much.

No. He owed her everything.

Kate turned her head, and her gaze locked with his. For an instant, unguarded warmth shone from amber depths, reaching out to envelop him. To hold him. Then a shutter dropped over her expression, turning it guarded —and Jonas's belly cold. His hands curled into fists at his sides. *He'd* done that to her. Hurt her. Betrayed her. Pushed her away so often...

Too often?

He hesitated. Then he closed the door behind him and

threaded his way across the room to her side. Every fiber in his being ached to reach for her on the spot, to fold her against him and hold her close and never let her go. But the rifle and her reserve made him pause. Told him he needed to go slow.

He cleared the tightness from his throat and forced a half-smile, trying for a lightness he didn't feel. "That was a pretty good shot you made just now, Constable Dexter."

Kate raised an eyebrow. "*Pretty* good, Agent Burke? I'm *pretty* sure that shot just saved your life."

Jonas's smile faded. "*You* saved my life," he corrected, his voice turning gruff. "Thank you for that."

She looked away, not answering.

Keep it neutral, his inner voice prompted.

"Why didn't you tell me?" He indicated the rifle, then shoved his hands into his pockets.

"It never came up," she said, shrugging. She carried the rifle to the desk and began to dismantle it.

"You mean I never asked."

Kate set the scope into its spot in the case, and he saw her hands tremble. Delayed reaction? Pain from her shoulder? Both possibilities made his gut clench.

"You never asked," she agreed.

"Because I was an ass."

"No," she replied. Then she smiled a tiny smile. "Well. Maybe sometimes."

A chuckle formed in Jonas's chest, but before it could escape, Kate continued.

"You didn't ask because you didn't want to know," she said. "You didn't want to care."

The amber eyes lifted to his, making it his turn to look away as his throat tightened again. She knew him so well. Better than he knew himself. And he couldn't keep up the pretense anymore.

"It didn't work," he said. "Not wanting to care, I mean. It didn't work."

Kate's hands stilled. Then she finished putting the rifle pieces back in their case and secured the clasps, her movements measured and precise. But her hands still shook, and from the corner of his eye, Jonas saw her swallow and close her eyes.

"You don't have to do this," she said. "I knew what I was getting into."

He snorted, thinking back over the past weeks. "I highly doubt that."

"You know what I mean."

No more pretending, Jonas reminded himself. "Kate—"

"Jonas, please." Kate's weary gaze met his. "Don't make this harder than it already is. You made your position clear from the start. Me choosing to ignore it was—"

"Your problem, not mine?" he interrupted.

A flash of pain crossed her expression, but she squared her shoulders and didn't look away. "Yes."

"But it's not," he contradicted softly. "And I realize now that it never has been. Kate—"

The office door opened.

"Oh, good. You're still here." Grant Douglas's voice cut between them, and Jonas flashed an irritated glance at the other man, who stood framed in the doorway. Douglas looked askance at Kate. "Am I interrupting?"

"No," she said.

"Yes," Jonas said simultaneously. A tiny spark of warmth flared in Kate's eyes.

"Uh—well, I just wanted to remind you about doing up a report, Kate," said Douglas. "And Jonas, we'll need a statement from you."

"Later," Jonas told him.

"It should be done as soon as possible, while everything is still fresh in..." Douglas's voice trailed off. His gaze narrowed on Jonas, weighing and assessing him in the same way he'd done at their first meeting. Then he smiled. "Later is good. Just make sure you see me before either of you goes anywhere."

The door closed behind him, and Jonas turned his attention back to Kate. She'd leaned against the desk, her arms braced on either side of her, waiting for him to continue. He took a deep breath.

The office door opened again.

"Kate? Oh, good. You're still here," said Dave Jennings. "I was wondering what your plans were for heading back to Ottawa. I'm booked on a flight tomorrow afternoon. Do you want me to see if I can get you a seat on the same one?"

Jonas muttered an expletive under his breath. He scowled at Jennings. "She's not going back tomorrow," he snapped. "She's not going anywhere until she listens to me, damn it!"

Kate stared at him for a second before looking at Jennings. "Can we figure it out later?" she asked. "I'll be out in a few minutes."

"Of course." Jennings shook his head at Jonas. "You've been up here for almost five minutes, Burke. What are you waiting for?"

"Peace and quiet," Jonas retorted.

Jennings chuckled. "Leaving now. I'll see you downstairs, Kate."

Kate thought she nodded, but she couldn't be sure, because Dave's words to Jonas had unlocked something in her that she'd given up on. A hope she thought had died. The door closed behind her old partner, leaving her and Jonas alone. Silence descended. The flicker of hope in her breast struggled to become more. To remember Jonas's words. To maybe begin believing them.

"Not wanting to care...it didn't work."

She curled her hands around the edge of the desk, trying to remember the fine art of breathing. She raised her gaze to the brilliant blue waiting for her. The office door opened again and several FBI agents filed into the room, chatting and laughing, oblivious to the two occupants already there. The flash of annoyance in Jonas's eyes found an echo inside her; his impatience became hers. Whatever he wanted to say to her, she suddenly— desperately—needed to hear it. She opened her mouth to ask the agents to leave, but Jonas beat her to it.

"Damn it!" he roared. Conversation ceased, and the agents turned as one to stare at them. Jonas glared back at them. "Can we *please* have an uninterrupted five minutes?"

Uncomprehending looks gave way to dawning awareness; awareness to knowing smirks. The group shuffled out again, their whispers interspersed with chuckles and sly looks, and the door closed once more.

Anticipation curled through Kate's belly and spread through her chest. The tension in the room soared to new heights. Jonas stood almost a dozen feet away, but his warm strength reached across the space between them to envelop her. To hold her. She thought that if she closed her eyes and listened, she might hear his heart beating.

In three long strides, he closed the gap between them to mere inches. His broad, muscled chest filled her vision. His warmth pulsated against her.

"Kate."

She tried, but she couldn't bring herself to lift her gaze to his. Couldn't face the possibility she might be wrong after all. Couldn't put her heart on the line again. Gentle fingers tipped her chin up. Somber eyes met hers.

"I hurt you this morning," Jonas said, "And I'm sorry. I never meant to. I hope you know that."

She did know. She'd known it even as she eavesdropped on the conversation she'd never been meant to hear this morning. Jonas might be a mass of conflicting emotions, but cruel he was not.

His deep voice continued, quiet and rich, vibrating with promise. "All along, I think I was afraid that if I touched you, really touched you, and if we made love, I would lose myself in you forever. That scared the hell out of me, because I didn't think I could live up to the responsibility of it. When I woke up beside you today, I panicked. I convinced myself you were better off without me, and that if I could just get you out of my life, things would be normal again. The phone call to Val was to prove to myself that was possible."

"And did it?"

"No. It just proved what an ass I am." Strong fingers swept back a lock of hair from her forehead, sending a tingle through her. Jonas's voice dropped a note deeper, rough and uneven. "Can you ever forgive me?"

"Maybe." Kate hardly recognized the husky murmur as her own. "On two conditions."

"Name them." Jonas's fingers tangled in her curls, tugging her head inexorably back, inch by exquisite inch. Kate's gaze lifted from the pulse in his throat to the stubborn chin, lingered on the fullness of his bottom lip, then met glittering blue eyes dark with need. Bright with promise.

"Cancel Saturday night," she said.

"Already done. I called Valerie back as soon as you left."

"And stop trying to be responsible for everyone else's life. Especially mine. If I stay, it's my choice. My decision."

"Your problem, not mine?"

"Exactly."

"I think I can live with that." His mouth hovered a fraction above hers, his breath caressing her lips. "Tell me, though—would you consider it undue influence if I told you I loved you?"

Kate went very still. She stared into velvet eyes, and felt rather than saw him smile. His lips brushed hers once, twice.

"That depends on what you're trying to influence, I suppose," she whispered. Shocking need quivered through her as Jonas's free hand slid down her spine, curved over her hip, drew her into him.

"Your decision to stay or not. How long you'll stay."

Another kiss, longer this time, made a sensual demand on her very center. The world drifted away from her feet, and for a long moment of utter bliss, Jonas's hard, muscled length became her only reality.

He pulled back slowly, then rested his forehead against hers. "Forever," he said. "That's how long I want you to stay. I love you, Kate Dexter."

Kate smiled with a quiet warmth that started somewhere near her toes, reveling in the sheer nearness of the man holding her. "Consider me influenced," she replied. "Because I love you, too."

EPILOGUE

Four years later

Kate caught hold of the little body barreling past her and swung her wriggling daughter into her arms. "Hold on, there, tiger. Where are you off to in such a rush?"

Jessica pushed at her chest. "Want *down*, Mommy. Jessie down!"

Kate looked past her armload as Jonas came through the living room, stumbling over a collection of play dishes and cursing under his breath. She hid a smile. "Hey, handsome."

"Stop trying to butter me up, lady," he retorted with mock ferocity, joining them. "You're late."

"Sorry. I got tied up in the office and then hit traffic because of an accident. Have you spoken to Mrs. Barr yet?"

He dropped a kiss on her forehead and poked Jessica in the belly, sending the two-year-old into a gale of giggles. Jonas's blue eyes lit up at the sound of little girl laughter, and Kate marveled again at the changes in the man she'd married. From tough, fiercely independent cop to doting, undignified fatherhood. Four years in, and it still didn't seem possible. She set the toddler on the floor and watched her run down the hallway.

"I have," Jonas answered her question. "I talked to the old battle axe after I called you. She's looping the principal in on the meeting this time. It ain't gonna be pretty."

"Did she say exactly what he'd done?" Kate watched her husband anxiously, knowing how close Jonas was to being at his wits' end with their fourteen-year-old foster son. Daniel had been with them now for almost six months, and as far as they could tell, they'd made almost zero progress with him. They were the third foster home the boy had been in during the last year, and Jonas took this one very personally. It was so close to home for him.

"Another fight," he replied. "What else?"

"Do you want me to come with you?"

"Nah. You put your feet up for a while. I can handle her...I mean, it." Jonas paused in his search for his keys on the hall table and narrowed his gaze on her. "You look tired today."

"Nothing that dinner and an early night won't fix."

He shook his head, looking doubtful. "Are you sure you shouldn't be the one at home? I see you like this"—he nodded at her ballooning belly—"and think about you having to work all day, then fight traffic to get back home, and I can't help thinking we made the wrong decision. I shouldn't have let you—"

"Burke." Kate crossed her arms and regarded him.

He paused.

"Remember that taking-too-much-responsibility thing you keep doing?" she asked.

"I'm doing it again?"

"You're doing it again."

He gave her a sheepish grin. "Sorry."

"Besides," Kate said, as she ushered him toward the door and his appointment with Daniel's homeroom teacher and the school principal, "how gullible do you think I am? You really expect me to believe that being home all day with the munchkin and all the housework and the animals to look after would be better for me than sitting in air-conditioned comfort and napping through meetings?"

He grinned. "Can't blame a poor househusband for trying."

"Well, you can stop trying, because it's not going to work. Now, are you picking up Sarah and Nathan as well, or are they taking the bus?" Their other two foster children were at the primary school on the way to the junior high that Daniel attended.

"I'll pick them up. By the way, dinner's already in the oven, but that early night you wanted..." Jonas turned to take her into his arms, trailing tiny kisses down the side of her neck to her collarbone. "I don't suppose we could delay that for an hour or two, could we?"

Kate's fingers tightened on his shirtfront as her knees turned to mush. Three years of marriage, a veritable parade of foster kids, a daughter of their own and another child on the way, and he could still turn her world upside down with just a touch.

Bemused, she stared up at him. "How do you do that?"

"What?" He nibbled on her lower lip.

"That," she said breathlessly. "Turn me into a puddle like that, just by touching me."

"Fair's fair. You can do it to me with just a look, sweetheart."

Kate smiled her satisfaction at the response, and Jonas chuckled. "Now you look like the Cheshire cat."

"And you've been watching too much television with Jess."

"Speaking of whom—"

"I'll find her. Give Mrs. Barr my regards."

"Yeah, right."

Kate watched the minivan drive down the lane until it disappeared behind the trees near the road. Jonas would handle Mrs. Barr just fine, despite his doubts. Just as he handled the million and one other problems that arose almost daily in raising four children, three of whom came with rather a lot of baggage. He had a knack for it, something that went beyond the understanding he'd gained from his own rocky start in life. Kate had known it instinctively, when he'd first suggested the farm and the idea of fostering to her.

It hadn't been a difficult decision to make. Hailing from opposite sides of the border as they did, they'd known from the beginning that only one of them could keep their career, and Jonas's dream of making a difference had been the deciding factor. And so here they were, living forty minutes from Kate's job in Ottawa, each working in their own way—and together—to make a difference.

As for Daniel, Kate suspected he'd come around eventually. He wasn't a bad kid, just angry and mixed up, betrayed and disappointed. But he'd come to the right place for healing—and found the right man. Just as they all had.

Kate closed the door and, still smiling at the last thought, went in search of their daughter.

ABOUT THE AUTHOR

Like most romance writers, Linda Poitevin is a firm believer in happy-ever-afters—especially since she's living her own. But she also knows how hard you have to work at those sometimes, and that's reflected in her stories about people who are as real to her as she hopes they'll be to you. People who live, laugh, cry, and love as hard as they can in this crazy life we all share.

In her other-than-writing life, Linda lives just outside Ottawa, Canada's capital, where she is a wife, mom, friend, avid gardener, walker of a giant dog, and keeper of many (many!) pets.

You can find Linda online at her website (LindaPoitevin.com) and on Facebook (where she posts many pictures of her many pets), and you can get a free story when you sign up to receive updates in her newsletter.